CLINICAL TRIAL

4

Also by Robert McMackin

Fiction
Delta Dawg
The Last Adagio
The Time Traveler
A Good Boy
Hope
Shrouded in Moonlight
The Dharma of Niall

Autobiographical Fiction
1967: Hitchhiking through the Summer of Love

Nonfiction
Trauma Therapy in Context: The Science and Craft of Evidence-Based Practice
(coedited with Elana Newman, Jason Fogler, and Terence Keane)

Understanding the Impact of Clergy Sexual Abuse: Betrayal and Recovery
(coedited with Terence Keane and Paul Kline)

CLINICAL TRIAL

4

ROBERT MCMACKIN

ISBN: 9798709316447

LCCN: 2021906929

Front cover photograph by Sheila Platt
Back cover photograph by Ashim D'Silva

For friendship

Optimism is realism.

CHAPTER 1

1

I have been away from the plangent drone and clank of rolling steel for almost three years. I thought I was inured to the whirring motor and *click, click, click* of the metal chain hauling the security door open, but I am not. I may have been once, but I am no longer. Simultaneously, it is both novel and commonplace, ominous and inviting—a sound that was part of the background noise in my life for nearly ten years.

"Hey, Doc, welcome back." The officer in the trap greets me while extending his hand across the small wooden desk onto which I have emptied the contents of my pockets.

"Just visiting," I mumble, refamiliarizing myself to the pale-green walls of the rectangular tunnel I must again pass down to enter the prison proper. There was a new officer at the front-entrance control room when I arrived moments earlier. While he eyed my license through the inch-thick security glass, the lieutenant running the shift warmly greeted me: "TC, my man, good to see you." It was Lincoln Grant. The surprise and pleasure in his voice evident. I watched the transformation of the CO's countenance at Lincoln's words. I was no longer an object of suspicion. He was about to chastise me for holding my ID up to the window and not slipping it into the security tray for a closer inspection, but now he simply waved and requested that I sign in on the visitors' log.

Lincoln made his way out to the entry and was standing behind me as I completed the procedure.

"How you doing, Captain?" he asked softly and then embraced me with surprising tenderness. The last time I saw him was at my wife's funeral. A few days before that, we were racing down I-95 at a hundred miles per hour, siren blaring with a police escort and Lincoln at the wheel. Minutes before, the superintendent had entered my office to tell me Maura had been in a car accident and was at the Rhode Island Hospital Trauma Center. "She'll be okay," he assured me, but she wasn't. She died. I was able to tell her the baby survived and was a healthy boy. She was surprised. We were both surprised, expecting a girl. We had gone so far as to have picked out a name—Estelle, in honor of the stars she was conceived under on Block Island. While Maura was being wheeled off for emergency surgery, she murmured to me, "Take care of our son, TC. Take care of our son."

"You doing okay, Cap?" Lincoln asked a second time after releasing me from his arms.

"Yeah, yeah, I'm fine." I lied. "I haven't been here in a few years. You know, a lot of memories."

"Any chance we'll be seeing more of you?"

It took me a moment to decide if he was asking about returning to work at the Rhode Island Department of Corrections or reenlisting in the National Guard, where he was a sergeant. His using my former rank of captain added to my disorientation. No one had called me Cap, Captain, or Captain Phillips in a dog's age. "The super asked me to come in. He said there was something he wanted my advice on. We'll see what happens," I replied, figuring he meant the prison.

"We can sure use you," he said. "No one was happy with what went down—at least not most of what went down."

"We'll see," was all I could choke out. "Jim's waiting, so I better get in there." But more than anything else, I had to get away from Lincoln and the unexpected churn of emotions that was bubbling up within.

"New linoleum," I observe, gazing beyond the edge of the table where my wallet, change, and a pair of reading glasses sit.

"Yeah," the CO replies. "Your tax dollars at work, trying to turn a sow's ear into a silk purse. You still working here, Doc? I haven't seen you for a while."

"I've been away. I have an appointment with Jim Dwyer at nine."

I can tell from how the officer is staring at my belongings that he is wondering if he should tell me to go back out and put it in a locker. Even official visitors aren't allowed to bring money into the institution, but since I'm unescorted, that may indicate I am still viewed as an employee.

"Ah, screw it," he mumbles to conclude the internal debate. "You're one of us." He then waves me through the metal detector.

I'm grateful for the brief pause. It helps me recompose myself. Then, stuffing the wallet, change, and reading glasses into my pockets, I proceed down the corridor to the next security post. This door is operated by an officer thirty feet above me in a tower built into the eighteen-foot-tall concrete wall that encases the ten or so acres of Cranston State Prison. Looking up, I see him begin to spin the iron wheel that manually cranks open the door I am facing. Inhaling the crisp March air deeply, I step into the jail.

Looming before me is the Victorian gray-granite facade of the combined administration and health-service building. Constructed in the late nineteenth century, it is the last visage of the original workhouse/prison designed by the noted Providence architectural firm of Stone and Carpenter. It is also the first and last visage of grace one sees upon entering the grounds. All subsequent construction followed the building mantra of the most square footage for the fewest dollars—an assortment of boxes all designed to keep people caged up. Gone, too, is the Board of Charities nineteenth-century philosophy that most prisoners "are not naturally vicious but the victims of habit or disease, call it what you will, or intemperance…susceptible to reformatory influences.[1]" I break out of the mild depressive trance the building has cast over me to traverse the ten yards to its entrance.

I again hesitate on the granite stoop to take it all in. Turning back, I note that the steel door I exited resembles a tiny mousehole in a massive wall that fans out to my left and right. In the distance loom two guard towers at each far corner. I've crossed into the admin building thousands of times in the past, but today this, too, is new. I expect to see an inmate in his state-issued jeans and work shirt sweeping up or preparing the flower beds for spring planting, but I am alone on the walkway. My office was adjacent to the health-service unit, where I spent much of each day. Someone else is probably using it now. I shake my head rigorously to dispel images from the past, links in a chain that binds me to the prison.

I expect to see more familiar faces when I push open the original oak door to the building, but the foyer is empty. Inmates don't have free access to this side of admin or health services, so there isn't a security post beyond the main entry trap. Jim Dwyer is Cranston's superintendent. His office sits on the top floor so he can survey the camp from its windows. I climb the two flights rather than take the rickety elevator.

Nothing has changed in the time I've been away. I saw myself as a different person, but now I am not so sure about that. Fifteen minutes earlier, when I pulled into the parking lot, I was uncertain whether I should take a visitor's slot near the entrance or continue to the staff section. The hesitation was brief, and I automatically drove beyond the ten visitors' spaces to find one designated for employees. There wasn't a lot of thought involved; I just did it. And then there was seeing Lincoln and the trap officer's "Screw it; you're one of us" comment. It was as if I had not officially turned in my resignation and

---

1 1869 Annual Report of the Rhode Island Board of State Charities and Corrections

walked away a couple of years back; I've simply been on an extended vacation.

Entering the superintendent's suite, I again feel like a foreigner. Jim's longtime administrative assistant, Jane Donning, is no longer at her desk, and it's a slight jolt. She had been a fixture at Cranston for years and knew where every skeleton, as well as all the missing files, were buried. I am taken aback, but before I can answer her replacement's "May I help you?" Jim appears from his office.

"TC, thanks for coming in. I knew I could rely on you," he says while shaking my extended hand and placing his left firmly on my right shoulder. He swivels me to the new administrative assistant and continues, "This is Dr. Thomas Phillips, Alma. Whenever he calls or stops by, it's okay for you to interrupt me." I nod to Alma as Jim hustles me into his suite.

"Where's Jane?" I ask as soon he shuts the door.

"She did her thirty years—even more, closer to thirty-five. She went out at 80 percent six months ago. Didn't anyone call you for her retirement party?"

After I shake my head, he observes, "That's one more reason why you shouldn't have left." Then more seriously, he adds, "Do you want to know what happened, or do you want to know why I asked to see you?"

Jim never beats around the bush, and nor did I. "No one was ever charged based on what I saw in the papers, so I expect Fahad has returned to population, or you swapped him out to another state."

"I left him here. Hell, all the Black inmates and half the officers would have revolted if I shipped Milton's ass out."

I don't respond. Fahad—or Jonathan Milton, the name he was born with—likely murdered Leon Alexander as a favor to me. It took a while for me to accept that, but it's where all the evidence pointed, and sometimes, even when you don't agree with the data, you must listen to it. I had worked closely with Fahad. He was one of the first people to complete the Medical Assistance Training Program I had initiated to train inmates to be aides in the hospital. Alexander, a two-time loser, was loaded when he drove his pickup into Maura's Nissan. His lawyer insisted he be held in Cranston's protective custody unit, more to protect him from guards than other inmates, because I worked for DOC. He was stabbed to death in the chow line when the supervising officer had to assist in quelling a disturbance at the far end of the tier. Fahad, although not assigned to help serve the meal, was filling in for a sick friend. The shank was a large shard of Plexiglas wrapped in surgical tape. The video surveillance showed a blur of people, and no one saw anything—or anything they were willing to comment on—amid the confusion. The Rhode Island State Police brought me in for questioning a few times, trying to squeeze out a confession that I somehow orchestrated the whole thing. Eventually, they believed I had nothing to do with it after I called a friend in the FBI for a character reference related to work I did with them in the past. That all led to my working with the FBI on an undercover matter, an unexpected cash windfall, and my resignation from both the DOC and National Guard.

Jim snaps my chain of automatic associations. "What happened, happened. It's in the rearview mirror and, if the truth be told, not many people are all that upset with what went down," he concludes, echoing Lincoln Grant's words apropos of Fahad's murder of Alexander.

I want to change the subject. I wish the whole thing were out of my mind, but I am equally certain it never will be. "Jim, I'm no longer here, so why don't we leave what happened in the past in the past. There is some other reason you asked to see me, right?"

"Right. I want you to come back for a special project. Actually, I need you to come back. It doesn't have to be into a state slot; you can be a consultant, and I can pay you top dollar. It will be temporary, in the six-month range, but it's critical that I have someone I can rely on totally, and you're the one person who came to mind."

I am studying Jim as he speaks. When he didn't go back behind the wide oak expanse of his desk after we entered his office, I expected it was something personal, not professional. He tended to lean back in his desk chair, flanked by the Rhode Island and American flags, whenever he discussed official prison business, merging with the desk, flags, and other correctional paraphernalia on the walls to create a tableau of authority, and it worked. When Jim was leaned back with others ringed before him, he expanded and grew—the most alpha of all the alpha males in the room. Today we are in the two wing chairs set off in a side corner, separated by a small rough table that was reportedly constructed from pieces of the last scaffold ever used in the Ocean State. The topic isn't some personal issue, as I had expected.

"You want me to come back…back to work on a special project?" I reply to his opening, curious yet guarded.

"That's what I said. You know those boarded-up old mills and foundries that dot the Woonasquatucket River?" he asks.

"Sure. There must be a dozen or so. I heard they're planning on turning them into condos."

"They've already started," Jim says. "But they want some industry to anchor the project. Apparently, a new biotech company may locate both its offices and manufacturing facilities there. It could be a major boon for Providence, the same way Biogen is for Cambridge and Boston. The Albert School of Medicine at Brown is equal to Harvard or any of the Boston schools, plus Boston is only an hour away."

I interrupt him with a laugh. "Jesus, Jim, you sound like a developer, but I still don't see what this has to do with me."

He chuckles along with me. "I am trying to sell you, TC. I guess I'm even trying to sell myself."

"Sell what?"

"There's this biotech start-up, Adams Pharmaceuticals. It's been around for five years but is now on the verge of taking off. You've heard of Carlo Poletti, right?"

"The president of the Senate, but isn't his name Carl, not Carlo?"

"He uses both," Jim explains. "He used Carl early in his career, but for the past couple of years, it's been Carlo. Anyway, his district includes North Providence and pretty much follows the course of the Woonasquatucket.

Apparently, he was approached by Adams, or he approached them, on locating to the river area. It's part of some larger renovation and expansion plan for that section of his district. Adams has some products in the pipeline that they are optimistic about. There is one in particular that is an antipsychotic/antidepressant mix, whose initial clinical trials indicate it can reduce impulsivity and anger. Now they want to do more extensive research, and they want to do it here."

"You mean inmate research? They intend to set up a clinical trial with prisoners?"

"That's not the whole of it. They have requested to do it by managing an entire unit, a specialized mental health unit devoted to reducing aggression. Inmate participation would be voluntary, and it will go through DOC's Institutional Review Board. In fact, the IRB has already given its initial approval. The cons will get the medication along with some other therapy—substance abuse, anger management, and the usual stuff. They're big on using us as a site so they can then market it nationally to state correctional systems. From what I've been told, they plan to emphasize how it can reduce anger and impulsivity."

"For a management tool?"

"You might say that, but they don't ever mention that in their write-ups. They focus on helping people stabilize their moods, better control their thoughts, and be less aggressive or impulsive. But a calmer inmate is certainly easier to manage, and everyone is aware of that."

"There are already several drugs that have similar properties, like Abilify, but they must already know that."

"I expect they do, but it's the prison angle they're focused on. My issue is that I don't believe they understand corrections, although it's pretty clear that's what they're aiming at. It's a big nut. Health care already eats nearly 15 percent of each state's overall correctional budget. This past year almost seventy billion was spent nationally on keeping people locked up, including ten-billion-plus for health services. That's big money. If they can show they can manage a highly secure unit where each inmate voluntarily takes Adams's new med, they'll be in the driver's seat. Poletti is after it for his district as well as the state, and Adams is after the money. The DOC commissioner has been pressured to make it happen, and since shit rolls downhill, he's been on me."

"I'm still not sure why I'm here. Do you want me to tell you if it's a good idea or not?"

"No. We're beyond that. Even if the idea sucks, I'm stuck with it. We've already begun setting up a modular unit by the eastern wall."

"Isn't that the rec field where the Spanish guys play soccer? They'll protest if you take their field."

"There will only be two modular units with a capacity for thirty inmates and offices. We'll set them right against the wall. It will mostly be in no-man's-land between the wall and the inner perimeter fence. We've already cut a separate entrance into the wall on the outside. The people that work there, especially the Adams people, will be able to bypass the main trap."

"You'll still require some recreation space, and that will mean extending into the soccer field unless you put it outside the wall, and I'm certain you don't intend to make a rec area outside the wall. Low-security guys or not, the risk is too big. And how about job assignments? Do you plan to let guys keep their jobs inside the camp?"

"This is why you need to help us out, TC. We identified the rec space issue, but no one raised the job question. I assumed they'd keep their regular job assignments. There's no way I'll set up a separate work program for one unit, but we do have to make a decision on it."

"I'd be happy to look over the plans and review their IRB material, but I'm certain that if they're linked to any academic institution, all of it will be in order. I expect it's the prison issues, anyway, that will cause the biggest concerns. Do you know if they're planning to use other inmates here as a control group, or will they be giving half the guys a placebo? Are you planning to have a captain or a lieutenant as the unit manager?"

"Half the guys will be taking the medication and the other half not, but I have no idea how they'll be selected or the other ins and outs of their study design. They requested the authority to operate a thirty-bed unit for six months to a year, depending on how long it will take to collect all the data. As far as running the place, that's why we're here. The job's yours if you want it."

"Me?" I smile. "I doubt it, Jim. It's an interesting project, but they'll have their own researchers who will be more qualified than me to run that type of study."

"I don't mean the research," he clarifies. "I mean you being the unit manager. You already said it's the corrections issues that will be the diciest, and I agree with you."

"But I'm not security. Unit managers are generally lieutenants. Plus, I'm not all that sure I want to do it, even if I wasn't living out on the island and had a three-year-old to take care of."

"Well, you are a captain, and everyone in this place—"

"Hold on, Jim," I interrupt. "I'm no longer in the Guard. I got a waiver for an early discharge. This—"

"And I'm certain it was honorable and that they would take you back in a heartbeat," Jim breaks in. "Look, TC, I totally realize that the past few years have been rough. I heard that the Mounties tried to shake you down as the mastermind behind Alexander's murder but backed off when the FBI recruited you to work on some type of project for them. You know, my head's not too far up my ass."

We pause as silence fills the room. I feel a bit like a fighter going into a neutral corner, yet I don't feel remotely angry. I am certain Jim's concern is genuine. He knew the state police—or "Mounties," as most corrections officers call them because of their ornate dress uniforms—brought me in for questioning. At the time, he warned me of the possibility, and his connections in the staties' hierarchy would have kept him apprised of what had happened. I am a little surprised he heard about the FBI, but I shouldn't be. He may even be aware that they fabricated a bogus charge of entering the country illegally from Canada to get me into a federal joint outside of Bakersville,

California.

"I need your help, TC," Jim says, breaking the quiet. "Give it some thought. You can have three sergeants to operate the place—your pick. The commissioner wants this up and running ASAP. I expect he is getting heat from Poletti and possibly the governor's office. Adams already requested input on the unit manager, but I said if it's happening in my joint, I own the position. I don't mean to pressure you, but this being so high profile, it's important that there is someone there I can trust. You're the person I'm most comfortable with, which is why we're here talking and why I want you onboard."

"I'll consider it," I reply, moved by the obvious affect in Jim's voice.

"How's Matt and life out on Block Island?" Jim asks, signaling that he is willing to let it rest.

"Good. I was able to get a house built, Matt's healthy, and my mom helps out with him. I do some work in a boatbuilding shop and a lot of fishing."

"Commercial fishing?"

"No, not commercial, although a buddy and I run a summer charter service. It's mainly sport," I explain.

"Are you doing any work as a psychologist out there?"

"Not right now, but I've considered hanging out a shingle. I've kept my CEUs up, and I am still in good standing with the licensing board." I don't mention that the thoughts of opening a private practice have been few and fleeting, nor do I mention that I go out on benders periodically, and if I wasn't friendly with every cop on the island, I'd have easily picked up one or two DWIs by now.

"Sounds as if you started retirement a couple of decades early," he observes.

"It's a life," I say defensively. But he's right. Out on the island, it doesn't feel like retirement, yet as I listen to myself describing what I do to Jim, it does sound like it.

"If you're interested in a George Foreman–type comeback, TC, we're here," he offers.

"What if it turns out to be more like Ali than Foreman?" I laugh.

"Hey, Ali had a great career and was past forty when he climbed into the ring for the last time. You're not even thirty-five," Jim counters. "I'd take an Ali at thirty-five any day against Foreman or anyone else. Think about it, Dr. Phillips."

2

On the ferry back to Block Island, I do think about it. Initially, I had planned to stop by the hospital unit after my meeting with Jim to visit the nurses I used to work with, but I decided not to when we finished. I was too preoccupied. If I stopped by, I would have to explain why I was there and listen to everyone's opinion on what I should do. Only a few boats are bobbing in the harbor as the ferry pulls in, but I know people are getting ready to launch their various crafts. During the next two months, I'd have as much work as I wanted in Izzy Fellow's shop, refinishing hulls and rigging out the off-islanders' yachts that were stored in his yard. I drive directly to the liquor store from the ship, hoping there may still be a twelve-pack of Sam Adams Winter Brew stuck in the back of their walk-in cooler. I luck out, and when I plop the box on the counter, the young woman at the register says, "The usual, TC?" while reaching for a pint of Old Forester from the rack behind her.

"I'm set," I reply, but I can feel the urge for whiskey. The hesitation is because *The usual, TC?* is echoing in my mind. I have no idea of the girl's name. Her older brother is Len O'Hara. That much I do know. He was a few years behind me in high school, but I have no idea who she is. Nonetheless, she knew *the usual* for me was a pint of Old Forester.

"Thanks," I mutter while tucking the beer under my arm and heading out to my car. *Jesus, I need to slow down,* I tell myself, and I simultaneously wonder about hitting a different package store for the whiskey. Instead, I drive right to Old Harbor and park so I can gaze out across the rippling incoming tide. The rising sea has already flooded into the salt marsh, dampening the pungent aroma of the mud that greeted me earlier as the ferry ran a beeline along the northern side of the island toward the outer breakwater.

"Jim, it's TC," I say to the voice that picks up on the other end. I had punched the super's direct line into my cell almost immediately after parking.

"That was quick. Are you still in Providence, or did you already make the crossing?"

"I'm back on Block Island. I caught the noon ferry, and I have a couple of questions."

"I'm listening."

"Are there any vacancies in the old staff residences out back by the potter's field?"

"They're all empty, but a couple are still habitable. The original warden's house is in decent shape, and maybe one more. We no longer offer them to staff, and no one's all that interested in living there anyway. Why?"

"If I do this, I'd like to use one of them. It will allow me to avoid renting an apartment in Providence for six months, plus keep me nearby if any issues arise on the overnight, which we both know they will. I'd also need a four-day workweek, so I will only use the house for three nights, and on some weeks, just two nights if I can catch the last ferry back on a Thursday."

"That may be an option. I'll have to check on the house. It's not in use currently except for storing dead records in the basement, so I can probably manage that, but being on site four days may be an issue. Your ability to manage the unit while you're out on the island half the time creates a serious accessibility problem."

"Not if you give me a lieutenant along with those three sergeants as shift supervisors. And it definitely won't be a problem if you assign Lincoln."

"I have Grant running the out-front operations, and on top of that, he chairs the disciplinary board. He's busy, and I don't want to lose him. He keeps an eye on all the loose ends. I doubt there's been any drugs coming in either on visits or any other way since he's been in charge. What about someone else? Wasolski's good."

"I'm sure Wasolski is good, but I have total trust in Lincoln. He's in the Guard, and we go back. My health-service unit used to occasionally drill with his company. If this is as important a project as you were saying, then Lincoln's our man. Why not make him the unit manager and me a consultant?"

"No. It won't work. You need to have some weight. They can blow you off if you're simply a consultant. I don't mind paying you as a consultant, but having staff authority is essential."

"Then why don't you have codirectors because of the special nature of the unit? I don't mind working Sundays. What if I did Sunday to Wednesday, and Lincoln worked a Tuesday to Saturday? We'd have a two-day overlap, and you'd have a manager on site every day. Lincoln is active in his church, so he would get his Sundays, which he would appreciate."

Jim pauses to ponder the idea and then responds, "If I can swing this, TC, how serious are you?"

Now it's my turn to pause. I initially called because of the girl at the package store asking me if I wanted *the usual*, not because I was interested in the position. But I do have to get my ass into gear. Once the fishing season starts, the drinking will likely taper off because I'll be busy, but it will be just as likely to pick up again in the fall.

"TC."

"Yeah, I'm here. I'm thinking; that's all." At that moment, the whistle for the ferry blows in the distance.

"What was that?" Jim asks.

"It's the first boarding call for the ferry, but yeah, you can count me in. I have to confirm with my mother that she can take care of Matt the days I'm away. Other than that, I'm set to go. When do we start?"

"Can you make it in two weeks? The modulars will be in place by then, and it will give me time to get the warden's house cleaned up and check with Grant. If he's not interested, should I assign him anyway?"

"No, it has to be his choice. If he says no, let's go with Wasolski."

"What about the money? Does seventy-five an hour work?"

"You mean seventy-five an hour for me? That equals a hundred and fifty grand a year," I reply, doing a quick computation in my mind. "You have that kind of cash available?"

"A lot of people are interested in this project working. When I tell them you're my guy, the money won't be a problem. Remember, it's only for six months or so."

"Lincoln and I report directly to you and not to a deputy, right?"

"I wouldn't have it any other way."

"It sounds good, Jim. Once I clear up a few things on the island and run it past my mom, I'll be good. I can't imagine my mother will have any problems with it, so two weeks should be fine," I say, certain that my mother will both jump at the opportunity to spend more time with Matt and be pleased I am finally doing something professionally.

Rather than driving to my mother's house to pick up Matt, I stop by Izzy's. Entering the shop, I see him leaning over the table saw carefully ripping some teak while Lester is grinding down a lead skeg that I had helped them attach days earlier to the keel of a sailboat. Izzy had made a mold, following the exact lines of the keel, and then they had poured almost a ton of metal to make the new ballast.

"No drag." I compliment Lester while running my palm the length of the keel. He is doing an excellent job in smoothing all the burrs out of the lead so it will glide effortlessly through the sea.

He grins. "A full gale won't turn her now."

I laugh and say, "I wouldn't want to test that," remembering the owner felt the boat wasn't stable, which is why they removed the former skeg and then modified the keel to accept the additional weight.

"Let's do the shakedown, TC," Lester suggests. "We'll bury the gunnels, and you'll see for yourself."

"I'll take a pass on that one, Les," I reply. I then head over to see Izzy as he shuts down the saw and shakes the dust out of his curly gray hair.

The tropical aroma of the teak greets me while I'm still more than twenty feet from the machinery. As the saw's whirr dies down, I tell Izzy that I may be returning to work.

"So what have you been doing these past few years?" he asks. "Building a house, starting a charter service with Woody, helping me out here, and taking care of a baby. You've been working plenty, as far as I can see."

"I mean back to being a psychologist. I was on the mainland today, and they asked me to return to Cranston for six months to help them start up a new program at the prison."

"Where will you live?"

"I'd stay here and spend three or four nights a week on the other side. They'll give me a four-day workweek."

"Do you want to do it?"

"When they initially offered, I wasn't that interested, but now, yeah. I have all this education, Izzy, and feel I should be using it better."

"Your dad had a master's degree in marine architecture from MIT."

"But he used that in the shop with you, especially on the restorations of Herreshoffs or other classic boats. It doesn't take a doctorate to catch fish or drive nails."

"Help me lay out the teak," he says, changing the subject.

"Flooring?" I ask, and he nods yes while motioning to an area on the concrete that has been swept clean.

Silently we position the wood and then test that the white holly joining splines fit the grooves he has cut into the side of each board. Without being asked, I mix a small batch of two-part epoxy, which we apply to the holly before refitting the pieces. A half hour later, we finish tightening the pipe clamps in place to make a large slab of teak with gleaming streaks of quarter-inch holly running between each board. In a day or two, Izzy or Lester will cut out the flooring pieces they require for an Alden restoration they are working on. Most other builders simply use marine plywood with a veneer that mimics the original decking that Izzy just fabricated from scratch.

"What does Lil think?" he asks as I finish adjusting the tension on the last clamp.

"It only happened today. I got in on the noon ferry and haven't been home yet," I reply, realizing that I continue to call my mother's house *home*, and my own place I usually refer to as *my house*. "My guess is she'll be okay with it and will enjoy any excuse to spend more time with Matt."

"A man has to work, and if that's what you want to do, then you should do it. You know this business is part yours, TC, and there is always work for you here. But you've got to do what you've got to do," he concludes in true island fashion.

His words—*You've got to do what you've got to do*—resonate within as I leave the shop. I decide they are a lot better than the other words that recently echoed within me: *The usual, TC?*

Matt's down for his afternoon nap when I arrive home. I tell my mother to let him sleep and then explain Jim's offer.

"Are you sure you want to go back into a prison?" is her initial response, and it surprises me. She has been nudging me toward using some of our connections to get a school psychologist job or open a private practice. I've shied away from each and any other type of mental health work, questioning what right I had to tell anyone, directly or indirectly, how to live their life. If they opted to screw up the works or even off themselves, part of me said to let them do it. If they were depressed or anxious, they needed to get a life and not tell me about it. And the same thing was true for me. Maura was dead, and that was that. But I couldn't follow my own advice and let it go.

"This time I'll be in charge," I reply, believing she is referring to my undercover stay in the El Camino Federal Prison outside of Bakersville, which the FBI had to explain to her three years ago because she was responsible for Matt the four weeks I was gone. "Plus, it's part of a controlled study on medication effectiveness."

"Hasn't research on prisoners been banned for some time?"

"Not banned, but there are strict federal and state guidelines that are more rigid than the guidelines for other populations. They even recommend placing an inmate, or an inmate advocate, on any review board granting approval for a study."

She doesn't respond, but I can tell she's not convinced. "Come on, Ma. You've been bugging me to get back to work, and then this thing pops up. The superintendent called me in because he believes I'm the most qualified person he knows to oversee the project, and you're not sure if it's a good idea?"

"I thought you were done with prisons—Guantanamo, Cranston, the FBI. When is it enough?"

I remind her that my stay at Guantanamo was part of a National Guard deployment, Cranston was my regular job for ten years, and the stint at El Camino was brief and part of an FBI operation I was uniquely suited for and inadvertently fell into.

"Prisons are such a waste of human potential for both the jailed and the jailers. You've done your part. You have a family now."

"I have a son, Ma. That's not exactly a family."

"All I have is a son, and I consider that a family," she counters.

I sigh deeply in frustration and try to control my anger, momentarily lost amid memories of Maura's and my father's deaths. While I struggle to form a response, she provides me an exit by asking me to describe the project at Cranston in greater detail.

"Are the researchers affiliated with the Albert School of Medicine?" she asks when I finish.

"I'm not sure. They may be linked to Brown, Yale, or one of the Boston schools. UMass is also a possibility; they have a large correctional health division. Why?"

"The academic oversight will ensure the research is unbiased, and future opportunities may open for you in one of those settings."

"Right." I chuckle at her ability to shift so quickly and now see the possibility in a positive light. "Maybe they'll offer me a position in their correctional healthcare division, and I'll get to go into even more prisons."

My mother smiles at the irony of my words and then asks if the project is valuable.

"I don't know enough yet to say, although Jim believes money is a big factor. If the trial is successful, Adams plans to market their product to correctional systems, and Poletti is interested in what it will do for his district and the state."

"What about the prisoners? Who watches out for them and ensures that they're not used as guinea pigs so those others can make money?"

"Remember, it's all voluntary, and there will be plenty of safeguards. If it won IRB approval, all of that must have been already assessed."

"If there are large sums of money involved, and you already said north of ten billion is spent annually on correctional health, then there will be a lot of pressure to make the results positive. Jim is right to have people he trusts keeping an eye on things."

My mother's conspiratorial side has moved to the fore, which doesn't surprise me. She is a big advocate of Deep Throat's maxim to Woodward and Bernstein: *Follow the money.*

Our conversation is interrupted by Matt stirring from his nap.

3

My next trip to the mainland is to meet with Alain Vos, the medical director of Adams Pharmaceuticals. In reviewing materials for the project, I saw two clinical social workers assigned to the unit were to be paid by Adams, which surprised me. When I called Jim about it, he said that Adams offered to fund them, and DOC accepted because of budgetary reasons.

"That doesn't make any sense to me," I said. "What do you think is really going on?"

"My guess is that they plan to kill two birds with one stone," Jim responded. "While they do a clinical trial on their medication, they can simultaneously field-test their ability to manage all the mental health services for a high-risk group. Besides marketing the meds in the future, they may be trying to break into the whole correctional healthcare management arena."

"Then why doesn't DOC just let them run the entire unit? They could pilot everything at once."

"That's what they first proposed, but I said that if it was run at Cranston on my watch, the administrator had to report directly to me. There's no way I'll have a unit in my shop that I don't control, and that's what would happen if the manager reported to someone at the central office, or worse yet, if they reported to some doctor or executive at Adams. You said it earlier: all the problems are likely to be on the corrections end. Them not understanding the inmate or officer cultures is a set up for disaster. I didn't make any friends insisting on the organizational structure that I did, but I can't have cowboys running around this place."

"Why didn't you tell me this before?"

"It didn't occur to me when we met."

"Bullshit!" I said immediately. "You didn't want me to know, did you, Jim? These people, at least the Adams people, may view me and Lincoln as potential obstacles, especially if they had hoped to control the management of the place. That's why you didn't tell me, isn't it?"

"Partly, but don't forget Poletti either," Jim cautioned. "He wasn't all that pleased they didn't get to be in control and applied a lot of pressure. This is a potential gold mine for his district, and he wants it to work. As for Lincoln, he'll be there but only as a lieutenant. Everyone agreed that having codirectors may be confusing in respect to lines of authority."

"Is there anything else you've yet to tell me?" I asked in frustration.

"Adams's name will be on your check, but we're paying the freight. It's too difficult for us to have a contract for you approved as a consultant during the hiring freeze. It's strictly accounting. They'll be reimbursed for your cost, and I'm still your direct report."

"I get paid by them but report to you. How long do you expect that will last? If they write my check, even if they get the money back from the state, they will try to control me. You—"

"That will not happen, TC," Jim said firmly, cutting me off. "There is too much riding on this working out right. You may think I deliberately misled you, and you're correct to some degree. I didn't mention their request to manage the whole thing, but I had already dealt with that. On Lincoln not being the codirector, I just lost that one. Both DOC downtown and Adams were against it. They prefer to deal with one person, but if Lincoln is on board, then as far as I'm concerned, he's your deputy. The money is out of my control due to the hiring freeze. None of this changes anything, and if it works out, who knows what kind of doors it might open?"

Bundled up in a down coat on the ferry's upper deck, I reflect on my conversation with the super as the ship makes its way to Point Judith. When he told me his logic, my anger rapidly dissipated, and we discussed how the building was proceeding. Jim said the modulars took up more space than he had initially planned for, in part because he decided the unit needed its own recreation area. As I expected, the Spanish guys were upset by the intrusion into their soccer field, but Jim was confident he could address their concerns. He expected that within a month, it would be ready for occupancy.

After I meet with the people at Adams, I'll go to Cranston to settle into the warden's house and survey how the construction is progressing. Then, for the remainder of the week, I will be working with Lincoln on staffing issues, identifying the three sergeants who will be our primary shift commanders, and revising the screening protocol Adams had developed. But the biggest thing I'll be doing is getting used to is being back inside a prison.

A shift in the rumble of the ferry's twin diesels vibrating up from the engine room, accompanied by a belch of smoke, tells me we are approaching Point Judith. A moment later the ship's first whistle confirms this, and I make my way down to the car deck.

Adams's offices are in a restored brick warehouse down a couple of blocks from the Rhode Island School of Design on Benefit Street, occupying roughly two thousand square feet on the second floor. The space is modest but nice, and I can tell as I enter the foyer that any manufacturing or research labs must be located in a different facility.

When I give my name to the receptionist, she smiles and says, "Oh, Dr. Phillips, welcome to Adams Pharmaceuticals. Dr. Vos is expecting you."

Moments later a man I judge to be in his early fifties emerges from the office area to greet me warmly. "Dr. Phillips, thank you for coming in. This is a critical project we are embarking on, and I am so glad we can speak. Can I get you a coffee or tea?"

After I say I'm fine, he invites me down to his office, which has a clear view of Providence's inner harbor.

"This next study will be highly significant for Adams, as I'm sure you have already been told," he begins once we are comfortably ensconced in two chairs. "Our initial trials on a new medication with antipsychotic and antidepressant qualities have shown that the drug is particularly effective in reducing hostility and anger in patients. We are anxious to run a double-blind trial with a population that has a documented history with management of aggression issues, and as you can guess, that is not a population readily available in most hospital or outpatient settings. Therefore, last year we requested to have a trial within the state prison system."

"Was this medication developed for any particular diagnostic group?" I ask, surprised he made no small talk whatsoever but rather delved into a description of the medication and clinical trial in clear layman's terms.

"Before I answer that, I have a brief question for you. Do you prefer to be addressed as Dr. Phillips, or may I use Thomas?"

"Most people call me TC. It's short for Thomas Carlyle."

"Fine, and please call me Alain. You asked about diagnosis, and in truth, I believe diagnosis to be highly overrated. We approach our work at Adams to improve one's quality of life, not to eliminate symptoms, although that is most assuredly important. Eumonia is the medication we will be field testing at Cranston. The patient population Eumonia was developed for is individuals who may have disturbances or distortions of cognition, which can affect their perception of reality and often lead to paranoia. Certainly, they may have accompanying difficulty with mood regulation and frequently histories of self-destruction. Outer-directed anger or rage as a component of their presentation was not our initial focus, but it has come to the fore, particularly for patients with a history of paranoia. In our initial field tests, many subjects met bipolar or PTSD criteria due to their trauma histories and an assortment of other Axis II diagnoses. Schizophrenia was an occasional diagnosis some carried, especially when their distorted cognitions became hallucinatory.

"But our focus has been on their well-being, not their diagnosis. We are interested in a prison population because we genuinely believe that a combination of Eumonia with therapy can be pivotal in helping many of these men turn their lives around, and we want to be part of that process. Our previous trials showed Eumonia to have a much greater impact on the lowering of agitation related to aggression than we expected. This factor could greatly benefit persons who have become criminally involved due to aggression. Obviously, from the commercial perspective, we must be fiscally successful for ourselves and our investors. This led us to consider the correctional area, and the more we evaluated that application, the better it appeared. In fact, Adams has made a significant investment for the past two years in the development of Eumonia, along with other medications that may assist in the management of behavior. Additionally, the entire field of correctional health is a central aspect of our strategic plan for the next five years.

"We are a young company and view ourselves a vital part of Providence's emerging biotechnology sector. Our strong interest in the correctional market is because the needs there are so great, which is why this project we are embarking on is of such importance to Adams. Our experience in working with correctional populations is limited; therefore, the expertise you bring to our group is critical."

Dr. Vos seems to be both reiterating a marketing pitch while simultaneously ingratiating himself to me, but his last phrase of my being part of his group sets off an alarm bell.

"Your work sounds both important and interesting, but my role will be to manage the unit for the Department of Corrections, not for Adams. I will not be part of the research group or team in any formal manner," I comment.

"Understood. But as a specialized treatment unit, we are all on the same team. We initially requested that we be able to administer all aspects of the unit, but corrections, and particularly Jim Dwyer at Cranston, stated that was not possible. Their opinion was that we simply did not have adequate correctional experience, and I now believe they are correct. It was our naivete. We did request that whoever they placed in charge of the unit was psychologically minded, so having an actual psychologist with correctional experience surpasses our expectations. That is what I meant, and I do hope you will have a professional interest in our work."

"I will need a working knowledge of the project to manage the facility effectively. As you said, we will all have to work together as a team—security, clinical, and in this case, research—for the unit to function properly."

"Absolutely," he agrees. "My experience is mainly in academic research. As I previously said, it was naivete on our part to think we had the skill set required to manage the entire thing, but we do want to learn."

I realize that I had entered the meeting with Vos from a defensive position, searching for ulterior motives to their endeavor and somewhat intimidated by their linkage to a major research/academic institution. One reason I spent ten years in corrections was that I was comfortable there. The rules, the male culture, even access to the gun range—it all appealed to me. The demeaning of others, the constant low-level threat of violence, the power dynamics were all things I could do without. But what Vos was saying I agreed with, and his immediate explanation of my role was refreshing. Unconsciously, I had been prepared for someone more condescending.

"If part of Adams's strategic plan is to explore opportunities in correctional health, then this will be a great opportunity for you to do that. But balancing the security and treatment concerns is not always easy. It is a prison, and part of my responsibility will be to ensure it remains a safe and secure environment."

"I may be an academic and more of a theoretician than a practical clinician, but I certainly recognize that safety and security are foundational for effective treatment. If you can help ensure for us that the hospital—or, rather, the facility—is safe and secure, it will greatly enhance our ability to do our work. I am aware you want to review the selection of clients criteria, our interventions, and a timetable. I have assembled our key staff to meet with you, but if you don't mind, I'd first like to introduce you to our CEO, Ralph Olken, and Senator Poletti's chief of staff, Anthony Vorenzi. They are in Dr. Olken's office, and in light of the importance of this project to both Adams and Senator Poletti's district, they asked to meet with you in advance of our sitting down with the others."

Olken's office is twice the size of Vos's, although Olken himself is barely half Vos's size. He is a short, lean man a year or two older than I am who is vaguely familiar. His receding hairline accents a slightly large, aquiline nose, making it appear more prominent than it is. When he rises from his desk, I judge him to be a few inches under the six feet that both Vos and I are. Rather than circle the desk, he leans across its polished glass top. His handshake is firm, and as I reach out, I notice a pair of flat-screen computer monitors fitted snugly beneath the glass. I expect with a flick of a switch, a small motor would whirr to life, raising them from the glass plane they sit beneath.

"Great desk," I say spontaneously. "I've never seen screens built into a desktop except on an evening news set."

"Ralph is very tech savvy, to say the least," Vos comments.

Olken shoots Vos a glance and then says, "In medical research, the latest technology is a necessity, Dr. Phillips. I'm sure you realize that."

His condescending tone is evident in the pause between his two sentences and the inflection he uses when stating, *I'm sure you realize that.*

While I am considering my response, it occurs to me why he is familiar. I've run against him in the past. I'm uncertain if it's been in a 10K or half marathon, but I always keep mental notes of the guys I tend to pack up with so I can use them for pacing in future races. Olken is in that group, and one thing I am certain of is that I will burn his ass the next time we meet on the pavement.

"Mr. Phillips," I hear from my right. Turning, I see a stocky man in his mid-to-late forties. Earlier I wondered if Vos had let himself go to seed a bit. We are near the same height, but he has me by an easy thirty pounds, although he carries the weight well. It is obvious that the new guy, with his hand outstretched, has fully gone to seed.

"Tony Vorenzi, Senator Poletti's chief of staff," he informs me. "The senator hoped to be here himself, but urgent business has come up. He asked me to convey to you how important this project is to him, the governor, and many others. We do hope we can rely on you to do all you can to make it successful."

He continues to grip my hand the entire time he is talking as if we're long-lost pals.

"As I explained to Dr. Vos a moment ago, my responsibility will be to oversee the safety and security of the unit. I don't expect to have direct involvement in the research, other than to ensure that the site at which it is conducted operates properly."

"Do you know why you were asked to take the position?" he asks.

"Jim Dwyer, the superintendent at Cranston, called me in and offered it to me. You'll have to ask him why."

"I have," Vorenzi continues. "He said you have a unique blend of correctional and mental health experience and that you were familiar with the institution. He said your wife died three years ago and that the man who drove the car that killed her was murdered at Cranston, and you resigned after those events. You told him you required some time to absorb all that had happened."

"Your point being?"

Before commenting further, Vorenzi pauses for apparent dramatic effect. "This is a critical project for our district and Rhode Island. If successful, Adams will be a cornerstone in the new Knowledge District that is being planned for the Woonasquatucket Watershed area. In light of that and your importance in this, we must be assured that you are up to the task."

"And I may not be because of?" I ask, unable to keep an edge from my voice.

It's Vos who responds. "I am not a clinician, Dr. Philips, but I do wonder if the prison may be linked to many bad associations for you related to your wife's death and the death of the driver who hit her."

"His name is Leon Alexander. The guy that was loaded when he killed her," I interject. "I expect you also know that I was held by the state police for a few days and questioned to see if I was complicit in any way."

"Yes," Olken replies pointedly. "You were totally exonerated, but nevertheless, you resigned from both the Department of Corrections and the National Guard. On a project of this magnitude, we have to be certain that all the key personnel are stable."

"I needed some time. I had a child to care for and a house to build on Block Island."

"But you didn't continue to work professionally, if I'm not mistaken," Olken presses.

"As I said, I needed some time."

"Where did you get the money to support yourself and build the house?" Vorenzi questions.

"I don't think that's any concern of yours," I shoot back, more visibly irritated. "If I am not mistaken, I've been hired by DOC, not Adams."

"We are covering your pay," Olken puts in.

"And you are being reimbursed for that," I clarify.

"We still have related administrative costs."

"Then you should request an adjustment from corrections."

"Please," Vos says in his most calming, professional tone. "Our goal is to not upset you, Dr. Phillips, but to impress upon you the importance of this study."

"I realize I'm not your first choice to run this unit. In fact, I'm not your choice at all; I'm Jim Dwyer's choice. If you have issues with that, ask corrections to find someone besides me."

Then, turning to Vorenzi, I continue, "You're familiar with how the state system works better than any of us. Have your boss tell the DOC commissioner you want to select the person in charge of the unit."

"Senator Poletti would never meddle in such a matter," he replies, but before I protest such an obvious lie, Olken speaks up.

"The fact is, Dr. Phillips, that you are correct. We did want to rigorously question you on why you accepted this position, and we have investigated your background. We were uncertain as to what your motivations were to take the position, but your answers have been fully explanatory. As I understand it, you wish to return to your profession and that an opportunity unexpectedly arose via this project. Additionally, you had the chance to do a former colleague a favor as well as work in a familiar environment while continuing to maintain your primary residence on Block Island. That makes complete sense to me. Please excuse us if our questions were at all upsetting to you."

I study Olken, who is leaning forward, elbows resting on the field of glass, which reflects the underside of his face. The condescending tone is not so readily apparent, but I still plan to bury him the next time I see him on the blacktop. My ambivalence about the position has disappeared; now I want it.

"My job is to have that unit operate smoothly, and that's what I plan to do. If your research ever interferes with that, the safety and security of both the staff and inmates will take precedence. I may be paid out of Adams, but I report to Jim Dwyer, not to you or anyone else in your company. Professionally, I am interested in the project and agree with Adams's focus on measures of well-being, but my responsibilities are first safety and security. For me, the clinical and research goals are secondary. If that's a problem for you, then you should request someone else."

I try to keep the condescending tone out of my voice but can't manage to do so any better than Olken could.

"I believe what you are offering is exactly what we require." Vos mediates. "As the primary investigator of the trial and Adams's medical director, I believe what you offer complements what we can provide. As I already mentioned, it was with some naivete that we made the offer to manage the entire facility. That may be in our eventual future, but our current need is to have access to an inmate population in a safe and secure treatment environment. Perhaps I should now introduce Dr. Phillips to the others involved in the project and get him registered with HR."

Olken rises from his chair and extends his arm to me for a second time as we prepare to exit.

On the way out the door, I notice a framed Boston Marathon number on the wall. I can tell it's a vanity number, one of a thousand or so given to runners who race for various charities. Turning back, I say, "Did you run Boston?"

"Three years ago," Olken responds.

"What was your time?"

"Three hours and fifty-six minutes. Have you ever run it?"

"Someday, maybe. The nearest I've come to date are a couple of half marathons in the ninety-minute range. We'll see."

"Possibly you and Ralph can go running together sometime," Vos offers when we're out in the corridor.

"Possibly," I agree, knowing it will never happen. I was under seven minutes a mile for thirteen with gas still in the tank. Olken was over nine for twenty-six miles. You have to be in the seven-and-a-half range to qualify for a regular number. I'm near the mark, and he isn't.

4

Driving back to Cranston, I replay the conversation with Olken, Vorenzi, and Vos in my mind. The subsequent meeting with the social workers and research assistants on the project went smoothly. The main issue requiring resolution is related to subject selection, but I am sure we can figure it out. The IRB proposal stressed that participation was voluntary, and individuals must meet various criteria related to their mental health, aggression history, and behavior. It made no mention of security levels, the possibility that two participants may be enemies or in opposing gangs, and other correctional issues. I was relieved that they easily grasped that such concerns were valid when I brought them to their attention. I had already reviewed their interview protocols, measures, and data collection plan, including their means of securing the data, and saw that they were well designed. It was how Olken and Vorenzi, along with Vos to a lesser degree, envisioned this as fitting into an elaborate plan, linking the revitalization of Providence to the success of Adams Pharmaceuticals, that made me uncomfortable. Their ideas were rather grandiose and premised on a foreordained successful outcome. I let thoughts sift through my mind as I weave my way along back roads toward the prison.

The super not only had the warden's house swept out but also gave it a fresh coat of paint in preparation for my arrival. There are eight spacious rooms, but I tell him I'll keep my use to the two on the first floor and the kitchen, which is the most recently renovated room in the house.

"It makes no difference, TC; you can use the whole place," he informs me as we tour the building. "Why don't you cart in some of your own furniture to make it homier? Everything in here is trash: leftover state issue or junk the last people who used the place left behind. One oddity is that there are no showers. The bathrooms haven't been updated since it was built, so you'll literally have to run a bath and sit in one of those antique claw-footed tubs to clean up."

"I may join a health club, and then I'll be able to shower there. I plan to get back into working out as well as keep up with the running. I may even take a shot at a marathon next year."

"What do you think of the mods?" he asks after we finish the tour.

"They sure as hell were put up fast," I remark.

"It's no more complicated than connecting LEGOs. There was a week of site prep and another week to drop them into position and bolt them together. The plumbing and electrical are embedded in the walls. We'll have the power on and the perimeter fence done by the end of next week. We also plan to place a small prefab on the outside of the wall for the entrance. We'll be in business in no time."

I laugh. "All we need now are some customers." Then, becoming serious, I ask Jim how he managed to get the modulars up so quickly.

"Poletti. The contract wasn't put out to bid because of some emergency clause. Undoubtedly, it's the fastest I've ever seen the state build anything. Plus, they're doing a good job."

"I met his chief of staff earlier today."

"Tony Vorenzi. He's been with him for years. I never had to deal with him before this. He's the one who makes things happen. He worked for Buddy Cianci during his first term as Providence's mayor in the late '70s but wasn't there in the second term when Buddy was indicted and put away."

"He didn't look that old to me."

"Midfifties easy, maybe older. He's connected to everyone."

"How connected?" I ask sarcastically, and Jim laughs, clearly reading my meaning. Providence is notorious as the home of the Patriarca crime family. Buddy Cianci was convicted for racketeering and extortion a few years back, and you'd be hard pressed to find anyone who didn't think the Mafia was involved. You'd be equally hard pressed to find anyone who was all that upset about it. The Patriarcas are Rhode Island's favorite gangsters. People take pride in Providence being big enough to have its own crime family. The closest thing we have to a professional sports team is the Pawtucket Sox, so having our own branch of the Mafia is kind of cool.

"Hopefully, those days are long gone. They are seriously focused on re-habbing those buildings on the Woonasquatucket. If they have some sweet-heart deal on the side, who's to say?"

"He and the president of Adams did some research on me. They were aware of Maura, Alexander, and the state police questioning me."

"I know. They quizzed me on those things too. I told them to ask you di-rectly. In the end, TC, it's all about money. If this works, they'll be marketing their drugs to corrections as means to help cons deal with aggression, which translates into a management tool for most administrators. And if they make the unit work, they'll set up some type of correctional-health-management division."

"Yeah, it's *Follow the money*. They already told me correctional manage-ment was part of their strategic plan. But I'm not here to help them make money; I'm here to make sure this unit runs properly, right?"

"As far as I'm concerned, that's why you're here. This is my joint, and that will be your unit. Have you and Lincoln started to identify sergeants?"

"He has, and we'll review the list tomorrow."

"Excellent. I can assign the sergeants, but by union rules, we have to put the line officers out for bid. Try to get job descriptions posted ASAP. The announcement has to be up for two weeks as part of the bidding process. I'll make assignments as soon as I can, and then you can begin training."

"That won't be a problem. We'll have it done by the end of tomorrow."

"*You'll* have it done, TC. Remember, Lincoln is your deputy, not the co-director. You're the one responsible, so when I need something, I'll be knock-ing on your door."

"No problem. I'll have job descriptions and the names of the three ser-geants we want tomorrow. On a completely different topic, I'm heading out to a grocery store later. Is it okay for me to pick up a six-pack of Sam Adams? I realize the warden's house is state property, but if I decide to have a beer after work, is that an issue?"

"Not for me. I expect whoever previously lived in those buildings drank. I'll double check, but I'm sure it will be fine. Anything else?"

"Not now. I'll see you by the end of tomorrow with the job posting and sergeants' list."

5

"Dad, when are you getting home?"

"I'll be there in a few days, Matt."

"But you've been gone so long," he whines.

Glancing around, I am completely unfamiliar with my surroundings and flinch at the blast of a horn. I am in the middle of traffic. Cars are whizzing past on either side of me. I have to get out of here, I decide, searching for a break in the flow. Briefly, the vehicles thin out, and I make a dash for the sidewalk but don't make it. A pickup is bearing down on me, and I leap from the ground, careening off the windshield. Tumbling through the air, I think, *I'm going to need a doctor—no, a nurse!*

I awake tangled in my sheets, vaguely hoping that the nurse will be Maura.

I spoke to Matt and my mom a few hours before I went to bed, but he never asked me when I would be home. He didn't seem particularly bothered that I was away, only taking the phone at my mother's insistence that "Daddy wants to talk to you." It didn't upset me due to his age. I wasn't expecting more, but more would have been nice.

The city in my dream was New York or some other metropolitan area. It made sense in the dream was that I was hit by a pickup like Maura was. That may have been due to my being at Cranston, where Leon Alexander was incarcerated and eventually murdered. He was stabbed within shouting distance from where I was sleeping, behind the walls in the protective custody unit. I had blocked out memories of that day until Olken, Vorenzi, and Vos questioned me, but it must have been lurking in my unconscious, waiting for an opportune time to appear.

I stumble down to the kitchen and see the microwave clock glowing 2:45 a.m. If I had bought that pint of whiskey, this would be the time to take a slug. But I didn't. When I had stopped by the liquor store, the girl's words from a few weeks back still resonated in my mind—*The usual, TC?*—as I reached the counter. The bottle of carbonated spring water is a poor replacement for Old Forester, but I take a long swallow and then head back to bed.

Lincoln and I quickly agree on the sergeants, and I complete the job posting the next morning. I have no question several officers, particularly among the Black staff, will bid on the posts because Lincoln is the senior lieutenant. I'm also hopeful we'll pick up a few guys who are in the National Guard. I know most of them from the times when my former health-service unit conducted joint exercises with the infantry.

The referral procedure is more convoluted, but we are able to work it out by the end of the week. Inmates will be identified and initially approached by a prison mental health staff person, who will provide them with literature about the study/unit. They will have a follow-up meeting a few days later, and if the inmate is interested, they will be referred to the program. They will then be interviewed by Dr. Vos or Andrea Boden, a psychiatrist who has worked with Vos on the previous trials. She is to be the senior Adams clinician and have some on-site responsibility for the mental health services. In the process of working out the details, I realize the program must have a name. It will quickly acquire one from the inmates, the way they refer to the Rhode Island State Hospital as "the Bug House" and to a trip there as being "tuned up" or "debugged." Rather than having it labeled by the cons—which it will be, regardless of whatever we do—it is better if we first give it a name.

"Do you have any ideas for a name?" Vos asks me after I explain why one is required.

"Why don't you ask Dr. Olken and the people at your office?" I suggest. "I expect the superintendent will agree to most anything. If it gets done sooner rather than later, then Cranston clinical staff can use it when they solicit referrals. Plus, it should be on any literature or forms that get printed.”

The next day Vos tells me about the rationale for the name that Olken recommended for the program. “We believe the Adams Pharmaceuticals Integrated Treatment Program explains the overall mission of what we are trying to do here,” he concludes. Yet I am already chuckling as he completes the final sentence.

“I don’t think that’s a go, Alain,” I say while composing myself. “The inmates will give us a name within the first few weeks if they haven’t already, and I don’t intend to give them any free ammunition. How long do you expect it will take for the Adams Pharmaceuticals Integrated Treatment Program to be shortened to A-P-I-T?”

“A-P-I-T?” he repeats quizzically, spelling it out as I did.

“Right,” I say. “A pit, as in a hole in the ground or a dump. You guys need to go back to the drawing boards on the name.”

“I hadn’t considered the acronym.” And he laughs despite himself. “What would you call it?”

“I’d keep it simple. I’m partial to nautical symbols. When I was here full time, I started a program to train inmates to be medical assistants in the hospital and called it MAST, the Medical Assistant Training Program.”

“That has a nice ring to it,” he replies. “Is it still operating?”

“It was, up until one of my graduates became the leading suspect in the murder of the guy that drove the pickup into my wife. That’s why the state police were so interested in questioning me.”

“I’m sorry; I was unfamiliar with those details. What happened to the man?”

“Fahad Milton. He’s listed as Jonathan Milton in the DOC records, but he converted to Islam some years back and changed his name to Fahad. The department doesn’t recognize name changes, even if an inmate files papers to do it formally. The name they have when they get booked in is the name they have when they serve their time. He’s still here, but the program was discontinued."

"Do you believe he was the killer?"

I hesitate momentarily. During the two weeks I have been working with Alain, I have grown to respect him. His initial, rather rote presentations on the benefits of Eumonia and Adams's grand plans have disappeared. Outside of their offices, he has become more human and adapted with ease to the correctional environment. He remains more of an academic than a clinician, but his heart is in the right place.

"You're the researcher. What happens when the data contradicts your hypothesis?"

"You must listen to the results, revising any hypothesis or preconceived ideas accordingly."

"Right. And all the circumstantial evidence points to Fahad as the murderer, but there is no smoking gun, so to speak. From a research perspective, I'd say his culpability was at the .10 level, yet there can be Type 1 errors. In this situation there's a 90 percent probability Fahad did it, but I hope that's a false positive. He was one of my star students. Therefore, if he did do it, it was likely as a favor to me. That's how the state police saw it, except they concluded that if he did it, I must have been the mastermind. They reasoned that most prisoners aren't that smart, so I had to be involved. The flaw in their logic was that Fahad is unusually bright, way at the far tail of the IQ curve for prisoners—or anyone else for that matter."

"That must have been an awful situation for you to be in."

"It wasn't fun, but at least it didn't unfold until sometime after my wife's death. I forget the exact timetable, but Alexander was murdered roughly two to three months after the crash."

"What happened to Fahad?"

"No charges were ever filed, but DOC moved him from medium- to high-security status, placing him in the max building. Not many people around here, staff or cons, were that upset. In fact, many, if not most, were happy Alexander was dead. This is a different culture. From the staff perspective, Alexander got what he deserved. From an inmate perspective, a high-status inmate, Fahad, killed a low-status guy and won the appreciation of the jailers. It was too weird for me, too many conflicting emotions, so I resigned."

"Why did you return?"

"Jim Dwyer called me. I came back first as a favor to him, but I wasn't doing a lot on Block Island anyway. Idle hands are the devil's workshop and all that. It was time for me to get back to work. It was an ambivalent decision, but now I'm glad I made it. This is an interesting project."

"I, for one, am glad you are here. The hands-on perspective is certainly different than it is from an ivory tower."

"It certainly is," I repeat, drawing out the word *certainly*. I had noted how often Vos used it to make a point and had kidded him about it a few times.

We both laugh, and then he asks if I have any nautical ideas for a program name, agreeing that the Adams Pharmaceuticals Integrated Treatment Program doesn't make it.

"Nothing comes to my mind nautically. The best thing is to keep it simple. If the idea is to provide guys with an 'alternatives to aggression' program, call it the Alternatives to Aggression program, ATA."

"How about the Adams Pharmaceuticals Alternatives to Aggression program?"

"You'll have to lose the Adams part. It sounds too much like an ad, and DOC would veto that. Plus, if it doesn't work out, your name will be linked to a failed project."

"Those are excellent points. I'll bring them back to the office. ATA is simple. I think it will work well."

We return to our focus on the referral process but immediately hit a sticking point. The model Adams proposes calls for admissions to be made in three groups of ten, with the full count being thirty. "We have planned for each group to be in all the same treatment interventions together, to participate in the program as a class," Vos explains.

I had read this in their write-up but didn't reflect on it until now. "It won't happen. Besides there being glitches that will turn up in the admission process, it's not viable from a security perspective. The officers on the unit require a day or two to monitor each new man to see how he fits in. We may be able to bring in an initial group of ten, but after that, it will be a rolling admission."

To Vos's protest that it will alter the study design, I remind him it's a prison, and security is the first priority. Nonetheless, to assuage his concerns, I tell him I will bring it up with the super.

Later in the day, when I discuss progress with Jim, he agrees that the rolling admission is better for security reasons. He's willing to make an exception for the first ten guys in but not beyond that. "After them, let's restrict it to no more than five or six admits a week. That will allow your count to be at full capacity by week four."

"What if we don't get enough referrals to fill the place? In the end we don't have a lot of incentives."

"I've been considering that too," he says. "Referrals won't be a problem; it's getting inmates to accept being there where the problems will arise. Any guy that has a single will never give it up to live in a two-person room. You will need more perks than a specialized program to reel them in. We can't use the classification board to mandate participation. For the initial study, it has to be voluntary. If it is successful and continues as an ongoing program, we can then classify people into it."

I am taken by Jim's fishing metaphor: you need the right bait for the right fish. "Can we make enhanced family contact part of the program by giving participants an extra visit per week as well as more phone time? We can even build in some type of family therapy. If you give us a green light on conjugal, we could load it up in a heartbeat."

"Girlfriends or wives in for the night is a no-go, but allowing more contact than the peck on the cheek that the other cons get is a possibility. I can see that, as long as guys aren't groping the hell out of their women. We'll begin at one visiting day per week like the rest of the joint but make it four hours rather than two. Later we can move it up to twice a week, plus the therapy visit."

"That will be good, but seriously, what's wrong with conjugal? We're only accepting guys within two years of wrapping up or parole, we have a separate entrance that's been cut into the wall, and we could set up a trailer outside that's linked to our outer control building. It may help keep down some of the weird sexual stuff that goes on. After all, we're not running a monastery here. What if we made conjugal part of a second phase that guys are eligible for once they successfully completed their first six months?"

"Let's kick that one down the road. I'll run it past the commissioner, and we can take it from there," Jim decides.

"What about after Adams leaves?" I ask. It's a question that's been lingering in my mind. Initially, I had put the question out of my mind, believing I'd be gone in six months, but now I am becoming more invested in the project and curious about what will happen once the research ends.

"The DOC agreement with Adams is for them to be in here for up to a year to conduct the study," he explains. "I expect they are hoping the findings will be so positive that by the end of the year the department will contract with them to operate the unit. You remember that's what they initially requested. As I see it, they are both angling to get approval for their new medication and to tout the unit's success as the cornerstone of a correctional healthcare division, and Poletti wants it all to work as the cornerstone for the Woonasquatucket revitalization. For now, what will happen after this year is an open question. But I expect when the time comes, the decisions on that one will be made at the commissioner level and above."

CHAPTER 2

1

Monday, May 1, 2007, is the official ribbon-cutting ceremony for the Rhode Island Department of Corrections new Alternatives to Aggression program. The press release I am holding reads, "This innovative project, assisting men to better manage aggression, is a joint venture between Adams Pharmaceuticals and the Department of Corrections. It represents Rhode Island's commitment in fostering public/private sector partnerships to address even the most difficult of problems."

Poletti is there. In his brief speech, he reiterates the importance of joint public and private ventures. "This collaboration brings the insight and knowledge of Adams Pharmaceuticals to bear on a significant social concern: the better management of aggression. The Alternatives to Aggression initiative is a research-based intervention. It is not innovation for the sake of innovation but a studied approach to a major social issue, bringing together the best aspects of the public and private sectors. It is the type of well-reasoned, evidence-based approach to problem solving that we wish to foster within Rhode Island's growing knowledge-based economy."

After he makes a few additional comments, we adjourn for refreshments. Poletti exited prior to the reception, but his chief of staff, Anthony Vorenzi, catches my eye and motions for me to join him. He is having a conversation with Jim and Ralph Olken, the president of Adams Pharmaceuticals.

"Good morning, Mr. Phillips," he begins as I near the group.

"It's Dr. Phillips," Jim corrects him as I shake his and Olken's outstretched hands.

"Yes, my apology, Dr. Phillips. I have been told that you are off to an effective start with the identification of men to participate in the program?" he says. His manner indicates it is a question.

"We've had a couple of glitches here and there, but nothing we can't work out. I expect the initial group of ten men will be entering within the next week or two. Our staff is in place, we complete our training program this week, and soon we'll be ready for business."

"Excellent! I believe that to solicit volunteers, you have recommended additional privileges, such as more family contact and perhaps even the possibility of conjugal visits?"

From the questioning glance that passes from Jim to me, I can tell that he was not the one who mentioned that to Vorenzi.

"Since this is a voluntary program, Dr. Phillips has conferred with me on ways to make participation attractive to inmates," Jim explains. "Any decision, such as conjugal visits, or other decisions of that magnitude, requires a commissioner-level policy review."

"Of course," Vorenzi agrees. "In fact, it was the commissioner who mentioned to me that the conjugal contact was one of the motivational…how shall we say…carrots that you were evaluating to insure there is participation."

"It's not simply a carrot," I interject, feeling slightly caught between Jim and Vorenzi. "All of the men in this program are eligible for release within the next two years, and it may help some participants reunite with families. Yet, as Superintendent Dwyer stated, this requires a major policy review, and we already have a variety of other motivational tools available to us."

Vorenzi nods as I speak. "We certainly understand and agree that all correctional protocols must be adhered to."

Olken then directs a question to me. "Dr. Boden has informed me that there has already been some difficulty in the recruitment process. Should we move to some enhanced forms of motivation at this time?"

"We have not had any recruitment difficulty, although we are proceeding cautiously to enroll a diverse population that is representative of the institution," I respond. "In addition to meeting your study criteria, we have to be certain that various security parameters are met. I have already explained this to both Drs. Vos and Boden. I do recognize they believe the recruitment process can be accelerated."

"This is a prison first and a research site second," Jim adds, unable to keep the edge from his voice.

"I am certain Dr. Olken has no desire to interfere with any of your security protocols, Superintendent Dwyer," Vorenzi says. "But we do become concerned when one of the Adams psychiatrists indicates there may be some difficulties in the recruitment. As you may have guessed from Senator Poletti's comments, the success of this is of the utmost importance to him. It is our desire to foster a stronger knowledge-based economy in Providence founded on public/private partnerships. If there are ways I can be of assistance, including asking the corrections commissioner to consider any motivational tools you may wish to deploy, don't hesitate to call the senator's office."

"I have a regular biweekly project meeting with Drs. Vos and Boden on Wednesdays at ten; why don't you join us if your schedule permits? We can then address concerns as they arise," Olken offers to me.

"I have been meeting with Dr. Vos regularly for the past four weeks, so I am not sure that's necessary," I reply.

"Yes, but once the study program is operational, Dr. Vos will be spending more time at our offices and attending to his academic responsibilities. Dr. Boden will be the senior Adams staff person here two or three days per week," Olken points out. "If you joined our biweekly meeting, it will enhance our overall communication."

I hadn't thought of Alain pulling back from the project. We had developed a respectful working relationship, yet in the short time I had worked with Boden, I had not found her all that user friendly. She was tight as a drum with an aloof, pompous quality to her presentation—rigidity without creativity, seasoned with an absence of self-awareness.

"If I came, I wouldn't be able to make any decisions that impacted upon security until I reviewed them with Superintendent Dwyer."

"And in a prison, that is practically all decisions," Jim puts in.

"Undoubtedly," Olken agrees. "It would not be to make decisions that affect security, but for communication in order to stay abreast of the data collection and the project as it relates to Adams."

I knew Olken was referring to a discussion I had with Boden a few days prior. She had requested to announce at the ribbon cutting that the first ten inmates to meet the study criteria had been selected, along with the day they were scheduled to enter the ATA. I nixed the idea, sensing something was wrong but unable to put my finger on it. The name that inmates had given to the program was "the Zebra House," reflecting that most of the officer staff in the unit are Black, and the majority of voluntary referrals are White. I told Boden I wanted the ATA population to represent the prison population, but she pushed to accept those who met the criteria.

"There is a higher documented incidence rate of mental illness among Caucasian incarcerated populations than African Americans or other racial groups," she explained. "Therefore, we should accept those who meet study criteria; otherwise, you are influencing our randomized design."

"Before I can approve that, I first need to understand the referral process better from a practical level," I responded.

"The referral procedure is quite clear," she countered. "All these men were referred by your own psychological service staff people or volunteered when they heard of the program, per our protocol. The individuals who volunteered were subsequently interviewed by me or Dr. Vos, and we accepted those that were appropriate, which were, in fact, all who were assessed. That they all are of European descent may be a simple artifact of the distribution of mental illness among racial groups and the greater acceptance of medication as a way to manage mental health concerns by Whites. This has all been documented by prior research. I do not believe the current subject selection process will interfere with the study design, whereas altering it may interfere."

I had presented my discomfort a day earlier to Alain, and he appeared okay with holding off on the opening of the unit, so her posturing both took me off guard and irritated me.

"Dr. Vos and I discussed this yesterday, and he appeared fine with the delay."

"Yes, he mentioned that to me when I expressed my concerns regarding the study design. Nevertheless, I would like us to announce a designated start date at the ribbon cutting to demonstrate our commitment to this project. Dr. Vos recommended I speak to you directly about this," she countered.

I told her I appreciated her concerns on the study design but that the ATA was not about to accept clients until I gave the green light, and I wasn't ready to do that yet. When she tried to mount an additional protest, I said I was expected at another meeting and left her in Adams's small office suite in the same modular that housed my office.

Standing now with Jim, Olken, and Vorenzi, I knew she had run to Big Daddy Ralph after we met to tell him her concerns. He was more diplomatic and took a tack of bringing me into the Adams fold with the invitation to the biweekly team meeting. I guessed she bypassed Alain when she contacted Olken. She wasn't to be trusted, and I became more uncomfortable with Olken's statement that she was to be the senior Adams person on site.

"After all, you really are an Adams staff person to some degree," Olken is saying as I return my focus to the conversation. "We hope that besides assisting corrections as a funding conduit for your consulting fees, you will begin to see yourself as part of the Adams group. Your grasp of the many nuts-and-bolts correctional issues is essential. As a group that is involved in basic research, we can sometimes be blind to real-world concerns. I want to reiterate Adams's commitment to see this project through and collaborate fully with corrections."

"And I'd like to reiterate Senator Poletti's promise to help foster that success in any manner possible," Vorenzi adds.

Jim glances at me and then says, "Well, it appears we're all committed to make this successful."

"Yes, we are committed," Vorenzi agrees. "But what happens when Dr. Phillips is not here? If I'm not mistaken, you are commuting from Block Island, are you not?"

"Dr. Phillips spends three or four nights in one of the former staff lodgings outside the wall," Jim answers quickly, masking his irritation. Like me, he probably thought the conversation was concluded a moment earlier. "We have coverage rotations, and I have assigned one of my senior lieutenants to be on site any day Dr. Phillips is off. I am also available by cell phone, as is Dr. Phillips. We can readily manage any concerns that arise on off hours."

Vorenzi nods at Jim's explanation. "Excellent. Yet I am sure you remember that when this project was initially developed, Adams Pharmaceuticals offered to assume the management of the facility as an initial step in developing expertise in the correctional management area. Clearly, it was the right decision to not pursue that at this time, although there may be a middle road. In light of Dr. Phillips's frequent absences, Dr. Olken wondered if Dr. Boden can be appointed the assistant director of the project."

"That should not interfere with any corrections operations but provide us with greater experience in the correctional management area," Olken adds. "Andrea is extremely bright and anxious to learn. I'm certain you'd enjoy collaborating with her, Thomas."

"This is neither the time nor place for us to be having this discussion," Jim interjects. "As I have already stated, this is a prison first and a research site second. Nonetheless, I will bring the idea up in my next meeting with the commissioner."

"Please do," Vorenzi replies.

Believing I had detected a slightly smug tone in Vorenzi's last words, as we walk away, I tell Jim that I expect either Vorenzi or Poletti had already spoken to the commissioner.

"We'll see, but in my shop, we do things my way," he replies.

2

I'm glad to have the two ferry rides between Block Island and the mainland each week. Since I bring my car, I cannot take the high-speed boat, but that is fine by me. I prefer the hour-or-longer crossing to the thirty-minute one. Summer is approaching rapidly, and the ride over in the warming sun helps me shake off my hangover. Jim called me to his office the day after the ribbon cutting.

"You were right, TC. Poletti got to the commissioner with a request to make that Dr. Boden the assistant director of the ATA. He realizes it's absurd; in fact, he wasn't all that pleased I brought you in. He wanted a DOC employee in charge."

"So did he tell Poletti that?"

"No. He made nice. He'd never give a non-DOC group that much control of a new program in a DOC facility, but we need to make nice, to throw them some type of bone."

"What's that supposed to mean? We've got enough on our hands getting this launched. Right now, inmates are calling it the Zebra House because the cons that signed up are all White, and most of the staff is Black. Lincoln has tried to drum up more volunteers, but most guys just shrug their shoulders."

"I know. Once Mario Zorello signed up, you picked up all the eligible gangsters and the wannabes. The word in the camp is that it's a gangster program. You have to get some of the serious Black or Spanish guys in there, or at a minimum have them give it their blessing."

"That was Lincoln's and my take too," I agreed. "I'm surprised Mario is short enough to be eligible."

"He's only doing a five-year state bit for fencing stolen property. The feds tried to get him to roll over on some of the Patriarca family, but they couldn't, and they couldn't find anyone to implicate him on federal charges. He actually got a stiff sentence for stolen property, but he'll be out in eighteen months."

"When I was here, he never signed up for psych services; none of the organized crime guys did. They're similar to the Asians: they do their time and stay below the radar."

"Then they all get out and go back to doing what they were doing before they came in," Jim said.

"Well, I guess the Zebra House is better than the Mafia House. I'll keep reviewing potential referrals with Lincoln to see if we can get some additional diversity in there. But how do you plan to make nice with Boden and Adams?"

"It's more how do *you* plan to make nice. There is no way either the commissioner or I will agree to her as the assistant director. But what if we call her the medical director? She gets a formal title, Adams can learn more about corrections, and I'll sideline her on the organizational chart. The clinicians can report to her, but that's it for authority, and I'll include her once a month in our regular supervision time. The real responsibility to operate the unit will continue to go from me to you to Lincoln."

"I can live with that as long as she realizes who has what authority," I consented. "It's pretty much as I already saw it anyway. The clinicians will report to her, and when I'm not on site, Lincoln remains the go-to guy for everyone else. Go ahead; call her the medical director if it will make them happy and get Poletti off the commissioner's back. Whatever floats your boat."

"You'll also have to go to those meetings Olken mentioned."

"That's fine. For the program to be successful, we do have to develop an ongoing working relationship. He is right on that one. What bugs me is how we appear to be but one small cog in some grand plan that Olken, Poletti, and whoever else has to revitalize Providence. I worry they want to make it work a little too much."

"Which is another reason why you should be there," Jim pointed out.

I agreed with Jim's plan, but it still nagged at me that Adams and Poletti pressured us. We're approaching the starting blocks, and they have already declared Adams the winner of the race. When I stopped at the liquor store that evening to grab a six-pack, the girl's inquiry—*The usual, TC?*—was still there, but I overrode it, snatching a pint of Old Forester off the shelf. At least I didn't pick up a quart, I told myself in some type of twisted logic. I ended up passed out watching TV.

Waking up at 5:00 a.m., I stumbled into bed and then missed the early ferry back to the island. I'd have missed the noon ferry, too, if it hadn't been for the racket an inmate crew was making outside the house cutting the lawn. After waking, I splashed a little water on my face, tossed a few things into a duffel, and shot down to Point Judith to catch the noontime transit.

The early afternoon sun has baked most of the alcohol out of me by the time the north end of the island comes into view. After the first whistle blows, I hesitate before descending to the car deck. Passing the outer breakwater, I can identify the majority of the boats already out on moorings. Most islanders have theirs in by Memorial Day or mid-June at the latest, whereas many of the summer people don't get theirs in until July. I can see Woody Kent's twenty-foot Whaler, *Kathy's Klown*, riding high on the light swells that are rolling through the harbor. Its twin Mercury 125s raise the bow against the encroaching tide. I am comforted knowing the next couple of days will find us out chasing blues in Block Island Sound once or twice.

After a brief stop at Izzy's, I swing by my house on the way to picking Matt up at my mother's. I open a couple of casements and then check the liquor supply, automatically making a mental note that I'm out of whiskey. Part of me recognizes it as a bad sign, so I call my mom and ask her if she can watch Matt until five o'clock. I need a run to stomp out the urge.

For the first three weeks at Cranston, I had an excellent conditioning routine, getting in a seven-to-ten-mile training run each morning with strength and speed conditioning at the health club, but for the past two weeks, I've been slipping. Besides relying on the sun to burn the booze out of me, I had to sweat some out. I decide on a ten-mile course that will take me out past the Southeast Light on a coastal route that will loop back to the ferry landing and finally up past the airport and Dodge Cemetery on the return to my house. It takes a long mile for me to get my body into rhythm, but then I switch onto automatic pilot at a seven-minute-a-mile pace. It settles me down as the miles tick by. I push up the small grade leading into Dodge Cemetery, making my way over to the grave site where Maura and my dad are buried. I can tell my mother has been by recently—pansies are planted by the base of the marker, and any debris has been removed.

"Three years, three goddamn years," I say to the dark, unresponsive granite. A few mere feet beneath me are the skeletal remains of my wife and father, but they are silent. There is a slight rustle and clatter as a light breeze lifting off the water sets the branches of a nearby tree trembling. Glancing back to the stone, I see some purple and yellow crocuses mixed in among the pansies, and by adjacent graves, daffodils, tulips, and narcissi are also poking through the earth. *Spring is here*, I think while dropping the pace to six-thirties for the final mile and a half to my house.

As always, my mother is happy to see me, although Matt doesn't act so thrilled. He gives me a big hug followed by "Daddy, Daddy, Daddy," and that's about it before he returns to navigating a toy fire truck across the floor. I had picked up two cod filets at the harbor and grill them up with rice for dinner.

"We always eat the best when Daddy's here, don't we, Mattie?" my mom says as we sit down.

"Nana doesn't like to cook, Daddy," Matt announces.

"I figured that one out a while ago, honey. But she's still the best nana in the world!"

"Can we stay with Nana tonight?"

I'm amazed at his fluency. It seems to have changed within the past week. I'm unsure how to reply, but my mom interjects, "No, sweetie, you should go home with Daddy to sleep in your own big bed. You still have the baby bed here."

"That's okay, Nana. I like the baby bed."

This time I respond before my mom. "We have to ask Nana if she doesn't mind. She may have to work at the health center tomorrow. But if she says it's fine, we can stay here."

My mother is looking to me for a clue, and I mouth, "We can stay." She then says she doesn't have to work the next day and asks us to spend the night.

Once Matt is asleep, I drive back to my place for pajamas. My mom has made a pot of tea by the time I get back. Passingly, I have an urge for a shot of whiskey but then attempt to banish the desire as best I can.

"I saw you already put some pansies in at the grave," I observe.

"They're biennials. I mulched them with marsh grass for the winter and took it off last month. Are they blooming already?"

"Yeah, and a couple of crocuses are too. What do you think, Ma? Should I come back to the island? Matt didn't even want to leave here for my place."

"He will tomorrow; you'll see. Are you worried about him, or is it the job? It must be hard to go back there after all you've endured with prisons."

"It was hard the first couple of days, the first week, but then it was almost as if I never left. I stopped down to the range, and when I picked up a weapon, the officer asked where I had been. For all he knew, I hadn't been down because I had been assigned to another part of the institution. So I told him I'd been busy, and that was it."

"Are you glad you're there? It's approaching six weeks, isn't it?"

"It's interesting. I've never had to pay so much attention to security protocols. I'm sort of the superintendent of this miniprison or treatment unit. I used to take all the security issues for granted, seeing most of it as overkill. A lot of it is, but when it becomes routinized, there is less room for error."

"What do you mean, 'routinized'?"

"For example, if I show up without my official DOC ID, they won't let me in, period. Everyone knows me, but they still have to call my supervisor to have him approve it. If a visitor shows up without a photo ID, they can't get in. There are no exceptions. It's a machine, and when the security runs smoothly, it allows the entire institution to run smoothly."

"It sounds like overkill to me."

"Sometimes it is, but it keeps things safe, and that's a big concern in a jail."

"Safe and dehumanized," she concludes.

I catch myself from responding reflexively in a defensive manner but realize she is right. Camp Delta at Guantanamo, where I was assigned as part of a National Guard deployment a few years ago, was the safest yet most dehumanizing institution I have ever been in.

"You're right about it being dehumanizing, and I guess you could go as far as to say it conditions many inmates to act even more pathological when they are released than when they go in. You lock people in a crazy, potentially violent, hypercontrolled environment for a few years and then expect they will act normally when they get out—what do you think will happen?"

Now the urge for a drink is back, and I excuse myself to grab a beer from the fridge. "Do you have any beer around, Ma?" I call out, seeing the refrigerator is empty.

"Check the bottom cupboard," she replies, and I find three cans of light beer. I hate warm beer, I hate light beer, and I hate beer out of a can, but I pop the top on one anyway and head back to the living room.

"What if Matt doesn't attach to me?" I ask. "You're spending more time with him than I am."

"You're being crazy, TC. He's already attached. You'll see tomorrow. He'll be stuck on you like glue. Something else is bothering you. You're not meant to be a prison warden or superintendent or whatever they call it. It's not you. You know that."

I do know it. I first took the position as a favor to Jim and then to get back into my profession by managing a demonstration treatment program, not to break into the DOC administration. I told my mother that Adams now asked me to participate more in meetings at their offices, but I resented the patronizing attitude of their CEO and how the results of the study were somewhat foreordained in their minds.

"That's not surprising," she responds. "Having already completed a series of preliminary trials, I expect they've allotted millions of dollars of investor funds to the project. They would never move forward with a prison study unless they expected it to succeed. They may be jumping the gun on planning to enter the correctional-health-management field, but if that's their long-term business objective, use it to your advantage. Don't interpret it as if they're trying to co-opt you by asking you to participate in their staff meeting, but rather, see it as them trying to learn from your expertise."

"That's what their president, Ralph Olken, says, but the way he says it bugs me. And it's clear that Poletti's chief of staff sees me as an inconvenience who doesn't display the proper awe of all the powerful people he's connected to. The whole thing rubs me the wrong way."

She sighs. "Listen to yourself, dear. If they rub you the wrong way, then show them what you can do. Maybe you're still a little depressed."

I finish off the rest of the lukewarm swill in my hand rather than respond.

"It's been a grueling few years for you. I'm glad you're back to work. You were busy out here with the house, working with Izzy, helping Woody on the charter service, but for the past six months…"

She doesn't have to say more. I let her words trail off into oblivion as I consider a second warm beer to avoid their meaning. I try to fool myself into thinking how refreshing a cool frosty would be but can't. It's warm piss, with alcohol's numbing effect its single redeeming feature.

3

My mother's assessment of Matt rapidly adjusting to my being home is accurate. I need a crowbar to pry him away from me the next day, and even then, I'm not successful. He insists on running with me in the afternoon, so I have to dust off the jogging stroller, and we do eight miles on back roads. That night Woody Kent stops by so we can plan a fishing trip for the next day. It is a good excuse to drink for a couple of hours, as the maximum time it takes either of us to plan a fishing trip is five minutes. My gear is always clean, my reels oiled, and my tackle box stowed in the entry. My mother will be home by 2:30 p.m. to watch Matt, which works out perfectly on the tide. We'll head out on a slack high tide to fish for blues that often congregate on sandbars halfway between the island and the mainland. Somehow Matt is aware that a fishing trip doesn't include him. Woody and I took him out in the *Klown* two weeks earlier, and I could tell the rumble of the twin Mercs unsettled him, but that wasn't the only reason. When Uncle Woody comes by, Matt must sense that aspects of our thirty-year friendship don't include him.

My mother is able to get out early and arrives home by two o'clock, so I call Woody to let him know I am ready. He tells me he figured I would be and is already bringing the boat into the town pier to gas up. Thirty minutes later, we're making our way beyond the inner harbor's last five-miles-per-hour sign. As soon as we pass the outer breakwater, Woody pulls back on the throttle control, and the Whaler surges to life as all 250 horses kick in. The briny salt spray pulses around the craft and over the bridge each time we slam into a small wave. Woody's a former Coastie who loves the sea, like me and almost every other guy we grew up with. We decided on blues the night before, but he still screams, "Blues?" above the engines' din as we clear the breakwater.

"Good by me," I call back. "Blues or stripers. I've got gear for both. Beer?"

He nods, and I go back to the cooler. While we're finishing the beer, Woody begins to power down.

"Close?" I ask.

"I'd say we're here," he replies.

There is a light chop with the mainland's distant shores to our north and west and Block Island to the south. The east holds the open waters of the Atlantic. It's a crisp May day, and the clean aroma of the ocean envelops us.

Occasional whitecaps snap atop the brilliant blue, only to disappear just as quickly.

"You planning to turn on the fish finder?"

"Are you a paying customer?" he responds. I laugh. As a rule, Woody and I don't use sonar unless it's with a charter client. We are bobbing along on the vast expanse of lapis when Woody announces that we are over a sandbar where baitfish tend to gather. I'm uncertain whether he triangulated off the distant horizons or noticed a slight surface disturbance or simply feels it in his bones, but I expect it is the latter. As the tide is drawn out in a few hours, the sea will begin to tremble in a long riff line that parallels the edge of the hidden sandbar.

"It never gets old," I say as we stand by the stern, preparing our lines.

"In winter, in the North Atlantic, it can get old," he responds, referring to his time on a Coast Guard buoy tender. "But I'll still give it to ya; these days don't get old. How's it working out on the mainland?"

"You know, same old, same old. I'm back here for three or four days each week. The first day I don't want to go back, but by the third or fourth, I'm ready to leave."

"The ocean may not get old, TC, but the island sure as hell can. You have the right balance happening with your feet in both worlds."

On cue, my cell goes off. "Apparently, someone from that other world is calling." I chuckle while checking the number on the display. It takes me a moment to register it as the super's mobile.

"It's my boss, so this may take a few minutes," I tell Woody as I sit down on the cooler. "You may as well start fishing."

"Hi, Jim," I say into the receiver.

"TC, are you on the island or in Providence?" Jim Dwyer immediately asks.

"Neither. I'm out on the sound, fishing. What's up?"

"We have a problem, and I need you here ASAP. I can send a state police helicopter out to the Block Island Airport. How long will it take you to get there?"

"The airport? I'm not sure exactly; I'd guess forty-five minutes. What's going on?"

I can tell from the tone in Jim's voice that it's serious, and Woody can tell the same from mine.

"We have a hostage situation."

"A hostage situation?" I mumble incredulously. "You have a hostage situation," I repeat more firmly. "Who's your lead negotiator?"

"We've been rotating it since you left. You're the most experienced guy we have. Can you get to that airport so I can send the chopper?"

"Wait a sec, Jim," I respond and then ask Woody how long it will take us to get to Point Judith.

"Twenty, twenty-five minutes max if I open her up,"

"I can be on the dock at Point Judith in under a half hour," I tell Jim.

"That's even better. I'll have Lincoln on the dock in a car with a state police escort to meet you."

"Hold on, Jim. Who was taken hostage and in what unit?"

"I have calls to make, TC. Lincoln will explain what happened when you get to Point Judith and then call me on my cell. But it was in your unit."

"My unit!" I exclaim, but it's into an empty receiver. Jim has clicked off.

"Point Judith," Woody calls to me from the small bridge.

I nod, still slightly in shock at Jim's last words that the hostage situation is in the ATA. We have yet to accepted inmates into the program, and we already have the most serious breach of security one can have in a prison—a hostage situation. It makes no sense. I try to talk to Woody, but it's impossible to hear anything as the *Klown* slashes and hydroplanes over the rolling surf on the way to the mainland.

Woody powers down as we enter the outer harbor but still keeps the Whaler significantly above the five-miles-per-hour speed limit. A line of flashing red-and-blue lights is strung out the length of the ferry pier.

"There's a hostage situation at the prison, and I used to be the lead negotiator. I still have more experience than anyone else they have there," I explain to Woody. "Tell my mom I'll call her as soon as I can, but I doubt I'll get back until tomorrow or the next day."

"You got it, TC. Anything else you need me to do?"

"Just run her in tight, and I'll jump from the bow," I reply as I clamor along the port side, flipping the safety bumpers down while making my way toward the front of the boat. There is a blue knot of state police by the squad cars, and I spy Lincoln among them. He breaks from the group and trots up to the dock area as Woody throttles down to skim past its edge.

"Thanks," I holler, leaping the two-foot gap between the boat and the dock's planking. I hear Woody slightly gun the engines as I land. Turning back, I see he is giving me a thumbs-up sign. I return the signal and begin to jog up to meet Lincoln, who had hesitated when he got halfway down the wharf. Unable to help myself, I begin to laugh at how unsteady Lincoln is on his feet. The wake from Woody's approach has set the dock swaying, and he has no sea legs.

"Need a hand there, buddy?" I ask, drawing close.

He laughs warmly. "Only if this was all we had to worry about, Cap," he says, using my National Guard moniker.

We make our way up to the pier, where three state policemen and two cruisers are waiting next to a pair of DOC cars and a couple of locals. "Decent fishing?" one of the cops asks.

"Never had a chance to find out," I reply, feeling incongruent in my fluorescent-yellow foul-weather gear and BC baseball cap, compared to their impeccable dress. Nonetheless, I was pleased the statie, true angler that he must be, asked the most important question first: *Decent fishing?*

"Too bad," the cop replies. "Looks like you're getting an express escort to jail—Do not pass Go. Do not collect two hundred dollars."

I smile, his good humor calming the rough sea within. "How long will it take?"

"Twenty minutes, and we should be there, sir," another cop replies to me.

"Well take 108 to 112 to 95; the locals will have all the major intersections blocked off for us, but it's still a good thirty miles."

"Let's do it," I say. Lincoln circles to the driver's side of the DOC vehicle, and I make for the passenger's.

"What happened?" I ask Lincoln as soon as we begin down the pier.

He has to almost yell his reply due to the state police cranking their sirens to full volume as soon as we roll onto the pavement and begin to scream out of Point Judith.

"Antonio Lopez took a hostage in the ATA."

"Lopez? What was Lopez doing there? He's a sex offender. Was he on a work detail or something?"

"Boden called for him."

"Boden brought Antonio Lopez onto the new unit?" I ask, totally puzzled.

"It gets better, TC; Boden's the hostage."

"Jesus H. Christ." I sigh, partly to myself but loud enough for Lincoln to hear, as the siren's blare has been dampened by our speed and the space between each vehicle. "Sorry about that, LT. Why don't you take it from the top for me?"

"No problem, Cap. We can always use a little help from the Lord in this type of situation. As best as we can make out of it, Boden requested a list of inmates who were eligible for the ATA from psych services this morning. She told them she was interested in diversifying the participants to more accurately reflect the prison population and asked them to identify the Black or Spanish guys who were within two years of release and had a history of aggression."

"Lopez is a Cape Verdean sex offender; how did he get picked?" I interrupt.

"The Cape Verdeans probably got lumped in with Blacks, and technically, he's not a sex offender. It was a rape that got reduced to indecent A&B, and he eventually pleaded out to simple assault and battery. We know he's a skinner, but everyone else doesn't."

"Psych services should have known it."

"They should have, but they didn't. At least the one who gave Boden the records to review didn't know. Anyway, Boden reviewed the records and then had Lopez brought over right as the second shift came on. He was signed in by the gate officer at two-fifty-five."

Checking my watch, I do a rapid calculation. "That's less than an hour ago."

"Right. I was doing a walk-through a little after three and saw that there was no sight line into her room. It would have been better if those office doors were ordered with larger panels. She was able to block the whole thing with only one or two sheets of paper, so I knocked on the door to tell her to take down the paper, but there was no answer. Then I tried my master to open it. When it didn't budge but an inch, I had a bad feeling and asked the gate officer if anyone was in the building. He told me Boden was in her office interviewing Lopez, but otherwise, it was empty. The work crew was already gone, and no other staff was nearby."

"Are you certain she covered the panel?"

"Absolutely. The officer said that when he escorted Lopez down, he questioned Boden about the window. She said she was the medical director of the ATA and had the authority to cover her window due to privacy concerns. The officer told me it seemed odd, but he knew it was a new unit and figured she was right. He wasn't one of our regular screws who has been through the training. They're not scheduled to come on board until we bring in prisoners."

"How long was he in there alone with her before you figured it out?"

"Ten, fifteen minutes at most. As soon as the officer mentioned Lopez, I knew it was bad. I paged the super and told him I thought we had a possible hostage situation. He was there in a heartbeat. You were the first person he called. After he got off the phone with you, he shut down all access to the ATA and ordered Paul Craven to activate the tactical team and internal perimeter security. He and I went back to Boden's door and were able to make initial contact with Lopez. He must have gagged Boden because he had her grunt but would not let her talk. We've been kind of lax on the negotiator training since you left, rotating it among three different sergeants, and none of them is on today. That's another reason the super called you first."

"Paul is still head of tactical?"

"Yeah, they were suited up and moving into positions as I was leaving. They'll have the entire place secure and cut the phone in case he tries to call out."

"I doubt that will be an issue. If I'm not mistaken, his victim was his teen-age niece. I met him once or twice when he first came in. I can't remember a lot about him. He was bright enough but refused to attend a sex offender group, saying the sex was consensual with the kid. He didn't strike me as a particularly violent guy."

"People change, especially in this place," Lincoln observes.

"You have that right," I agree. I then ask Lincoln if her panic button was on.

"It was on, but they don't work unless you press them. Hers is in the standard place under the desktop. She either never hit it or didn't sit behind her desk. They may have used two chairs in front of the desk."

I nod at Lincoln's answer while saying I better call Jim.

"Hit star-seven. It will ring directly to the super," Lincoln tells me while handing me his DOC phone.

"Dwyer," Jim says on the first full ring.

"It's TC; we'll be getting onto 95 shortly. I'd say we should be there in ten minutes. Lincoln filled me in."

"Excellent! It is a definite hostage situation, and there's no easy access except by the door. I've spoken to him a little bit and told him you will be here shortly. Apparently, you've seen him in the past?"

"A couple of times right when he initially came in, but that's it."

"It's something. That he doesn't view you as a threat is a potential plus. You and Captain Craven will be in charge; let me put you on with him."

In the pause that follows as the super gets Paul, I feel a sudden accelera-tion. Lincoln is starting down the ramp onto 95, and my pulse begins to race.

The last time I was with Lincoln Grant on Route 95, we were blowing down the highway at a hundred miles per hour to the Rhode Island Hospital Trauma Center, where my wife later died. Lincoln hears the hitch in my breath and glances over as my name is thinly called from the distance.

"Yeah, yeah, I'm here, Paul," I say into the receiver. "Looks like we have a real one this time."

"As real as it gets, TC—one hostage, an Andrea Boden, and one hostage taker, Antonio Lopez. They're in Boden's office in one of the new modular, and the only real access is the hallway door. There is a small twenty-four-by-thirty-six exterior window, but it has a heavy security screen over it. No side doors. The door's not locked, but it is barricaded. When we applied light pressure, it moved an inch, and then nothing, no movement whatsoever. We put a mini-periscope-camera to the exterior window and saw that he rotated her desk, so it sticks lengthwise away from the door. He then pried a metal bookcase between the desk and the wall. It's not going anywhere. We need to get him out by the door."

"Can we pop the hinges?"

"Flush mounted. That's a no-go."

I pause to weigh the information Paul has given me. "Gas?"

"Not a good idea. The door and exterior window are both safety glass. It will take too long to bust through either one to be safe for the hostage. Talking's the best thing."

"Who approved doors that swing in anyway?"

"Don't ask me, Doc. The design's for shit."

"What's the story on the hostage? Did you get an eye on her?'

"No, she wasn't in any of the sight lines we had with the camera. She must be against the rear wall."

"Okay, we'll be there in five. I'm in my fishing gear, so I'll stop by the old warden's house first to grab a pair of pants or a sweat suit."

"I'll send one of my guys to get the clothes. It's better if you come right here so we can do some planning."

4

The state cops shut down their sirens when we turn onto Cranston's access road. I'm glad they don't make a grand entrance, as it may simply agitate Lopez and alert the rest of the institution that something major is taking place. Thankfully, the ATA's entrance is clear of vehicles, news crews, or anything else that can get in the way. Besides the state police cruisers and DOC cars, the only other vehicles are two ambulances that sit idling. Jim has done an effective job of keeping it quiet. He knows it's counterproductive to turn the hostage taker into some type of celebrity.

Jumping from the DOC car, I pull off my slicker and toss it onto the front seat. That will keep me from being mistaken for a giant banana, I tell myself as Lincoln and I make our way up to the entrance, where we are waved right in by the officer manning the post. We pass security and then go through a sliding steel door cut into the wall, joining the outer control area to the modulars on the opposite side. We are standing in a large foyer that contains three doors in addition to the one we entered through. One is a security post for entry into the prison, which was the door Lopez initially entered by. The second leads into the living space and treatment rooms for the cons, while the third opens into the administrative suite, where my office is located and where Boden is now being held hostage. In addition to the officers securing the entrance to the administrative area, there are four paramedics with two rolling gurneys off to the side.

"ID, Doc," one of the two tactical officers who are watching the door says. Then more softly, he adds, "Sorry, rules."

"No sweat," I reply, reaching for my wallet as Lincoln says he will go in to get the super.

"Need to pat you down first, LT," the second officer says when the lieutenant moves toward the door.

"Right," Lincoln acknowledges, extending his arms out. The bulletproof vest and other gear members of the Corrections Emergency Response Team wear make the officer's movements awkward as he runs his hands over Lincoln's body. As soon as he finishes, he speaks softly into a shoulder mike: "Two outside the gate. We're unlocking the door to let one in, Lieutenant Lincoln Grant. The second, Dr. Thomas Phillips, requires a formal ID."

The officer then keys Lincoln in. As soon as he passes into the hallway, Superintendent Dwyer looks out, gives me a brief, studied glance, and then says, "Thomas Phillips, he's okay."

"Pat down," one officer instructs while the other relocks the entry.

I extend my arms to either side as the officer begins his search of my body. He pulls the fabric of the suspenders holding up my foul-weather bibs and says, "You better take those off. If you go in with Lopez, they can easily be used as a weapon that he could strangle you with."

"Can't. They're sewn right into the fabric. He'd need scissors or a knife to cut them free."

The officer ponders what I said for a few seconds and then says, "No problem."

As each moment passes, my years of training in hostage negotiations have shifted more and more into focus. I'm anxious to get inside but appreciate how they are following their protocols. Once he completes the pat down, he again uses his shoulder mike: "Man coming in, Dr. Thomas Phillips." He then opens the door to the administrative area. My old National Guard training mantra enters my mind as I step into the hallway: *Prepare, prepare, prepare, and then expect the unexpected.*

Jim is waiting on the other side of the door for me and motions me over to him, away from the group farther down the hall. "You're sober, right?" he asks.

Perplexed, I respond, "I'm sober?"

"The officer that picked up your clothes said there was an empty bottle of whiskey on the kitchen counter," he explains.

"I haven't been there in two or three days, Jim. I was out fishing with a buddy and had one beer an hour ago."

"So you're good to go?"

"Yeah, I'm good to go," I confirm, unable to keep an edge from my voice.

"Sorry, TC, I had to ask. This one isn't a drill."

"That's okay. You caught me off guard, that's all. I wasn't expecting the question." As I finish, the Guard's mantra flows through my mind, *Prepare, prepare, prepare, and then expect the unexpected.*

"Understood. Now it's up to you and Captain Craven. The two of you are in charge."

Starting down the corridor, I notice five tactical officers chatting quietly in the social workers' office. Their Lexan body shields are all neatly stacked off to one side. In the room adjacent to Boden's office are two more officers, with some type of listening device attached to the wall. Paul Craven has watched me come down the corridor. As I draw near, he mouths, "He wants to see you." I nod and then motion with my head toward my office at the far end of the hallway.

Paul passes me a black-plastic trash bag as we enter the room. Peering inside, I see it holds my Adidas sweat suit. "At least I'll be comfortable for however long this takes," I say as I pull the first and then the second suspender strap free before stepping out of the rain gear. "What do I need to know?"

"Nothing much new to add. We've contacted his unit officer, and he saw no unusual behavior during the past few weeks. Lopez is a low-maintenance guy, stays to himself, few visits, and no recent mail or phone call with bad news that we are aware of. We can't find anything that may have set him off."

"I believe he's a sex offender who pleaded down to A&B. His victim was in his family if I remember right, so there are no positive hooks we can use there."

"You're right." Paul agrees. "He's in four years on a six-year sentence. I have his record if you want to review it."

"That's okay; Lincoln briefed me. But let me see his booking picture and any others you have."

Paul opens the folder to Lopez's face page. The photo is four years old and shows a late-twenties light-skinned Cape Verdean man with a round face and close-cropped hair. His wide-set dark eyes reach across the intervening years with a blank stare. The picture was taken when he was booked into corrections and still in partial shock. My first impression of the image is that of a Black Charlie Brown. He had three tattoos at the time, and there is a blowup of each. Tony and a simple cross are inked on his upper left arm, and a sea serpent encircles his left forearm. I remember that when I interviewed him, I asked him about the snake on his arm, and he immediately corrected me, explaining it was a sea serpent he got in Newport with his first big commercial fishing check. It was beautifully done, whereas the other two were clearly homemade. After studying the picture, I ask Paul if Lopez is active in any religious groups, if he has a lover, or if he has recently picked up any disciplinary reports.

"Nothing on the first two, and he only has two D-reports, and they were both minors in his first year—disrespecting an officer."

"Were they the same officer?"

"No, but wait a sec," Paul says as he scans Lopez's folder. "The officers were both women, and on each occasion, he told them they didn't have the right to give him orders. He may have a thing with women."

"Possibly, but whatever that thing is, he's been able to keep it in check for the past three years. You said he asked to speak to me?"

"When the super told him you were our official negotiator, he said he knew you and requested to see you. That was it until ten minutes ago when he asked when you would get here. Other than that, he's been quiet. From the window camera, we have observed him sitting on the edge of the desk and periodically talking to the hostage, who appears to be on the floor beneath the window. We have a listening device in the adjacent room but can't pick anything up."

"Well, we've done this plenty of times in drill, Paul, so now's our chance to try it out for real. My job will be to engage him. If he has to vent, I'll let him vent. I will show empathy for his concerns and reassure him whenever possible but make no promises, particularly unrealistic things like he can take a ride to McDonald's in Providence; he'd know it was BS. I'll be searching for a common interest and make a point to stay away from family, as with his history that may set him off. I'll reinforce any positive ideas he has, particularly on how we can end this. It's almost chow time, so I'll offer him some food and suggest the hostage needs food, too, or to go to the bathroom. I'll work to ingratiate myself as a type of friend or confidant and may recommend exchanging myself for her, say, to let her use the john. Does that all make sense?"

"Right out of the book, Doc. If you do go in, we have the camera by the exterior window. They'll observe him and keep me posted by an earpiece. If you can get him to let her out, we can be through the door and have him subdued within thirty seconds. He would never have time to get the desk back into position. I'll station my guys to either side of the doorway against the wall, so they won't be visible if he takes down the paper blocking the window."

"What if he asks me to come in before he lets her out? That's what I would do. Do you have a marksman in position?"

"Two. We've pretty much had him in our sights for the past half hour, but that's something we want to avoid."

"Agreed. We definitely want to avoid that." I sigh and then shift quickly into professional mode. "If there's nothing more to say, let's get started. Do you mind taking your gear off? If we get him to remove the paper, you'll be standing near me, and seeing you in all that stuff is prettying intimidating. If none of this works, what's our fallback plan?"

"I have two guys in facilities practicing how quickly we can cut a hole in the door. We're lucky it's wood, not metal. In the worst case, we pump in some gas while they rip a hole in the door large enough to put someone through. It could take as long as two or three minutes to cut the door and get someone in, so we want to avoid that too."

As Paul speaks, he pulls apart the Velcro securing his bulletproof vest and places it on the table along with his utility belt, kneepads, and helmet. He no longer resembles a storm trooper, but all in black, he remains intimidating.

"I've no idea why we wear all that garbage anyway," he comments, eyeing the paraphernalia now laid out on my desk. "Do you think the super will give us a free hand or try to get involved?"

"He told me we were in charge, so we'll see," I reply as we leave the office.

Jim approves our plan, as vague as it is. After we review it with him, we brief the tactical squad members, four of whom take up positions against the wall on either side of the entrance to Boden's office with their Lexan shields leaning back against their knees. At the same time, the remainder stays in a small knot at the end of the corridor adjacent to my office. Lincoln and the super are positioned by the hallway entrance, beyond any field of vision Lopez has from the door. Finally, we remind the group that all cells must be off or on vibrate. They have all been drilled on protocols and know that keeping out of the way is often the best thing they can do to help out. We've been told that two guys with circular saws are now in the entry area if we're forced to slice through the door.

Paul and I survey the hallway and exchange a glance. He nods and gives me a thumbs-up. Somehow, he's turned a switch on, and I feel myself click into a different internal mode.

I lightly tap on the door and then softly call into the small crack in the doorway, "Tony, it's Tom Phillips. We met a couple of years ago." Next, I wait.

There is noise emanating from the inside, and I glance back to Paul, who is standing on the far side of the corridor. "He's coming," Paul whispers.

"Who is it?" a voice asks.

"Tom Phillips. We met a few years back."

"You're a doctor, right?"

"Right, a psychologist."

"Do you remember me?"

"Sure do, Tony. I saw you a little while after you came in."

"What did we talk about?"

"I explained some of the programs we have here, and you said you weren't that interested in programs. I believe I asked you about the sea serpent too. Remember, I thought it was a snake."

There is a hesitant laugh from behind the door. "I remember that."

"Didn't you tell me you got that tattoo in Newport or Portsmouth after a fishing trip or something?"

"It was Newport after my first big trip."

"How long were you guys out for?"

"Almost two weeks."

"What month was that, Tony?"

"Late April. It was my first time on Georges Bank. My share was just shy of a thousand."

"Decent money. Is that what you used for the tattoo?"

"It didn't cost that much. Three fifty, cash."

"You know, Tony, I've always wanted to fish Georges Bank, but I can't say I'd like to be out there in April. The weather can still be a little rough at that time. How was it on your trip?"

"We had a couple of squalls pass through, but nothing we couldn't handle. She was a seventy-three-foot Novi trawler, banged up but a solid boat. What did I tell you when we talked?"

His question catches me off guard. I had been trying to find common ground and often used his name in the conversation to develop initial trust, and now I can't hesitate to respond. "You told me you weren't interested in any of the counseling services we offered."

"Why? Why did I say that?'

"If I remember right, you told me you weren't interested in talking about things you didn't do."

"What did you do when I said that?"

"I told you that was okay and that if you changed your mind, you could ask to see me. I may have also told you that parole looks favorably on guys who get into counseling. Why are you asking, Tony?"

There is a long pause. "She just kept bugging me about my crime. I told her to back off, but she kept asking and staring at me."

"Who kept asking?"

He laughs at my question. "Who do you think? We both know you're not here to talk fishing, Doc."

"Hey, Tony." I chuckle in response. "When they called me, I was cruising a sandbar for blues a couple of miles off Point Judith."

"No way!" he replies, but I hear the surprise and curiosity in his voice.

"Kid you not, sir. I was even in my foul-weather gear when I got here and changed into a sweat suit that they gave me."

"Did you catch anything?"

I flash back to the state cop's first question on the pier: *Decent fishing?*

"My cell phone went off before the first cast."

"Sorry, Doc. I didn't mean to blow up your day."

"No problem, Tony; I'm glad to be here." As we talk, Paul hands me a note that says the commissioner, Boden's boss, and someone else are outside and asked to come in. After scanning it, I whisper no to Paul and then turn toward the super and shake my head from side to side.

"I'd rather be fishing," Lopez replies, but my concentration has been broken.

"Yeah, I guess I'd rather be fishing, too, but here we are." I'm not satisfied with my response, and there is a long pause from behind the door.

"How are we going to get out of here, Doc?" he finally replies while lifting an edge of the paper from the window to stare out at me.

"Good question, Tony. Were you ever out in a heavy sea?"

"Plenty of times. Too many."

"How'd you get out?"

"We'd ride it out. Turn the bow into the bitch and ride her out."

"I bet that was rough. Now we have to figure some way to ride this thing out and get you back into port."

"You mean back into a cell, don't you?"

I pause. "Yeah, I guess you're right, Tony. This place is a prison."

He has pulled more of the bottom sheet of paper away and now turns his head back to the far wall where we believe Boden is. Suddenly, he turns back to me and smashes his palms against the door, which is slightly ajar. The slam of the door, combined with the slap of his hands, sends a shock wave down the corridor, stiffening all of us. The tactical officers grasp their shields; Jim and Lincoln start toward me, as do Captain Craven and the officers by my office.

"Easy, easy, Tony," I say, holding up my arms, with my words are as much for the guys approaching me as they are for Lopez, and the tension dissipates.

"I didn't do anything to her, Doc, I swear. I told her to shut up, but she wouldn't. All I wanted was for her to shut her fat fucking trap, and she wouldn't do it." He has worked himself into a lather and is screaming by the time he finishes.

"Easy, Tony," I say again. "Why don't you open the door a crack so we don't have to yell?"

There is a lengthy pause, and then a calmer Tony reopens the door. "I told her to read my record to find out what I did, but she said she wanted to hear it from me. She said it was better in my own words or some other stupid thing. Then she said it again and again and again. I told her to shut up, but she didn't listen. I said it nicely, and she still went on and on. She wanted me to say I raped my niece; I'm sure she did, but she said she didn't. She lied. I wanted to scare her, that's all. She said she was a doctor. Is she really a doctor, Doc?"

"Yeah, she's a psychiatrist."

"Don't they teach those idiots how to talk to people, to know no means no?"

"They're supposed to, Tony. How are you doing?"

He laughs, and I'm relieved. I feared he was getting himself worked up again.

"I've done better."

"I would imagine you've done a lot better."

"I lost it. All I wanted to do was shake some sense into her, and then she screamed, so I had to put my hand over her mouth. Christ, she pissed herself, and then I knew I was in a jackpot. But she kept ragging on me even after I told her to stop. I finally stuffed tissues in her mouth to shut her up and used her stockings or tights or whatever you call them to tie her arms and legs. I didn't do anything to her. You believe me on that, don't ya?"

"If that's what you tell me, Tony, I believe you."

"I'll have to do ice time, right?"

"We'll see. You'll get a D-report and then have to deal with that."

"Will it make any difference that I told her to stop?"

"I can't say. I've never been to a D-board."

"Will it make a difference, Captain Craven?" he asks, looking beyond me to Paul, who is across the hallway.

"We listen to what an inmate has to say, Mr. Lopez," Paul answers. He then continues, "But I can tell you one thing that will make a difference is if you leave there quietly. That will make a difference."

"How big a difference? What about new charges? Will I pick up new charges or only a D-report?"

"We really can't answer all of that, Tony," I reply. "But like Captain Craven said, if we end this nice and no one is hurt, that will help you. I expect it will help you a lot."

"If I'm put in the hole, will you come see me?"

"Without a doubt."

"How often?"

"Once a week. I'll be there once a week. I'm usually here Sunday to Wednesday. I'll come by one of those days each week."

"When I told you to stop, you stopped. She didn't. She didn't stop. She kept it up and up and up."

"You mentioned that, Tony. What do you say we figure how to get you on out of there?"

"Today's Friday, right?"

"All day long."

"Did you come in on your day off?"

"Yeah. Remember, I was fishing for blues off Point Judith when they called me."

"That's right. Hey, Doc, I didn't mean to ruin your day off."

"No problem, Tony. I'm glad they got ahold of me. Why don't we see if we can get you out of there now?"

"Is the goon squad outside?"

"There are a couple of officers here with Captain Craven. He can make sure you don't get hurt. He's a good guy."

"I'll escort you out, Mr. Lopez," Paul adds. "You'll be safe."

"I didn't hurt her, Captain, so they shouldn't beat my ass down."

"No one will lay a hand on you. You have my word on that," Paul assures him.

"You won't forget. You'll see me every week?" he again asks, turning back to me.

"Every week," I confirm. "Now how shall we go about getting you out?"

"I have a bookcase pried between her desk and the back wall. I need to close the door to be able to move the bookcase, and then I can slide the desk. Once I do that, I can come out, okay?"

I defer to Paul, who responds, "That works for me, Mr. Lopez, but I will have to cuff you when you get out."

"Yeah, I know," he replies dejectedly.

"Tony," I call as he begins to move away from the door he has just pushed shut. He stops to glance back at me through the window. "I have to move away from the door now to give you and Captain Craven some room. I'll see you again after the weekend."

He nods and then lifts the bookcase free from behind the desk. A moment later he pushes the desk to the side and opens the door. As he is working, Paul tells the two officers to the left of the doorway to immediately restrain him if he refuses to be shackled, but it's not an issue. Once Lopez opens the door, he slowly exits with his arms extended before him to be cuffed.

"Next week," I tell him as he starts to move up the hallway surrounded by a phalanx of officers.

"Yeah, thanks, Doc."

He has gained some weight since I last saw him. His face is now fuller and rounder, making him appear more of a Charlie Brown caricature than he did four years ago.

5

As soon as Lopez clears the door, I'm in the room. Immediately, I'm taken aback by a familiar scent. It smells more like a hospital room than an office, and then I realize it's urine. Boden is hog-tied and has been pushed back against the wall, facing away from the doorway. The whole time Lopez was talking to her, she would have been unable to see anything. It must have been terrifying for her.

"It's okay, Dr. Boden. This is Tom Phillips. You are safe now." As I speak to her, I hear the other tactical guys moving the furniture to have a clear path to get her out.

Turning back to them, I say, "Get the paramedics with one of those gurneys in here." The bustle of confusion and voices outside the door draw away my attention as the superintendent asks someone to leave.

Suddenly, Olken is in the doorway, and he appears almost to be hyperventilating. "Is she okay? Is she okay?" he's asking, his voice steadily rising.

I remember the note Paul had passed me a little earlier about the commissioner, Olken, and someone else being outside. "He's unauthorized. Get him and anyone with him out now," I hiss at the three tactical officers in the room. "That is an order. I don't care who they are. Get them out and get that gurney in here ASAP."

"You got it, Cap," I hear Lincoln say as Olken begins to protest. The three tactical officers who are in the room with me immediately get up to assist Lincoln. Turning back to Boden, I hear them escorting the group out. Fleetingly, I hope I didn't get Jim in trouble before refocusing my attention on the psychiatrist.

Turning back to the huddled form against the wall, I identify myself for a second time and then say in the calmest voice I can muster, "You are safe, Dr. Boden. Antonio Lopez is gone. You are safe." I pause and then continue, "I am going to put one hand on your shoulder and one on your knee and then move you away from the wall. After that, I will untie you. We want to get you to a hospital to be checked out. I will now place my hand on your shoulder."

I place my hand lightly on her left shoulder, and she instantly cringes, so I hesitate and do not move her. I have no idea how much shock she is in or if she even heard a word I said. There is a clatter as two EMTs wheel the litter in. I notice one is a woman, and I motion to her with my head. As she kneels next to me, I whisper, "She may be in shock. Her name is Dr. Andrea Boden. Tell her things will be all right."

"Andrea, I am Cynthia Linden," the woman says in a slow, deliberate manner. "I am an EMT. You are safe, and you will be fine. We are taking you to the hospital."

A soon as the woman says her name, the tension begins to disappear beneath my hand and continues to dissipate with her every word. "Cynthia and I are starting to move you away from the wall now and will untie you," I say and then nod to the EMT. I grasp both her shoulders lightly but firmly while Cynthia grips her knees. We gently slide her from the wall while rotating her body toward us. The second EMT quickly positions himself between Boden and the wall and then begins to slice away the hosiery binding her arms and legs as soon as we stop moving her.

Cynthia briefly studies tissue paper that is bulging out of Boden's mouth before saying, "Andrea, I will now remove that tissue from your mouth." She strips off her latex gloves, tossing them to the side, and then pulls on a second pair. She then takes hold of Boden's jaw in such a way that she can prevent herself from being bitten if Boden panics. Meanwhile, the psychiatrist is saucer-eyed, her glance rapidly shifting from me to the woman now cleaning the tissue from her mouth.

The whole thing takes only a matter of minutes from when I first spoke to Boden to having her freed and her mouth cleaned out.

"You are safe now, Andrea," I say as our eyes lock. "You are safe." I initially planned to say "Dr. Boden" but switched to "Andrea," remembering how I felt her relax when the paramedic used her first name.

"We will be placing you on a gurney now," Cynthia says softly. "Okay?"

Boden nods and then croaks, "Yes."

"She could probably use some water," I suggest after they deftly shift her from the floor to the gurney.

"How about a little H_2O?" the male EMT offers as they position and then secure her to the cart. She nods yes, and while he removes a water bottle from the myriad of cargo pockets on his pants, Cynthia asks if I'm planning to ride with them.

"Where are you going?"

"The Trauma Center at Rhode Island Hospital. They can manage both physical and mental health issues."

Her words slam into my solar plexus. I should be accompanying them. My job's not done until the hostage situation is fully resolved, and that means until the hostage is not only freed but properly cared for. But I can't do it. I was last at the Rhode Island Trauma Center after Leon Alexander rammed Maura's car. It is a state-of-the-art facility, but my wife still died there.

"No," I mumble. "I need to stay here."

She studies me quizzically. "Are you okay?"

"I'm fine. I have to do a report. You know, paperwork."

My response satisfies her. She turns back to the gurney, releases the wheel locks, and says, "We're leaving now, Andrea."

Boden nods and then glances at me as they begin to wheel her out. "Thanks, Tom," she whispers as our eyes momentarily meet for a second time.

I am preoccupied with memories of the afternoon and night I spent at Rhode Island Hospital. "Sure, no problem" is all I can get out as they roll her from the room.

I'm swamped simultaneously by a huge sense of relief and melancholia as I stumble back a step or two until I hit the desk and then let myself collapse atop it. Sighing, I shut my eyes and instruct myself to breathe deeply while counting each inhalation backward from ten. At seven, I hear my name. Sitting up, I see the super standing in front of me.

"How long did that take?" I ask.

"Less than two hours from when she was taken."

"I'm exhausted. It was okay I told Lopez I'll see him in isolation, right?"

"No problem. If you want to see him in the can, we can arrange that. Now I'd like to introduce you to Commissioner Hanley."

I had noticed a person was standing next to Jim but never focused any attention on him.

"Yes, sir," I respond, automatically flipping into military mode in which you stand at attention in front of any senior officer regardless of how tired you are.

"Henry Hanley," he says, extending a hand to me. "Sorry I interfered by allowing those two men in. I should have known better."

He's a little guy, five-six or five-seven at the most. Commissioners are political appointments, but for corrections, the governor ordinarily tries to hire a person with some public safety experience rather than a politician's or campaign donor's brother. I remember Hanley's been on the job six months, but I forget what his qualifications are.

"That's all right, sir. We have protocols and must keep the area secured until the situation is resolved."

"Thank you again, Dr. Phillips, for your management of an exceptionally delicate matter."

We make additional small talk, but I'm unable to follow the conversation thread, periodically nodding my agreement to what they are saying so I don't appear completely lost. They are gone in no time, and I return to my office to grab my foul-weather gear.

The corridor has emptied in the minute or two it takes me to scoop the yellow bibs off the floor. The faint scent of urine has drifted out from Boden's office, and I think that we have to get facilities inside to clean the place up. Lincoln enters from the other end of the corridor as I'm standing by Boden's door.

"Nice work, Cap," he says as he nears.

"None of it had to happen, LT. Boden had the shit scared out of her, and Lopez is going to pick up a year or more of ice time in the Departmental Segregation Unit, and none of it had to happen. It was one big idiotic mistake!"

"It could have been a much bigger mistake if you didn't get him out of there. He could have been dead, or she could have been dead. You did a good job."

"Does it count when you prevent something that shouldn't have happened in the first place? Psych services never should have given her access to the referral list or records. She shouldn't have kept ragging on him to put him over the edge. And he never should have put his hands on her. I don't see anything good in any of it. To me it's a waste, one big fucking waste! I need to get out of this place. Is Craven still around? We have to debrief before I can go."

Lincoln doesn't respond, which is just as well. I've been through more than twenty hostage drills in both the DOC and the Guard, but it is different in real life. During the drill, you know it's merely a drill. No matter what happens, it's all make-believe. This wasn't make-believe. There is one tactical officer in the entry area, and when I ask him where Captain Craven is, he speaks into his shoulder mike.

"The captain said he is placing Mr. Lopez into an isolation cell. He asked me if you thought he required a one-on-one for the night."

The idea that Lopez may try to kill himself had never entered my mind. Reluctantly, I have to switch back into professional mode to consider the issues. He has no family support, appears to be somewhat of a loner, and must realize that he's facing potentially serious charges from assault to kidnapping or even attempted murder if a DA decides to throw the book at him or corrections to make an example of him. He may be staring down at another five years or longer. On the plus side, he has no history of self-injury, and that's always the biggest risk factor. I decide it's best to err on the side of caution and relay the message to Paul to place him on a watch until tomorrow when someone from psych services can evaluate him.

"The captain says thanks and will be out in about ten minutes," the officer responds after he gets off the radio with Paul.

I decide to wait in the entry rather than go out front. The super may be out there with the commissioner, Olken, and the other guy, who I guess is Poletti's chief of staff, and I would rather avoid them. Lincoln asks if I will need a ride after the debriefing. I check my watch and see it's 6:15 p.m. Gazing past the gate that leads into the camp, I see the late-afternoon sun is illuminating the chimney of the prison's power plant with a golden shimmer. My mind briefly drifts back to a few hours earlier when I was preparing to cast off the stern of *Kathy's Klown* for blues.

"I may as well stay here tonight," I reply to Lincoln, returning from my momentary sojourn into Block Island Sound. "It will take a half hour or longer for Paul and me to debrief and write an initial report, and the last ferry is at seven. I'd never make it. My cell is in my slicker. If someone can pull it out of the car, I'll call my mother to let her know I won't be home tonight."

"No problem, Boss," Lincoln says as he moves toward the outer control area of the ATA. Paul arrives a moment before Lincoln gets back. We all chat briefly, and then Paul and I go back into the administrative corridor.

"Lincoln can be quite the mother hen sometimes, eh?" Paul comments as we make our way to my office.

"He's a great guy. Big in his church and takes the Christianity love-your-brother thing seriously," I reply.

We hesitate outside Boden's office, studying the tumult inside. "Not a real auspicious start for this new unit," he observes.

"Yeah, and we've yet to open for business!"

"What was Lopez doing here anyway?"

I fill Paul in on what I believe happened, and he says, "So she exceeded her authority by directly requesting psych services for a referral rather than going through you?"

"Pretty much," I agree. "The super recently appointed her the official medical director of the program, so I guess she assumed that gave her the right to solicit referrals directly."

"What did Lopez mean when he said she kept bugging him about his crime and that set him off?"

"He's in for A&B, but it's a plea down from indecent A&B. He's short time-wise but wasn't eligible for the program due to his offense history. She never should have seen him, never mind been questioning him on his crimes, especially after he told her to back off. The whole thing was easily avoidable."

"That will all help him at a D-board. If he doesn't pick up new charges, he may only get a year or eighteen months of DSU time. Most hostages don't pursue charges unless something serious like a rape takes place. They don't want to go to court, and DOC wants to avoid the publicity. We still have to do the review. Do you want to write, or should I?"

"I can," I say, flipping on my computer and then calling up the DOC Serious Incident template. While we chat, I write, and it takes us until after seven o'clock to complete the report. I print up two copies, and after a few edits, we sign a finished one for Paul to slip into the super's box, and I email him an electronic version.

6

Paul has to use a master key to open the steel door separating both sides of the wall to let me out, and there is no one outside the entrance by the time I exit—no state police, no ambulances, no tactical squad members. No one.

Twilight has fallen as I follow the access road back to the warden's house. To my left the prison looms, a massive fortification lowering darkly and ominously over me while I make my way to the former staff housing area. It never dawns on me until I arrive at the building that my keys are on Block Island. Knowing we rarely lock up at home, I first try all the doors, but they are fastened. Fortunately, the first window I check is open. I can hear the cast-iron weights clank in the tracks between the sashes and studs as I force the antique frame upward. Then, hoisting myself through the opening, I land on the floor in the living room, where I lie for a few moments on the rug before making my way to the kitchen with the futile hope I left a beer in the fridge. Scanning the room, I see the bottle of Old Forester Jim had questioned me about. It is empty, so I run an inch of water in and then slosh it around to pick up any of the whiskey that may have been left clinging to the bottom and sides of the container. The slight taste does nothing to slake my thirst as I gulp it down.

I'm tempted to walk to the nearest package store but quickly ditch the idea as stupid. Instead, I change into a spare set of running gear and toss on a reflector vest. I'm familiar with various routes around Cranston and decide it will take a minimum of ten miles to get my head straight. While I'm lacing up my sneakers, my cell begins to jingle in the slicker's pocket.

"Dr. Thomas Phillips?" a voice asks after I answer the call.

"Speaking."

"Hi, doctor, this is Richard Santos from the *Providence Journal*. I have a few questions to ask you concerning the hostage situation at Cranston State Prison today. Can you tell me how many prisoners were involved and if there were any injuries?"

His words flow quickly and with a certain authority that automatically elicits a response, but I catch myself. "I'm sorry. All questions go through the Department of Correction's Information Office."

"They're closed at the moment and may not be able to provide a statement until Monday. If you can give us a little background for our next edition, that would be helpful. At what time did the situations take place, and in which part of the institution?"

"You really must call DOC on this; I am not authorized to provide any statements."

"Can you confirm that you were the primary hostage negotiator and that there were no injuries?"

"Sorry, call DOC," I reply, ending the conversation before he can get out another query.

I consider calling Jim's cell to give him a heads-up on the reporter but decide to call my mother instead. I give her a brief update on what happened, assure her I'm fine, and say I'll be returning home the next day. While we're speaking, the phone beeps once with an incoming call. Checking the number after we click off, I see it was Santos calling with more questions. I turn off the phone and run into the night.

The next day, a sign is posted on the ATA doorway directing all personnel to the main staff entrance. It's Saturday and my day off, so I was planning to put in as brief an appearance as possible to check for messages before trying to find a ride to Point Judith. As soon as I enter, the CO at inner control tells me the super is up in his office and has asked to see me. After he conveys the message, he says, "Big day yesterday, hey, Doc?"

"Yeah," is all I say as I make it through the gate. I'm the search of the day, so the gate officer gives me a thorough pat down before motioning me into the metal detector. I have not even been back for two months, and it's already completely familiar to me. None of the emotions I felt my first day back are remotely present, and I'm not sure if that's good or bad.

The super's door is open, and I call his name out as I enter the foyer to his office.

"Come on in, Dr. Phillips," he calls back, and I am slightly puzzled. He never calls me "doctor" except in formal situations. Entering the room,

I am surprised to find both the commissioner and Olken sitting in front of Jim's desk. He remains set back beyond a blond expanse of glossy oak framed by the American and Rhode Island flags, looking his official best. "I'm glad you're here, TC. I tried to call you earlier. I'm glad you're still on site."

Before I can mention that my cell was turned off, Commissioner Hanley is on his feet with an arm outstretched to me. "Allow me to again acknowledge how grateful the department is for your actions, Dr. Phillips," he says, gripping my hand tightly. "Your work averted a major crisis. I will see that you're recommended for a commendation."

"Thank—"

But Olken interrupts and also reaches out to clasp my hand. "For myself, Dr. Vos, and the entire staff at Adams Pharmaceuticals, you have our heartfelt appreciation but most especially for Dr. Boden. She spent last night in the hospital for observation and is expected to make an excellent recovery. She had no physical injuries, but as you can imagine, she has been traumatized emotionally."

"Thanks" is all I get out, somewhat overwhelmed by the unexpected displays of gratitude.

"I received the incident report from you and Captain Craven, and it seems totally in order," Jim says, shifting the subject slightly.

His words are followed by a pause that continues to extend until the commissioner clears his throat. "Superintendent Dwyer has shared your report with me. As you can imagine, an incident of this magnitude has caused us to reevaluate the Alternatives to Aggression initiative. I discussed the need to reassess the program yesterday evening with Dr. Olken, Mr. Dwyer, and others interested in this project. As I am sure you realize from the publicity surrounding the ribbon cutting, there are many parties who require assurance that the Alternatives to Aggression program can be operated in a safe manner. From your incident report, I noted that Dr. Boden appeared to not follow protocols in requesting that inmate Lopez be brought to her office. Is that correct?"

"In part," I reply. "Sex offenders are not eligible to participate in the ATA. She requested from the prison psych services a list of individuals who met basic entrance criteria: they were within two years of sentence completion, had a history of aggression, and may show an interest in participating. While Lopez met those criteria, he never should have been on the list since his A&B was pleaded down from indecent A&B. Psych services shouldn't have identified him to begin with, and she should have picked that up when she reviewed his record. My guess is that none of them checked his mitts."

"Mitts?" Olken interrupts.

"Mittimuses," I explain. "They're the court orders that indicate to a jailer why a person is being held. What a person is initially held for or charged with is often not what they are convicted of in the end, as with Lopez. I am fairly certain one of his original mitts was for rape."

Olken nods at my explanation. "I get it. Without examining the mitts, Andrea or someone else understandably assumed he was incarcerated for what he was convicted of."

"He was incarcerated for what he was convicted of," Jim interjects. "The problem is that many, if not most, inmates plead their cases down from more severe to less severe crimes."

"That's what happened with Lopez," I continue. "When she began to question him about his offenses, he thought she was referring to sexually assaulting his niece. He said he asked her to stop, and when she continued, he lost it. At least that's how he reported it to me."

"Is that what you think happened?" the commissioner asks.

"It's a possibility," I answer. "In the end, the only two people in the room were her and him. If I'm not mistaken, Dr. Boden is more of a psychopharmacologist rather than a clinician."

"She did complete clinical rotations in her training, but she is more of a psychopharmacologist in practice," Olken acknowledges.

"Had Dr. Boden done this before?" the commissioner asks.

"She or Dr. Vos had interviewed patients to confirm they met study criteria, but this was always after I had first reviewed the referral. I was concerned that the majority of our referrals and all the inmates accepted to the program were White. I brought this up to Dr. Boden prior to the ribbon cutting. She wanted to announce the day prisoners were entering the ATA, and I asked her not to do that until we had more diversity among those accepted so that the program better reflected the prison population."

"What was her response to that?" Hanley asks.

"She wasn't particularly pleased."

"I'm partially responsible for that," Olken puts in. "I asked her to try and get a firm start date."

There is another long pause in the conversation until the commissioner continues. "I believe everyone in this room knows there have been differences of opinion in respect to the administration of this project. I preferred a full-time correction employee, and Adams preferred one of their staff. Dr. Phillips, you were more or less a compromise candidate—and, I should add, an excellent compromise candidate, as recent events have proven. If this project is to continue, its administrative structure must be reviewed. Adams Pharmaceuticals is a collaborator, and we are providing them space to conduct a field trial of their medication Eumonia. I believe it important that all persons linked to this project, outside those directly associated with the field trial, must be DOC staff or contract personnel. This means Dr. Phillips and the two social-work positions will be paid by and report to us. This represents a change for the social workers but not so much for Dr. Phillips, as Adams is merely a funding conduit for him. It won't take longer than a week for me to secure an exemption from the hiring freeze and have these funds channeled into the Cranston budget.

"On another note, I realize Adams had hoped to use the field trial to both examine the efficacy of Eumonia as well as to gain experience related to correctional healthcare in order to enter the correctional-health-management field."

"That is part of our longer-term strategic plan," Olken concedes.

"Anthony Vorenzi, Carlo Poletti's chief of staff, discussed that with me late yesterday. We all appreciate that the Senate president is committed to making this successful, as he indicated at the ribbon cutting. Nevertheless, of paramount importance to me and Superintendent Dwyer is the safe and secure operation of the prison. If I am not mistaken, the intervention phase of the field trial is for six months. Should the initial results appear positive by our own metrics, such as a lowering of disciplinary reports, positive correctional officer climate assessments, and, at a later date, recidivism data, we will continue the program. Dr. Phillips has agreed to assist us for the initial year."

At those words, Jim glances over to me. We had agreed for six months, but he must have told the commissioner I was on board for a year.

"If Dr. Phillips elects to continue with us after that time, assuming the program is successful, we will move him into the same staff position he held in the past. Yet I know from what the superintendent has told me that because of living on Block Island and other commitments, Dr. Phillips prefers his independence and a part-time schedule."

After completing his last sentence, he turns to me, and I nod my agreement.

"Therefore, with no possible conflicts of interest, Adams may select to enter into negotiations with Dr. Phillips to see if he can provide consultation to their correctional-healthcare-management aspirations. He will be in a unique position to do so after managing the Alternatives to Aggression project for a year. Additionally, there would be no ethical concerns in Dr. Phillips consulting to Adams, as he would not be leaving a state management block to take a position with a firm of which he had some oversight. I recognize that this is jumping ahead with a number of assumptions, but it's the best way I can project a scenario where all our respective goals can be achieved. For the safety and security of the institution, particularly in light of what has recently transpired, we must have full control over all aspects of the program, other than the field study."

We have all deferred to Hanley, and after he finishes, Olken is the first to break the silence.

"Our first goal is to have a clinical trial of Eumonia within a correctional population with histories of aggression. That supersedes all our other objectives. Naturally, we want to do that in conjunction with the Rhode Island Department of Corrections. Our longer-range desire is to enter the field of correctional healthcare management. This incident rather dramatically highlights how much we must learn in that area. Our staff person exceeded her authority, and I am partially to blame for that by vigorously requesting that we be given greater responsibility for this project. I apologize for myself and Adams Pharmaceuticals. We were overreaching our level of competency."

There is a lull in the conversation, and I am uncertain whether Olken is waiting for a response. When none is forthcoming, he continues, "It is fortunate that this incident took place prior to the opening of the facility, as it will give us a chance to correct for our errors before patients are enrolled."

"When we initially spoke," Jim says to Olken, "I told you the biggest difficulties you would have are in understanding the differing cultures you encounter in a prison—the security, the inmates, and other staff."

"You accurately predicted we would have difficulty in those areas," Olken agrees.

"Although I never expected a hostage situation to develop," Jim continues. "Nonetheless, it was the reason I lobbied for Dr. Phillips to have the position as the unit manager. He comprehends and can move within each of the overlapping worlds we're dealing with better than anyone I know. For me to be comfortable with this continuing, it has to be clear that Dr. Phillips is the final authority on all issues that arise within the ATA, with the sole exception of matters related to the prescribing and administration of Eumonia. If he says we wait until there is a more diverse prisoner group interested in the program, then we wait. If he doesn't consider a particular Adams staff person suitable to be on site for any reason, then that person is no longer allowed in the facility."

"I'm not sure I want that level of authority, Jim," I interrupt. "For the unit to work properly, we require an integrated team. Dr. Vos fully realizes that, but for whatever reasons, Dr. Boden never grasped some of the dynamics at work in a prison and didn't show an inclination to learn. She was fully dedicated to the research, but studying people is different than rats or chimps."

"She is a dedicated researcher," Olken states, somewhat defensively. "But you are correct; interpersonal skills are not her strong suit. I can assure you, Dr. Phillips, that the Adams staff do wish to work with you and the Rhode Island Department of Corrections collaboratively on this project and to be part of a team."

"Are you heading back to Block Island, TC?" Jim asks, tactfully shifting the focus of the conversation.

"I was planning to. I'm not scheduled back until tomorrow, and I was going to try and get a ride to Point Judith."

"Why don't you take a couple of days? Let's let things simmer down. The unit's ready to go, your staff are trained, and several inmates have been screened. A lot has happened in the past twenty-four hours. Let's meet again on Tuesday afternoon after a bit more of the dust settles. Is that all right with everyone?"

"Two in the afternoon works best for me," the commissioner says, and from how quickly he offered the time, I suspect he and Jim had already determined it. Olken rapidly checks his PDA and then says he can be here.

"Good," the commissioner declares. "We are all committed to making this work, so let's discuss how to do that on Tuesday."

As we get up to leave, Olken offers me a ride down to Point Judith.

7

"Do you have to pick up anything?" Olken asks as I slide into the Lexus's passenger seat.

I shake my head and tell him I just want to make the noontime boat.

As Olken exits the prison's parking lot, he brings up our first meeting in his office six weeks earlier. "I need to apologize, Tom," he explains. "At that time I was still lobbying that Adams be given full responsibility for the administration of the program. Tony Vorenzi had represented Adams's request to the commissioner but was rebuffed. It was the reason he questioned you concerning your wife's death and your subsequent resignation from corrections. Ostensibly, we told ourselves it was to ensure you were the proper person for the job, but our actual goal was to make you reconsider the position. I'm glad you didn't. We were in much more over our heads than I realized at the time. It was a significant judgment error on my part."

I reflect on his words for a moment and then respond, "I don't care for people telling me what to do. If anything, it can make me more intransigent."

"If that is what it did on that occasion, then I am grateful. I have no idea how we could have handled the situation with Andrea if you weren't there."

"It wasn't yours to handle, regardless of my being there or not," I clarify. "DOC has other trained hostage negotiators. Jim called me because I knew the inmate slightly and due to my familiarity with the program."

"I expect he also viewed you as the most qualified."

I shrug. "Maybe."

"Whatever the reason, I'm glad you were available, and I'm sorry we previously underestimated you. I must say, Alain has spoken rather highly of you."

"We've developed a decent working relationship. Do you have any idea of Dr. Boden's role in the future?"

"It remains too early to say, but it doesn't appear that she is the proper person for the position. I wouldn't be surprised if she was more comfortable in an academic setting. Naturally, we are committed to her to help her get through this. Andrea is a gifted pharmacologist, but she'll have to do what's best for her."

Olken is now cruising down I-95 at a steady eighty miles per hour. I expect he will move Boden out of Adams as quickly as possible and try to discourage her from filing any charges. For him, any publicity related to a hostage situation is unwanted.

"I'm exhausted. Do you mind if I catch a little shut-eye?"

"No problem. I'll call you when we enter Point Judith."

I am tired, but mostly I want to avoid any more of a conversation. I want to escape Olken's oppressive cordiality. I've fished for a long time, essentially all my life. Olken is trying to reel me in, and I don't plan to take the bait. I'll accept his apology for now, but that's it. I have no interest in hearing how much he looks forward to me being part of the Adams teams or any other related blandishments. That can wait. Flounder are bottom fish. They skim along the seabed, periodically burrowing into the muck with only their eyes protruding above the mire to scan for predators. I want to lie low for a while, until Tuesday, anyway. I'm not interested in what Olken is selling.

⊹

"Live bait?" I ask Woody.

"Why not?" he replies, lifting the lid from the bait bucket. "Stripers love eel."

Inside the container is a churning mix of seawater and algae. Woody drops his hand in and plucks a squirming eel from the mess, inserting the hook into one of the fish's eyes and out the other.

"Time to eat, guys," he calls out while casting away from the stern. With the eel wriggling from its end, the line flows over the water in slow motion and then disappears below the surface of the waves.

"Aren't you fishing today, Popeye?" he asks while taking up the slack on his line.

"Just making sure you get things right," I reply, plunging my arm into the bucket. I grip a writhing fish in my left hand and then position the hook against one of its eyes with my right. Baiting the eel through its eye sockets provides additional skull support, forcing the striped bass to bite down harder to free the fish and, in turn, setting the hook firmly in the bass's mouth, yet I hesitate. The fish seems to be saying, *Why are you doing that? Why are you driving the barb into me?* I stare at the squirming animal, and it slips from my grip. Dropping the hook, I scoop the eel up with my right as it slithers along and then wraps itself about my forearm, squeezing tight. I go to grab the fish with my left when suddenly an air horn blares. I leap up, expecting that a cargo ship or some other large vessel is bearing down on us, but all I see is a brilliant blue dome above and a calm sea with several small boats gently rocking on their moorings.

I have been asleep atop a bench on the ferry's upper deck. An announcement calls for drivers to return to their cars as the dream returns to me. Pulling the sleeve of my jacket back, I study my right forearm. There is no image of an eel or other indication that one had recently been squirming over me. Then I remember Antonio Lopez's tattoo of the sea serpent encircling his left forearm. He's now in twenty-three-hour lockdown with only two showers a week, if he's lucky, and an hour of recreation a day. All his meals will be served in the cell, and initially, he'll have no TV, radio, or other stimulation. He might get a Bible, or a good-hearted screw may pass him an old newspaper now and again. I have no idea how he'll manage the ice time, but I had promised to visit him in isolation, and hopefully, that may help.

Driving off the ferry, I call Woody. "Sorry I screwed things up a couple of days ago," I say after we exchange greetings.

"Yesterday," he replies.

"Yesterday what?"

"Yesterday, TC. I dropped you at Point Judith yesterday, not a couple of days ago."

"It feels a lot longer than that."

"Do the math, genius. It's less than twenty-four hours."

I have pulled to the curb and am staring out into the harbor. He's right. It was only yesterday when we were setting up for blues.

"I'll be home for two days. How's your schedule?"

"I have an early charter for tomorrow. They just want to drop a line over the side, circle the island, and then land someplace for a picnic. Monday works, but the tides suck. We'd have to go early or late."

"How about you pick me up around five thirty at my mom's? We'll drink coffee instead of beer."

"See you then, sailor," Woody says before clicking off.

Rather than driving directly to my mother's, I park the car in order to walk along the harbor. Thoughts of Lopez linger in my mind as I unconsciously glance down at my forearm. The most he can walk is in a one-hundred-foot circle in one of the tiger cages the isolation guys are let out into, whereas I could circumambulate the entire thirty-five or so miles of island coastline if I felt like it. My Boy Scout troop did that once on a three-night camping trip when I was fifteen. Lopez is one of the reasons I'll stay at Cranston. That I told him I would see him each week is more important to me than any deal Olken tried to imply.

Jim and the commissioner now both want me to run the Alternatives to Aggression program. It is what Jim wanted the whole time, but I always felt the consent for me to manage the unit was grudgingly given by the higher-ups, and from what the commissioner said, I was right. Rather than simply reviewing the referral list, I will now meet with all inmates interested and then decide whether they should be seen by Alain or any replacement Adams chooses for Boden. Too bad if they say it interferes with their randomization model. I'll also meet with Mario Zorello and some of the other organized crime guys who signed up for the program to see why they volunteered for the ATA. Their participation doesn't make sense to me, although they do meet all criteria.

We'll formally accept inmates a week from this Monday, as long as the system is set up to move the social workers and me onto the DOC payroll. I'm certain the social workers will be pleased because the state positions offer a much better benefits package. If I am to run the unit, I can't view it as a field test location for Eumonia. It has to be a unit to assist men in reducing their level of aggression first and a study site second. Adams Pharmaceuticals will be an adjunct to the treatment, and if that means they have to modify their research design, then that's what it will mean.

Traversing the harbor, I realize I had been viewing my role primarily as establishing a safe correctional environment in which the study can take place. Unconsciously or not, I had abdicated the clinical oversight to Adams, and that has to change. I'll propose to Jim that Lincoln assume more authority for all security issues so I can focus solely on treatment. In our current model, Lincoln defers to me, while we all know he has greater expertise in the area. The reality will be nearer to the codirector design I had initially proposed.

I have passed beyond the harbor's commercial district and out to Corn Neck Road toward the island's north end. I am not dependent on the money from the Cranston job, giving me the green light to do what I deem right. Fortunately, money's not a problem for me, and I appreciate that freedom. Turning back to the harbor, I feel much better about the position.

CHAPTER 3

1

"I 've been around a lot of violence, Doc, and I'm not getting any younger. I've got family."

"But you're not doing time for violence."

At my words, he gives me a condescending eye roll.

"Well, you aren't doing time for violence, Mario, right?" I insist.

"You know what I'm doing time for, and you know what they tried to have me do time for. If the FBI had its way, I'd be locked away in Marion or some other federal joint on racketeering charges. How much time do you think that would be?"

"A lot."

"Yeah, a lot, a whole lot," he says, his voice rising slightly. "You could make a goddamn long-distance phone call with all the numbers they'd stick up my ass if they had half a chance. I've already pushed past fifty. That's half a century. I don't intend to give them that satisfaction. I've done all right for myself. I plan to retire when I wrap this bit up. So I figure I get in this program—maybe it can help me with aggression, maybe it can help me get out a couple of months early. Capisce?"

"How'd you hear about it?" I ask.

"Come on, Doc. There are no secrets in the joint. The word is that there is this new program opening for guys that got trouble with, ah…"

"Aggression." I help.

"Yeah, aggression. I was going to say for beating people down but knew that wasn't quite kosher. I've had some trouble with aggression. I've had a lot of trouble with it, so I looked into this program and signed up."

"You realize it includes a trial on medication too."

"That's okay by me. I'll try anything if it will get me out a little quicker and keep me out. I've stayed away from that in the past, the meds, the counseling, but it's time to try something new. When you spend fifteen of the last thirty-five years in the can, it may be time to switch gears. It's life on the installment plan, and I'm tired of it. When I was a little kid in the late fifties, that installment plan was called revolving credit, and San Souci's Department Store in Olneyville Square offered it. They gave out Green Stamps with each purchase, and those stamps were my first heist. When I was ten or eleven, we stole a couple of the big books the cashiers used to rip the stamps out of for customers; then we cashed them in, and I got a Japanese transistor radio. One of those little things with an earplug. Christ, I haven't thought about that in years."

"Life on the installment plan," I remind him.

"Right, right, that's what kicked it off." He chuckles. "As I was saying, I'm getting short, and if this can help me get out early, sign me up."

"The goal is not to help guys get out early, Mario. It's to help guys deal with aggression."

Instantly, an air of disquieting apprehensiveness fills the room. The reminiscing older man disappears, replaced by an intensely focused individual whose dark, lidded eyes stare out from beneath bushy salt-and-pepper eyebrows directly into mine. "I've done damage to a couple of people, Doc, serious damage. There are some people out there that don't deserve to live. That's something that's not news to you if I'm not mistaken."

His words unsettle me. I buy time by clearing my throat and then ask what he means.

The momentary foreboding that swept through the room has receded. The Mario Zorello sitting with me now is an older, slightly squat Italian man pushing sixty, not the imposing Patriarca crime family capo who had just made a brief appearance.

"You're saying this program, this Alternative to Aggression thing you have, can help violent guys. There's times when I was a kid that I was violent. So if you can help me, I'm here. That's what I'm saying, and that's what I told the doctor that spoke to me a couple of weeks ago, that's all."

"It means moving out of your unit, so you'd lose your single room. We only have doubles in the new building. You'll keep your job in the print shop and eat in the prison's chow hall but with the other guys in the ATA program. After the afternoon rec time, you'll be expected to participate in a minimum of two groups per week and one counseling session a week. Then after supper, you will be restricted to activities on the unit. Visits are planned for Sundays in a small area we will set up in the unit."

"There's a rumor that you may have conjugal visits?"

"You're right, Mario; it's a rumor. We have no plans for that at this time."

"Canteen?"

"You'll get the same canteen access as anyone else. There's a small kitchenette with a microwave, stovetop, dinnerware, and a sink."

"Can you skip the chow line and eat in the unit? I've got that diabetes and have a special diet."

"Lieutenant Grant and I haven't made a final decision on that yet. I expect it will depend on our staffing. If there are enough officers on, you'll probably be able to stay back to prepare something for yourself, but that would be for one meal a day at the most."

Mario ponders my responses. "I can live with that, Doc. Do I get to pick my roommate? I know a few other guys interested in the program."

"Lieutenant Grant will make all the room assignments. Any requests can be made to him."

"What about the tests that other doctor mentioned? What's the word on those?"

"There will be blood draws done weekly for the first month to monitor your blood level of Eumonia—that's the medication you may be taking. After that, they will be done at two-week intervals. Additionally, you will be given a series of questionnaires and interviewed by a staff person from Adams Pharmaceuticals when you enter the program, at three months, and at six months."

"What happens after six months?"

"If the program shows success, I expect DOC will continue it, and you'll be able to stay until you wrap up or are paroled. The whole thing is voluntary. You can withdraw at any time you wish, and it won't have any bearing on your sentence."

"Yeah, I realize that. The doc I saw from the drug company explained all that and had me sign a release that I understood. He told me pretty much the same things you did, except he wasn't up on the canteen and those types of things. So what do you say, Doc? You planning to sign me up?"

I hesitate and then respond, "Lieutenant Grant and I are reviewing all the applicants who were interviewed by Drs. Vos and Boden and will be getting back to you shortly. If it all works out, we'll be accepting the first group of ten next week, which will include you."

Zorello nods and then says, "How's that Dr. Boden doing anyway? I heard there was a little problem last week."

"I can't discuss staff, Mario."

"Just asking," he replies solicitously. "You know there are no secrets in this place. If there is anything I can do to help out, you let me know."

A slightly ominous breeze accompanies his words to momentarily fill the room as I tell him it is nothing for him to worry about.

"I wait to hear from you; is that it?" he asks as we stand out in the entry, waiting for the gate officer to key Mario back into prison.

"You'll hear from Lieutenant Grant or me in a couple of days," I confirm.

"Thanks," he says and then exits through the gate and into Cranston State Prison proper.

"He doesn't need an escort?" I question the gate officer as I watch him cross the big recreation field, where a group of Spanish guys is playing soccer.

"He's minimum," the officer reminds me, indicating Zorello's security level. I remember it is part of the entry criteria for the ATA. All inmates have to be at minimum-level status to move unescorted to their job assignments, chow, and other activities in the institution.

Heading back to my office, I easily follow Zorello's logic. If he can get a few months knocked off his time, why not participate in the program? He does meet the entrance criteria, and making his status as the highest-ranking member of the Mafia at Cranston an exclusionary criterion is impossible.

How he not-so-subtly brought up the murder of Leon Alexander was momentarily unnerving. It was as if we were coconspirators, both agreeing that certain people didn't deserve to live. The trouble was that I did agree with him, at least as far as Alexander was concerned. Some people deserved to die. Even Lincoln, the active churchman and elder in the Baptist Church, let me know the first day I was back that no one lost any sleep over Alexander's murder. It was as if Mario was saying, *Hey, Doc, you did what you had to do. You arranged the murder of the scumbag that killed your wife, and I arrange the murder of people who got in my way. Capisce?* But I didn't capisce, and I didn't order Fahad or anyone else to gut Alexander in the protective custody chow line. Zorello has merely made somewhat explicit an issue that will be in the back of many guys' minds—that the unit manager of the Alternatives to Aggression program arranged for someone to murder the guy who killed his wife. It's an issue that will have to be acknowledged in some manner.

I decide to only briefly interview the other candidates whom Vos or Boden have already cleared. They will likely say the same thing as Zorello, that they do have histories of violence and are searching for any way to shorten their time. I will have to bring up with Vos how the inmates' desire to lessen their sentences will be a confounding variable in their study. Adams is interested in seeing whether Eumonia reduces aggressive impulses by stabilizing subjects' moods and lowering paranoid or other ideation that can contribute to violence, while the subjects are most interested in presenting well and being compliant to get out of prison ASAP. To some extent, it is a win-win situation. Adams gets the results they want, and the inmates make early parole by appearing as if they have addressed issues that have led them into prison. Still, from a research perspective, the positive results of Eumonia may be a false positive, a red herring, an artifact arising from the inmate's desire to present well rather than any intervention done by Adams or the ATA program.

2

After Zorello leaves, I call the Departmental Segregation Unit to inquire whether it is a good time to see Antonio Lopez. "His schedule's fairly open," the sergeant quips in response to my question. Traversing the institution to see him, I reflect on my previous day's conversation with the super.

When I returned to the prison after the hostage situation, I was surprised that Jim agreed to my requests. They were not exactly demands, but he got the message. I was still the unit manager, but my focus was now on the programming rather than security, which was ceded over to Lincoln. We even revisited the idea of Lincoln being the codirector of the unit, which Jim did not immediately rule out as he previously had. But when we later spoke to Lincoln, he wasn't interested. "I'd rather try to make captain," was his response. I had forgotten that aspect. Becoming the codirector necessitated moving into a management block, whereas remaining a lieutenant, with the hope of making captain, kept him in a CO block. He was eligible for an earlier retirement as a correctional officer; plus, he got a military time bonus. With any luck, he could be out at fifty-five with 80 percent of his salary, not including military benefits.

Nonetheless, Jim and I concurred on my backing off from managing the security issues. I was relieved, as they had already begun to bore me. I wanted the unit to be safe and run smoothly, but I had minimal interest in arranging schedules, ensuring we were compliant with the department's overtime policy, monitoring training, negotiating with the union rep if an officer was disciplined, ensuring random strip or unit searches were done properly, as well as monitoring the other assorted surveillance protocols related to operational security. I was happy to hand it off to Lincoln, lock, stock, and barrel, and he was happy to pick it up, aware that it may accelerate his promotion to captain if he did a good job.

During my meeting with Jim, I asked him what the commissioner meant when he said I had agreed to manage the program for a year.

"I was waiting for you to ask me that," Jim said. "I know I told you it was for six months, but I figured once you got on board, you would decide to stay for the year. The commissioner wanted to be certain we had stable leadership for the first twelve months, so I told him you agreed to the time. He was taking a lot of heat politically to make it work from Poletti's office. In an indirect way, the hostage situation with Lopez got Poletti to back off, to back way off. They hope this thing works to promote their knowledge-based economy scheme, but they don't want anyone to get wind that their strong-arming of corrections led to a hostage situation or worse. If you leave after six months, I'll have to deal with the commissioner, but I'm hoping you'll stay. For now, it's all moot. Everyone hopes you to stay indefinitely because of how you got Boden out."

I pondered what Jim said for a few moments and then replied, "If Lincoln manages the majority of the security issues, you may not even need me all that much anyway."

Jim laughed at my response. "You don't get it. I never expected you to manage security protocols. That you're familiar with how we operate is important, but I've got a lot of guys besides Lincoln who can run a unit from the security perspective. You're here to keep an eye on Adams. That's the part you can do better than anyone else. I feel more positive now that we have got control over the social workers and that they've pulled back on trying to administer the entire program. When I said you were a compromise candidate, I was serious. Can you imagine if the commissioner had caved and gave the authority to manage that place to Adams? Can you imagine placing Boden or someone similar to her in both the medical director and unit manager positions?"

"A bad idea," I observed.

"That's the understatement of the year. It would have consumed huge amounts of my time to ensure it didn't get totally out of whack. Recruiting staff would have been a major pain in the ass, too, and all because of some politician's desire to help Adams Pharmaceuticals break into the correctional-health-management field. With you and Lincoln at the helm, we had guys lining up to work there. Then I gave Adams a little power by calling Boden the medical director, and the shit hit the fan. The silver lining is that the Boden situation has given us a free hand to run the unit the right way. I never wanted you in there to verify counts were done properly or shift changes took place. I wanted you in there to keep an eye on Adams. I can run a prison, but a unit where half the cons are on pills that are supposed to turn them into a herd of contented cows is a different animal. I need help with that piece."

"Why didn't you tell me this when we first talked?"

"I did. The one thing I wasn't square with you on was that the commissioner expected a year commitment, but I may not have even known that at the time. I forget if he said that before or after we first met. I told you I needed someone who was savvy on both the mental health and correctional issues. I expected you to realize that your emphasis was on the mental health part. I can manage the security piece, and I should have been more explicit on that. We've got plenty of male and female officers here who can handle that end. Remember, this thing is a work in progress, and I didn't put certain parts of it together in my own mind until we began to get it up and running. Although I am certain I made the right decision by getting you in here. You already prevented a serious incident from escalating to the point where it could have shut the whole project down without a con ever passing through its gates. As far as I can see, you're the best guy for this job, and I expect that Olken, Vorenzi, and anyone else who wants this to work will agree with me."

My irritation that Jim had misled me disappeared as he explained his logic in more detail.

When he finished, I said, "For me, Adams is an adjunct to the ATA. I've reviewed their programming ideas, and it's all standard cognitive behavioral interventions that were lifted from a bunch of workbooks on aggression management, substance abuse treatment, and social skill development. I'm planning to modify that for a prison population. It's a little too intellectual for inmates and doesn't include any trauma material—"

"TC." Jim interrupted me. "You don't have to explain any of this to me. I trust you, and I trust you'll make sure any interventions are appropriate for our population. Run the changes you make by the Adams people, but I have no doubt they'll give you free rein."

Arriving at the max facility, I'm roused from my reverie. The Departmental Segregation Unit is a forty-bed supermax facility. The prison within the prison is located in a special section of Max I. Inmates like Lopez may be locked down in the DSU on awaiting-action status until their disciplinary hearing is completed. This normally never takes longer than two to four weeks. They then can be locked up in the unit for the duration of their disciplinary time assignment, which in some cases is years. They can earn privileges, such as access to a small black-and-white TV, reading materials, and more recreation time, by not causing problems. Considering that most inmates don't read much and that rec time consists of pacing in circles outside in a tiger cage, the most appealing privilege is the TV. Not causing problems is understood to mean not destroying your cell, which is hard to do since, besides the molded concrete bed and desk, along with a wall-bolted steel hopper/sink combination unit, the only other piece of furniture is the thin closed-foam mattress. Flooding the cell by stuffing clothing into the toilet or throwing feces and urine out the food slot when it is open are the most common types of disruptions. Most prisoners are eventually transferred to Max I to complete part of their DSU time. That facility has common dining and recreation space for the inmates and some programming and job assignments. The DSU is on a regular twenty-three-hour lockdown, with meals served in the rooms and almost no interaction among the inmates.

To get into the max building, I must first be buzzed through an exterior security checkpoint that is video monitored. A thin, tinny voice asks me to identify myself and state my business.

"Dr. Thomas Phillips," I reply. "I'm here to see Antonio Lopez in the DSU."

At the sound of a buzzer, I pull open the gate and make my way down a cyclone-fenced tunnel to the Max I entry. The whole facility is a giant futuristic concrete-and-steel box transferred in from the *Clockwork Orange* set. Human contact is kept to a minimum, particularly in the DSU. Various human rights groups have documented how the isolation highly correlates with heightened suicide rates in supermax facilities and increased psychotic episodes among the inmates. To address this, Rhode Island Corrections instituted a policy dictating that inmates in DSU spend a maximum of three consecutive weeks in isolation at a time. Once the three weeks are up, they are transferred into a special section of Max I for a couple of days. It was developed to avoid lawsuits claiming the isolation was cruel and unusual punishment but had the side benefit of providing guys with a little light at the end of the tunnel.

There is almost no natural light in Max I. High-mounted narrow and heavily screened transom windows only allow a dull metallic glow into the large open area that separates the DSU side of the building from the two fifty-bed Max I high-security blocks. The obscured radiance from the transoms is overwhelmed by the banks of LED lights that glare down from on high. When Max I opened a few years back, a lot was made out of the fact that the lighting was the same type used in modern sports arenas. It was almost as if the staff and cons should be grateful that they lived and worked beneath the same luminaries that graced Madison Square Garden. The brilliant blue-white light was phosphorescent to me, enhancing the stark sterility of an already barren landscape. I hated going into the max facility and did my best to avoid it. There was no way to pretend you weren't in a brutal, dehumanizing environment as soon as you crossed the threshold.

Once the officer clears me, I cross the open space used as the common chow and recreation area for the two Max I blocks. Several inmates are idling about as I traverse the space. Some are on work details sweeping and cleaning up, while others are watching TV, playing cards or board games, using the two exercise machines off to one side, or making general chitchat with each other. I cross over a fluorescent-orange out-of-bounds line painted on the concrete floor that indicates the entrance to the DSU. At the second security post, I reidentify myself and then hold up my DOC ID to a video monitor. "Pull it open, Doc," a voice instructs from beyond the steel door that I now haul back. I know the door can be moved electronically, but the gate officers generally operate it manually to ensure it doesn't jam.

I haven't been in the DSU in years. It's high tech, except for the old-fashioned wire cage I am now standing in. A single guard peers out at me from a steel and Plexiglas control booth to my right and waves. I motion back as he presses a button, setting off the distinctive electronic snap of a lock releasing. I next push the wire mesh gate in front of me. The DSU has the same fancy overhead lighting as the rest of the max facility, but I've never been in it when more than a third of them are illuminated, and those appear to be on low. It is in perpetual twilight. On one of my first trips into the isolation unit, a lieutenant explained that most inmates deal with isolation by sleeping as long as possible, as much as twenty hours per day. The officers are happy to oblige them by keeping the lights dim, as the more they sleep, the fewer potential problems there are.

"I'd like to see Antonio Lopez," I tell the officer who buzzed me in.

"No problem, Doc," he says, from the DSU's mini-control-room. "He's down in cell 15 on the right side."

"Any chance you can bring him up to an interview room?"

"It might take a while; we're running shorthanded today. I can call for backup, but…" He trails off, not needing to complete the explanation.

I prefer to see Lopez in the privacy of one of the DSU's two interview rooms but realize that it may take as long as an hour to free another officer up from some other area of the institution to help out. "That's okay. I can use the food slot," I respond.

Walking down the dim central hallway the separates the twenty isolation cells on either side of me, I doubt that Lopez will want to chat for long through his food slot when all the other inmates can listen in on our conversation. I will be able to fulfill my promise to see him yet still be able to get out quickly.

Arriving at cell 15, I peer in the door's twelve-by-twelve-inch safety-glass panel to see Lopez asleep on his cot swaddled in sheets. I tap vigorously on the steel, and he begins to squirm within his dirty white chrysalis. A head slowly emerges, and he tries to focus on the doorway. I wave once but have no idea if I am visible behind the glass. I next kneel on the concrete, pull back the latch to release the metal door over his food slot, and then lean my head sideways so he will be able to see me in the eighteen-by-six-inch rectangular opening.

"Antonio," I call, "it's Tom Phillips."

Now he's groggily staring at the slot. From his perspective, there's a disembodied face framed by the peeling battleship gray of his door, calling out his name. "Eh?"

"Tom Phillips, the psychologist. We spoke a couple of days ago."

"Oh yeah, yeah," he mumbles. "Hey," he continues, brightening up. "How you doing, man?"

He's sitting on the side of the bunk now with the sheet pulled loosely about his body. I'm fairly certain he is naked under it. He no longer resembles Charlie Brown, but draped in bed linens, he appears to be more of a giant off-white Humpy Dumpty.

"I'm okay. Thanks for asking. I wanted to check on how you were doing."

"Tell me, Doc, were you straight with me the other day when you said they called you in from fishing?"

"Slack tide, casting for blues off the stern of a Whaler Rampage with twin Merc 125s when my cell started to ring."

"Eh," he concludes while gathering the white fabric around his waist. He then gets off the bed and shuffles up to the door.

"They're short staffed and aren't able to let us use an interview room," I explain as he approaches and kneels on the floor opposite me.

"They're always short staffed. No one got to go outside today because they were short staffed." Then, lowering his voice, he asks, "What are they going to do with me, Doc?"

"Have you had your D-board yet?"

"Nah, I bet they want to see if that"—he hesitates and then continues—"that lady's gonna file charges."

I expect he was planning to say "bitch" but caught himself.

"I guess you'll have to wait a bit."

"What do you think? Will she file?"

There is a hitch in his voice as he questions me. With our faces inches apart, separated by a thin plate of steel, I feel the warmth of his breath and hear the trepidation, even dread, in his words. He hasn't shaved in the five days since the hostage taking. He's grizzly and unkempt with slightly bloodshot eyes, having aged years for each day he's served in isolation.

"You know, Antonio, most people are happy when these situations go away. I can't say what will happen, but you didn't really hurt her. I mean, you tied her up, but you didn't do anything else, right?"

"No, no, no." He groans softly. Both of us have lowered our voices not to be overheard. "I got pissed. She wanted me to talk about my crime, my niece. Christ, it never happened, but she wouldn't let it go. I told ya years ago, she was sixteen…ah, fuck it! No one's gonna believe anything I say."

We kneel in silence. The darkness of the unit enhances the odd confessional aura surrounding us.

"Like I said, Antonio, if this goes away, I doubt anyone will complain. DOC doesn't want the publicity, and you don't want the time."

"What about her? What do you think she wants?"

I see Boden's terrified face in my mind as she is wheeled out from the ATA. "I have no idea what she wants."

"What if I write her an apology letter? What if I tell her I'm sorry? Will that help me?"

"If I were you, I'd give it a rest; let her deal with it on her own for now."

"But there's nothing for her to deal with, Doc. I'm telling you I didn't do anything. That's the God's honest truth," he pleads.

"You did keep her in there against her will, Tony."

"Christ, you know what I mean. I didn't screw her. I could of, but I didn't, okay? I just wanted her to back off, and she wouldn't." He moans in frustration. "That's all that happened. Will you be at my D-board and tell them I listened to you? I came out, and I didn't have to. I could have stayed in there longer, but I came out. I let her go. Will you come and tell them that?"

"Sure, I can be there. How are you doing now?"

"I'm not planning to off myself if that's what you're wondering."

We continue for five more minutes to go back and forth over the same material, and then I tell Antonio I have to go.

"You'll see me again, right?"

"Every week, Antonio. I'll be here every week."

"How about twice a week, Doc? Can you make it twice a week, eh?"

"I'll see what I can do," I reply, closing the food slot and rising to my feet.

Antonio's face is pressed against the safety panel. "Thanks for coming by, Doc," I hear, muffled by the glass and steel. Turning, I notice a dozen or more faces glued to the door panels of the cells on the opposite side of the block. I take a few steps toward the control room and hear a tapping on my left. A young Black guy is knocking lightly but steadily on his window.

"Hey, can I talk to you too?"

3

I lie restlessly on my bed in the warden's house that night. It took me the better part of two hours to get out of the DSU. I had to kneel at almost a dozen doors of the baddest badasses in the Ocean State, listening to their litanies.

"I haven't heard from my family in months, man. Can ya call my moms? Can ya tell her to get her ass up here to see me?"

"I didn't do anything. He tried to stab me first. Can you tell that to the D-board? I don't belong in the hole. Can you help me get out?"

"I have no idea who my caseworker is. Can you get his name? Please, I need to speak to him."

"This place is driving me loco. Can you get hold of my sister? She lives with my nana."

"I can't sleep. Can you get me something to sleep, Doc? I used to take Trazodone. Can you get me some Trazodone, 150 milligrams at night? That should do me."

All of them pathetic and pitiful in one way or another, all simply wanting to talk, all praying for the same thing: "Will you come back and see me again?"

I had to escape from their despair, to shake off the pleas, entreaties, and supplications that each one affixed to me with some type of crazy glue. The pint of whiskey I picked up helped, and I was able to pass out in my bed without their voices echoing in my mind. But now it is 4:00 a.m., and my head throbs. I want off the mainland. I want my island and to be coasting out beyond the breakwater in the *Lir*, Izzy's eighteen-foot gaff-rigged Whitehall, running wing on wing with a following wind. I would break beyond the turquoise of the coastal reaches for the deep sea's lapis, out and beyond Georges Banks, where Antonio Lopez fished, to the flowing warmth of the Gulf Stream. I'd leave them in their segregation cells, atoning for their miscellaneous sins. I fall back into a fitful sleep, trying to dislodge myself from their intolerable hopes.

I'm hung over in the morning but still determined to run. Lacing up my sneakers, I am out onto the access road that girths the prison at 7:00 a.m., and ten minutes later, I'm leaning against the wall, retching my guts out. It will only be a few minutes until I'm noticed by an officer in one of the guard towers, and he dispatches a car to investigate. But without something to lean against, I'd be kneeling on the grass or even collapsed into my vomitus. It takes less than two minutes to purge the toxic swill, and then I'm back on the move. I force one foot in front of the other, and after a mile, I begin to have some semblance of a rhythm, albeit at a sedate ten or eleven minutes a mile, but it's a pace.

The desires of the DSU guys keep pursuing me, and I decide I'll require more distance between myself and the institution if I plan to stay for a couple of months or longer. I thought I could manage things easier by staying out back in the warden's house for free, but it's not working. I can't escape the wall with all the yearning and frustration that lurks behind it, particularly on days like yesterday when I visit the segregation unit. I'll look for a studio or a room in Providence. It will also save me the worry of wondering who's inside poking around in my stuff. No more questions from the super about me being sober because some screw or maintenance guy, checking the plumbing or hunting for old records, notices an empty pint bottle and goes off running to him. I have an early meeting at Adams with Olken and Vos to review the status of the ATA. After that, I'll drop by a Realtor's office or check out craigslist and then start home.

The atmosphere at Adams Pharmaceuticals has changed since I was last there. Olken immediately comes out to greet me as soon as I check in with the receptionist. He brings me back to his office, where Vos is already awaiting my arrival. Rather than ensconcing himself behind his high-tech desk with the built-in monitors, he joins Alain and me by a small smoked-glass coffee table that sits on gigantic industrial casters.

"Again, you have our thanks for how you managed the situation with Andrea," he immediately says after we are seated.

"She spent one night in the hospital, feels much better, and is already anxious to return to work," Vos adds.

I study him for a moment. "Return to work where?"

"Why, here at Adams. She has been part of all phases of Eumonia's development, including the initial trials. I expect she will eventually return to Cranston as well to continue her work there."

I pause to gauge my words and then simply say, "I'm sorry, Alain, but that will not be happening. As far as I am concerned, she largely brought the hostage situation upon herself. She is too high a security risk for me to allow that. You'll have to find someone else to fill in for her."

He studies me with a mix of incredulity and disdain before replying, "That's ridiculous." Then, turning to Olken, he continues, "Andrea is familiar with all our protocols. She developed many of them. She's critical, and I'm certain she'll expect to continue her work."

I also turn to study Olken, but he doesn't respond. Finally, I say, "From a security perspective, she is too high risk, and from a clinical perspective, I have serious reservations in respect to her interviewing skills. On top of all that, she may be asked to testify at the disciplinary board for Lopez, and there is still the question of criminal charges. There are no secrets in a prison. All the inmates will be aware of the hostage situation."

"Who would have told them?" he asks accusatorily.

I shrug in response to the question. "It's a prison. It's incestuous."

Vos leans back pensively in his chair. "Tell me what happened last Friday."

I reconstruct the events of the day to the best of my ability. After my account, his demeanor has altered markedly. "You're right; she can't go back there."

"I wonder if hiring a nurse practitioner to do the work at Cranston may not be best. We can still retain Andrea here for the analysis and other responsibilities," Olken suggests.

"Knowing Andrea, I believe she'll expect to be on site some of the time."

"Is she teaching?" Olken asks. "It may be an opportune time for her to pursue some of her academic interests."

"Are you planning to let her go because she was held hostage, Ralph?"

"No, no, of course not." Olken backpedals. "But she does have a range of career interests. If she can't get back into the field site, it may be better for her professionally to evaluate other options, continuing with us on a consultation basis."

"I'm not sure what she told you, Alain, but she was seriously shook up," I say. "From a retrospective frame of reference, it may not seem that bad to her at this point, but to me, that is a form of denial. She was in a state of shock, traumatic shock. Doing studies with prisoners is not the same as working with college kids or other populations. She may appreciate the opportunity to bow out gracefully. Regardless, she can't reenter the prison until the disciplinary process is completed. It routinely takes a couple of weeks, but she doesn't have to know that. If she's committed to the study, she may realize that for it to progress, someone else must take her place. She'll get to bow out with her head high, and the study will move ahead. She doesn't have to be told that in the end, we wouldn't allow her back in."

"She was also responsible for supervising the social workers and to develop the group interventions that will be used in the therapy component."

As Alain speaks, I realize that Olken has not appraised him of the meeting he had with Jim, the commissioner, and me on Saturday to debrief what had happened initially. I again hesitate to give him a chance to enter the conversation, but he remains mum.

"Corrections has made some changes to the administration of the Alternatives to Aggression program," I begin as he casts me a quizzical look. "The social workers are being moved into DOC slots, and my pay will be channeled through the department as well. The commissioner believes that will be cleaner in respect to the chain of command. I'll be supervising the social workers and taking responsibility for all treatment aspects of the program, except for the medication distribution. I reviewed the group protocols Dr. Boden recommended, and they were an excellent mix of general cognitive behavioral interventions, but I believe they require tweaking in order to more specifically fit a correctional population, particularly the substance abuse and trauma components, so I have begun to do that."

"You didn't think they were very good?" he interrupts.

"I'd say there was clear room for improvement, but like you or Dr. Olken said, she is more of an academic."

Vos sighs. "When was all this decided?"

"I had a meeting on Saturday with the commissioner, the Cranston superintendent, and Dr. Phillips," Olken explains, finally entering the conversation. "I wanted to wait until the three of us met to consider how this impacts our trial. Eumonia clearly must be our total focus from here forward. Corrections has assumed full responsibility for all other aspects of the ATA."

"Will there be an on-site medical director?" he asks.

"I doubt one will be required on site," Olken speculates.

"I'm fairly certain there won't be," I add. "We plan to operate it under the same protocols used for the DOC substance abuse unit. The psychiatric services will be an adjunct and, in this case, an adjunct provided by Adams as part of a field test for Eumonia. That's one of the reasons they moved the social workers into state positions and directed my pay through the DOC. It's a standard model that allows me to have full supervision of the clinical component."

"This will have no impact on the clinical trial of Eumonia," Olken emphasizes. "That has always been our primary objective. The possibility of entering the correctional health-management field was a secondary goal for Adams."

"I understand that. I was never part of those conversations. They were between you and the board of trustees." Then, turning to me, Vos asks if I am certain that it will not affect the Eumonia study.

"As far as I can see, there will be no change. You'll still have a control group who attend the ATA and don't receive Eumonia."

Vos sighs. "As Ralph said, the field test has always been our primary objective."

Silence fills the room after Vos's remarks, but there is an acceptance in it that does not have the sharp edge of previous breaks in our discussion.

"If Andrea is told of the elimination of the medical director position and that revisions in the treatment aspects of the program were made by the DOC, do you think it may influence her decision to stay on?" Olken asks.

"It may," Alain replies. "She is exceptionally bright and will realize she's been marginalized and will have no influence in any decisions made by the DOC. She already has one standing academic offer based on her prior research of which I am aware. Continuing as a consultant to the Eumonia field trial may give her the graceful exit Tom mentioned to pursue her other interests."

We continue to assess how the program must be reorganized, deciding an ongoing weekly planning session is necessary to keep the project on track. Before today, I favored alternating the meetings between Adams's offices and the prison, but now I believe all the meetings should be at their place. It keeps the lines clearer in that they only come to the prison when there is a reason for them to be there, either as part of the study or for an appointment. Additionally, it will give me a reason to get out of Cranston once a week.

At the conclusion of our meeting, I ask Alain to give Boden my best.

"From what you've said, she's very indebted to you," he replies.

"I wouldn't go that far. It was more Hostage Negotiations 101. We were fortunate that Lopez wanted it ended as badly as we did."

Olken chuckles. "Virtue is its own reward. You won't get him to take any credit, Alain. I already tried."

I begin to protest, to explain myself, but then simply shrug. Neither of them has lived on an island. You do what you need to do to get by. I did what I had to do with Lopez, and now I'm doing what I promised to do by visiting him in segregation, and that's that.

Olken brings the meeting to a close as both of them again thank me for helping Boden. He then asks me to wait a moment.

"Tom, I want you to know how grateful I am and we all are for all you have done. I expect you easily could have shut down the entire trial on Saturday if you told the commissioner you viewed it as unworkable."

"I doubt that. You have some heavy hitters on your side with Poletti's involvement and Adams anchoring that Knowledge Center, or whatever it is, in his district."

"That's true," he concedes. "But you'd be surprised at how quickly a politician can distance himself from any messy type of situation. This trial is critical to Adams. We have a sizable investment in Eumonia, and if the results confirm our previous studies, it will be a major—and hopefully final—step in allowing us to bring the drug to market. In the world of pharmaceuticals, we're a small firm, and this represents a chance for us to move to the next level of competitiveness."

After our meeting, I ask him if there is a computer I can use for a little while, explaining that I plan to check craigslist for an apartment or studio in Providence.

"What about a condo?" he suggests. "Those mills by the Woonasquatucket, where we expect to relocate, are already being renovated for both residential and commercial usage. We have options on two for both our corporate offices and manufacturing. North Providence has gone to seed a bit in the past thirty years, but nevertheless, they are magnificent structures. Occupancy is six to eight months away, and spacious one-bedrooms with views of the river are now available at excellent preconstruction prices. I don't mean to come across like a real estate agent, but I was sold for those exact reasons."

"I'm staying in the warden's house right now. It's part of the former housing units for prison employees located outside the walls on the prison property. I really don't want to wait six months or more to move."

"That's understandable," he agrees. "It's too bad. They are exceptional properties, and as the river area continues to recover, the whole neighborhood will gentrify, which is precisely what we are counting on. Let me find you a space where you can work."

4

As we proceed down the corridor, I realize that Adams is a smaller operation than I initially thought. Overall, there are no more than half a dozen offices, plus a conference room.

"Where is your manufacturing located?" I ask as we enter a vacant office that appears to be shared by a few people, having no personalized decorations on the walls.

"Currently, we have temporary space at the University of Rhode Island, which we are able to lease at a highly favorable price as part of the new business and technology incubation program subsidized by the state."

"How many products are you currently marketing?"

"In addition to Eumonia, we have two other psychiatric medications in development. They have antipsychotic and mood-stabilizing characteristics, too, but have not shown the specific trait of reducing paranoid or other ideation that can be linked to aggression. We are hopeful one will be particularly effective on acute mania-related psychosis, but that is not a large market. The most commercially successful products are those developed to treat chronic conditions, which therefore require daily usage, such as insulin for diabetes, statins for cholesterol levels, or antidepressants. That is why Eumonia has such potential. Not only may it help stabilize mood and reduce cognitive distortions, but its reduction of related aggression provides a major social benefit. In light of the chronic aspects of the conditions with which our initial trials have shown it to be effective, it would be prescribed in an ongoing manner to patients.”

“Is your interest in correctional health management related to the use of Eumonia to reduce aggression, making inmates more compliant with their incarceration?”

“I wouldn’t phrase it that way,” Olken clarifies. “We are absolutely not interested in any type of social control via pharmacology. If that was the objective, Thorazine, Stelazine, and other first-generation antipsychotics continue to be remarkably effective, although their side effects are often unacceptable. We are hopeful longitudinal studies will confirm Eumonia has many fewer side effects than the first- and second-generation antipsychotics. In fact, we believe Eumonia should be viewed as a third-generation antipsychotic due to its relatively benign side effects. Our interest in correctional health management is related to the lowering of aggressive impulses so that the prison population will be more amenable to treatment, which is why our initial model called for Adams to manage the clinical interventions provided within the unit.”

As he speaks, I reflect on Jim’s comments when we first met to discuss my return to corrections. No matter how Adams presents Eumonia, correctional administrators will see it as a management tool, knowing that calmer inmates are more tractable than agitated ones.

“The management of correctional healthcare systems remains an element in Adams’s long-term strategic plan,” Olken continues, bringing me back to the conversation. “As the commissioner said last week, if we choose to pursue that area, perhaps you can collaborate with us on a consultative or more regular basis.”

“Perhaps,” I agree while remembering my first conversation with Jim. Possibly DuPont Chemicals was right back in the ’50s, ’60s, and ’70s: better living was possible through chemistry after all. If Antonio Lopez was taking Eumonia and did not have the overwhelming and inaccurate paranoid ideation that Boden was pushing him to reveal his sexual relationship with his niece, the entire hostage situation may have been avoided. Nonetheless, it is a definite two-edged sword. Part of me preferred pain. My mother and others suggested an antidepressant after Maura's death, but I rejected the idea. I even rejected therapy, although I happily recommended it to others in similar situations. I used the excuse that Block Island was such a small community it wasn't feasible, while the actual reason was more related to finding the solace offered by the bottle being more to my liking.

Olken points me to a desk and says he will log me in. I step to one side as he turns on the computer, and we wait a moment for it to boot up. As soon as the sign-in screen appears, he enters *rOlken* followed by his password. I note that his typing skills are excellent as his fingers fly over the letters and numerals that compose the log-in.

"Take as long as you need," he tells me. "Andrea shared this space with our data entry clerk and research analyst. Obviously, Andrea won't be in to-day, and the other two are on a per diem basis, and we have no work currently scheduled for them."

After Olken leaves, I root around in the desk for a bit. I find a Robert Parker novel, an open tube of Life Savers, and a couple of disposable pens and writing pads, but nothing of any real interest. It's an automatic behavior and curiosity I've had my entire life: checking the titles on bookshelves, studying the pictures people select to hang on their walls, examining furniture, snooping in medicine cabinets. The miscellaneous clues people strew about related to their hopes and desires. This room is vacant both of others and personality. When Olken stated Boden used it, I had hoped it might give me some insight into her, but it does not. She has left no trail behind to indicate where she is headed. I am tempted to try and enter Olken's electronic world. He has logged me on via his password, so I would likely have access to all the files on Adams's common drive as well as his more personal material. I decide that's a boundary I don't want to cross and open Internet Explorer.

The prices for studios aren't as bad as I was expecting. For $500 to $600, I can get into a decent spot on Federal Hill, where Maura and I used to live, and $1,000 will get me a place in one of the new downtown high-rises, which includes a pool and an in-house health club. Suddenly, as I'm studying the other young tenants frolicking in the pool, a wave of bleak melancholy floods over me. I realize I have not once considered Matt as I searched apartments. I have a tremendous desire to know how he is doing and immediately give my mom a call. Matt is down for an early nap, and we chitchat a bit before I confirm that I can make the three o'clock ferry home. As soon as I click off, the secretary enters to tell me Dr. Olken has asked to see me. I expect she was waiting outside until I got off the phone with my mother and tell her I'll stop by his office momentarily.

"Any luck?" Olken calls across his desk as soon as I appear at his door.

"Not yet," I respond, wanting to get out of there as quickly as possible, forgoing the apartment hunt to try and make an earlier boat home.

Olken rounds his desk with a manila folder, which he in turn opens. Reaching in, he withdraws a yellow lanyard with Adams Pharmaceuticals repeatedly stamped in black along the webbing. I had previously seen the lanyards around Olken's and others' necks but never looked at them closely. Now, I am immediately taken aback as I take the strand of polyester Olken has proffered to me in his outstretched arm. The color scheme is the inverse of a similar ID lanyard I wore at Camp Delta in Guantanamo while I was stationed there. That one read JTF—GITMO, for Joint Task Force—Guantanamo, silhouetted in yellow against a black background for the length of the half-inch-wide fabric. Two keys and an ID hang from the lanyard, and I'm half expecting to see my military photo taken at Fort Hill five years ago, but it's not there. Instead, I find the simple plastic ID card with my name emblazoned on the front adjacent to the Adams logo.

"You should have your own ID and keys if you'll be coming here at least once a week," he explains. "The slightly larger key is for the exterior door. If you happen to be here on the weekend or later in the evening, you'll need the exterior security code, as well. It's two-six-two. You have to enter it before using the key. The second key will let you into our offices. That space you used is usually left open, but if by any chance it is locked, a key box is kept under our receptionist's desk. Our most valuable assets are located on our computer hard drives, and all that material is password protected and kept on a secure server as well as backed up each night to a different server. If someone did happen to break in and steal our computers, they wouldn't be able to access our research."

I think of telling him the keys aren't necessary but instead simply take them and thank him for his hospitality. I am already cruising down I-95 in my mind trying to make the next ferry home.

5

I arrive at Point Judith as the cars are beginning to be waved aboard the 1:30 p.m. boat. I pay my fare and jump to the end of the vehicle line that is making its way onto the ship. With summer rapidly approaching, I'm lucky to drive on so easily, even on a Thursday afternoon. The final whistle blows just as a deckhand blocks my rear tires to stop the car from rolling back down the slight incline I parked on and then off into the drink. I immediately make my way to the upper deck as the boat's twin diesels thrum to life. Gripping the rear handrail, I watch two guys on the pier haul in the heavy bow and stern lines. The twin bronze screws begin to churn the water while the motors' dull vibrations work their way up from the engine room and are transmitted through the metal railing into my arms. A spume of roiling foam forms below the transom as we push off from the landing. From childhood, I have always had an urge to strip off my clothes and dive into the churning mixture of air and seawater that initially forms adjacent to the stern as any big ship begins to inch away from a dock. I imagine being tossed about in its tickling, bubbling froth, yet the nearest I ever came to doing it is sitting in a Jacuzzi that was cranked up to high.

Rounding the outer breakwater, the captain powers up, and I go to find a sunny spot to sit and call my mom. After telling her I made the earlier ferry, she mentions that Woody called to check my schedule. "He plans to invite you for dinner Saturday night," she explains. "Kathy has a friend visiting for the weekend who he thought you may like."

"Then why didn't he call me?"

"I've no idea. You'll have to ask him that."

I chuckle and ask her to put Matt on, who gives me an obligatory "Daddy, I miss you," which I expect is urged on him by my mom. After a slight pause, he adds, "Daddy, I love you."

"Did you tell him to say that?" I ask my mother when she is back on the line, and she laughs warmly.

"TC, you're his father. He loves you the same way you loved your dad."

I mumble a response and then tell her I'll be home in a couple of hours.

"Don't forget to call Woody," she reminds me and then hangs up.

I expect the reason Woody called my mom rather than me was to confer with her on why I should have a woman in my life. They have both let me know that it is time to move on, and I know it too. There was a woman I had met when I was in Las Vegas and have subsequently seen a few times during the past few years, but we both knew it wouldn't go anywhere. I cared for her, but in the end, I cared more for her touch, her skin, and her soft breasts than I cared for her. We parted amicably. Then four months ago, I spent a brief time studying the *Women Seeking Men* and *Casual Encounter* ads on craigslist but rapidly became depressed at the mix of desperation and perversity seen in the majority of the postings. I ended up settling on the imaginary women I could encounter via videos and late-night cable TV, meeting my needs in a temporary and unsatisfactory manner. The desire for a woman in my life was becoming more prominent.

"Kent's Matchmaking Service," I say into my phone as soon as Woody picks up.

"TC, what are you talking about, my friend?" Woody responds to my comment.

"My mother told me you're playing yenta."

"Isn't that some sort of animal in the Himalayas? Where are you, anyway?"

"I'm roughly at the same spot I was when we were after blues and my mobile phone rang."

"You must be on the ferry. How far out are you?"

"A half hour, plus or minus a few."

"Great! I have to take care of a couple of things. I'll meet you in the bar at the Block Island Inn and fill you in. Grab me a beer if you get there first."

Before I can protest, Woody is gone. I give my mom a quick call to tell her I'll be stopping for a beer but will be home by four o'clock at the latest.

"Stay at the inn," she suggests. "I'll come down with Matt, and we can all have a bite to eat together."

"Great. I'll see you soon," I agree. I click off and then make my way over to the starboard railing.

The northern tip of Block Island slowly gains form as we steadily advance across the sound. I scan the horizon for landmarks and try to locate where the sandbar was that Woody and I were planning to fish from. Crossing to the port side, I see a couple of boats around a half mile away. The location is right, and I'm pleased to detect the probable spot without a GPS.

Woody is already waiting at the bar with two drafts when I arrive. When I tell him my mother is coming down at four o'clock with Matt for an early dinner, he gives Kathy a call to see if she can join us. We find a booth that will accommodate the five of us.

"How's the little guy doing?" he asks.

"Who, Matt?"

"Who else? Kathy and I have been wondering if we should add a little guy to the family."

"He's doing okay. I spoke to him on the ferry, and he told me he loves me. That was definitely cool. I had been worried that my mom is taking care of him too much and that he may not attach to me. It felt good to hear him say he loved me. But tell me…what's up with you and Kathy on the baby front? This is the first I'm hearing of it."

"Actually, we've been trying for the past two years."

I smile. "Maybe you have to make like Avis and try a little harder."

"That's not the problem; we're getting in plenty of practice time. We had a preliminary fertility workup last month, and I've got varicocele."

"Isn't that an enlargement of the blood vessels, like varicose veins?"

"Pretty much. It's more a tangle of vessels. Nearly fifteen percent of all males have it, and if it is adjacent to the testes, the warmth can kill sperm. I have it more on the left side, but my total sperm count is still low."

"You've been doing your homework," I comment.

He shrugs. "I guess so. It has Kathy pretty upset. There are two different surgical procedures. They either go in through your femoral vein to shut off the blood flow or use a knife to remove the vein or cluster of veins."

"Which one are you planning on?"

Woody hesitates. "I'm not sure. They're both questionable in terms of effectiveness. Fertilization rates after either procedure only run around 40 to 50 percent."

"Is there a downside? I mean, it's not about to make you impotent, right?"

"No real downside that I've seen yet for either procedure. The noninvasive one is called varicocele embolization. It's day surgery that can be done on an outpatient basis."

"If there is no downside, why not take a shot at it? Unless there are better treatments, it's definitely worth a try," I conclude while waving down the waitress for a second beer.

"I'm set," Woody says when she arrives, and I notice that while I had polished off my beer, he's only drained a third of his.

"Since the studies show such variability of effectiveness, our insurance classifies both procedures as experimental, making it an uncovered benefit, according to the VA's guidelines," he explains after the waitress leaves. "The whole thing will run ten to fifteen grand and possibly more. We'll have to save for a while to make it happen. The clinics that do it aren't big on extending credit. We considered having it done in Thailand or Costa Rica. We can swing that, but the travel costs as much as the surgery, and neither of us are real big on that option, anyway."

We sit in silence for a few moments as the waitress places a fresh pint on the table.

"I'm not big on the foreign option either," I say after she leaves. "Where's your doc located?"

"New Haven. I've been to the fertility clinic at the Yale New Haven Hospital a couple of times. They did the initial workup and gave me some literature."

"Then screw it, sailor; they'll do the surgery. I've got plenty of money. I'll pay for it. If it may mean that Matt will have a Kent to grow up with on the island, then it's a good investment."

Woody laughs. "That would be fun, but I couldn't do it, TC. It may take a while, but I'll figure it out."

"Woody," I say earnestly, "do you have any idea where I got the dough to build my house?"

He pauses for a second time. "Maura…her insurance money."

I shake my head from side to side. "Wrong."

He studies me more intently, and I sense his question, responding, "Wrong on that one, too, and it's not the route to take. You don't want to do that."

We're both aware of what the other is thinking. Many of the guys I grew up with, including Woody, entered the Coast Guard after high school or college. Another large, and often overlapping percentage, used their nautical skills as drug runners or smugglers. It was no secret and not even all that frowned upon. As all islanders understood, *You do what you have to do.* If Woody needs ten to fifteen grand quick, he has to be weighing the risks. He has the perfect boat for moving midsized quantities from large ships to the mainland. At night with no cruising lights and 250 horses, the *Klown* would be a uncatchable ghost.

The air is vibrating between us. "One trip. That's all I'm—"

"Woody, it's not worth it," I interrupt. "The risk is too much. Plus, I have a lot of money, and I mean *a lot of money*." I repeat the last few words with a slow emphasis.

We drink quietly for a while, and then I motion to the waitress so Woody can have a refill.

After she leaves, I say, "Remember when those FBI agents came by to see you and Kathy a couple of years back?"

He quietly nods.

"They said I was being charged with entering the country illegally from Toronto for the time you picked me up in Lake Ontario a few years ago. Wasn't it a bit odd they brought charges after a couple of years and only against me? Remember, we got arrested in Rochester as soon as we landed, and we got arrested together, didn't we? And why do you think those charges got dismissed back then? I was helping the FBI. It was through an agent I met when I studied Arabic and Pashtu at the Quantico Language School before I shipped out to Guantanamo. I've worked with them twice, and they've even offered me a job. On the second occasion, I ended up in Las Vegas. They used me and one of those guys we ran into in Rochester to bring down a drug cartel, but that's another story. Two of the guys involved put in an IRS whistleblower's claim for a hundred-million-plus in unpaid taxes against the shell companies that laundered money. They walked away with fifteen million and passed a third of that on to me. It was all done legally and aboveboard."

"They gave you five million dollars?" he says, the incredulity evident in his voice.

"Closer to three million after taxes, but like I said, it was all done way aboveboard. That's how I built the house, and that's why I'll pay for your surgery if you'll let me."

"Why did they ever give you that kind of money?"

"One of the guys credits me with saving his life. He was shot, and I was able to get him out of a bad situation. That woman I've visited in Vegas was involved too. It's how we met."

"Is she the third person?"

"No. The third guy's currently in federal prison, but he'll be out soon, if he isn't already, because of his cooperation. That is all I can say, except that money's no object for that surgery."

"I knew something was up after the FBI put in an appearance, but then you were back in two or three weeks. I figured it was all a big misunderstanding."

"Yeah, it was more like four weeks, but that's what people were supposed to think—that it was a mistake. I could have got my job back at Cranston or been reinstated in the Guard, but I decided to stay here to build my place and take care of Matt."

"I don't know…" he ponders.

"What are you going to do? If you got bagged transporting, especially from some international freighter, you'd win some serious time in a federal prison. It's not worth it."

"I can sell the *Klown* and get more of a steady job. I'd be a shoo-in for assistant harbormaster, but it's seasonal. That's Kathy's solution."

"Harbormaster's a great idea. I'd always be able to bank on a decent mooring, but why sell the Whaler? That will kill our charter service."

Woody laughs. "Be serious, TC. You're not into chartering. The boat's almost paid off and worth a solid ten grand; plus, if I got the assistant harbormaster gig, I'd be too busy all summer for chartering."

"Then I'll buy the *Klown*. It's an investment. I can't charter regularly this summer because of the mainland job, but that's temporary. You do it this summer, and next year we pick up doing it together again."

He doesn't respond to my suggestion. Checking my watch, I see it is closing in on four o'clock. Kathy, Matt, and my mom will be joining us soon.

"Woody," I say in frustration. "What if the shoe was on the other foot? What if you had three million dollars and I needed ten or fifteen grand? Hell, what if I needed a hundred thousand? What would you do?"

"That's different," he says, but I can tell he is wavering.

"Give me a break! There's no difference except that you're too pigheaded to take the bread. Have you ever saved anyone's life?"

"I've helped pull guys out of rough seas a couple of times when I was on a helicopter rescue team. Why?"

"I bet they were pretty happy with you, right?"

"What are you getting at, TC?"

"I did save that guy's life and probably my own and the woman's. He wanted to pay me back and could. I expect many of the guys you saved wanted to pay you back too. But because you were in the Coast Guard, all you got was a letter of appreciation or commendation. It's payback time; you deserve the money, and I've got it."

"Let's finish this later. Kathy and your mom are here," he says.

Glancing to the door, I see Kathy and my mother chatting as they angle for our table. Matt is snuggled up in Kathy's arms.

"She looks good with a kid," I whisper to Woody, who smiles warmly as they draw near.

6

I knew I got to Woody with my last argument, and seeing Kathy with Matt sealed the deal. It would simply be a matter of time until he came around, but I was confident he would.

Neither Woody nor Kathy mention children during the meal, but my mom does, jesting to Kathy that since Matt is so comfortable with her, it may be time for her to consider having a child. I can tell by the glance that subsequently passes between Woody and Kathy that the issue consumes a lot of their time.

"We'll see," is all Kathy can say, and thankfully my mom backs off, likely sensing the emotions her comment evoked.

When we get to my mother's later that evening, Matt immediately asks if we are going home or staying with Nana. Before I can reply, he says, "I want to sleep in my big bed tonight."

My mother and I are both a little taken aback, as he usually requests that we stay with her. As we're organizing his stuff, he announces, "I need my potty." Surprised, I turn to my mother.

"He began to ask to sit on it a day or two ago, so I've been letting him. You're a big boy, right, Mattie?"

He beams as I rapidly calculate his age in my mind. A little shy of three years seems right for toilet training, but the idea had never occurred to me until now. I can't remember if I even bought one of the little plastic training toilets for my place, so I tell him we'll bring his potty along.

As we are leaving, I ask if my mother can watch Matt the next afternoon so I can go out running, and Matt immediately asks if he can run with me. "Sure, little guy," I reply, as I enjoy pushing him in the jogging stroller. Exiting out to the car, I'm struck by how much older Matt seems. It's as if he had another growth spurt in the few intervening days I've been on the mainland.

Later that night, after Matt is asleep in his room, Woody calls. "I spoke to Kathy," he says, getting right to the point. "She's okay with the money. I told her Maura had a million-dollar life insurance policy she took out with the Rhode Island Nurses Association after she got pregnant. I said you wanted to give us the money in her name, and she was okay with it when I explained it that way."

My eyes well up at his words, and I can't speak.

"TC, are you there? Did you hear me?"

"Yeah, yeah, I'm here," I choke out. "That is exactly what Maura would want, Woody. No doubt about it. I should have thought of that. I really appreciate it, man."

"No, we're the ones who appreciate it, you idiot." He laughs.

But I am still too touched by his words to join in the laughter. "No, you're wrong. You and Kathy are doing me the favor. I'm serious. Wherever Maura is, she's happy for you."

"Hey, if it works and it's a girl, you know what her name will be."

"Thanks, Woody, and thank Kathy for me too. I need to sign off; I hear Matt stirring."

"If your mom can't watch Matt on Saturday, Kathy said she and her friend will. Remember, we're catching dinner for Kathy and her college pal who'll be here for the weekend."

"Saturday should work. I'll check the tide and get back to you tomorrow."

"I already did. It's high around four, so we should cast off by two. Bring gear for stripers, okay?"

"Will do, but I still have to check on Matt. I'll catch you tomorrow."

"TC?" Woody calls through the receiver when I'm about to click off.

"Yeah."

"We appreciate it, buddy, both Kathy and me. We appreciate it big time."

"My pleasure," I half croak and cough out and then click off.

Matt's not stirring, but I had to get off the phone. The linkage he made to Maura completely blindsided me. She would want that for Woody and Kathy and certainly would have had no issues in fronting them the money with no expectation of repayment. Against my own will, I rummage about the kitchen, futilely searching for something to drink. I momentarily consider dashing down to the harbor to snag a pint of whiskey but abandon the thought just as quickly. Instead, I go upstairs to watch Matt sleep, pulling my dad's old Kennedy rocker next to his small bed. I attempt to settle into a rhythmic to-and-fro motion in time with his breathing but can't manage it. Matt's respirations are too shallow and rapid. I simply find a steady pace and linger there by his bedside, dozing in and out of sleep before eventually making my way to bed.

There is a distant voice calling to me. I strain to hear the words, but they're unintelligible.

"You better go see what it is," Maura suggests, but I'm too fatigued to move.

"Later," I grunt.

"You better go now," she presses.

"In a minute," I plea.

"Hey, Doc, any chance I can come fishing with you on Saturday?" another voice calls out. It's a familiar voice. It's Antonio Lopez.

"I haven't been out in years. Can I go out with you and your buddy?"

I'm momentarily disoriented as I open my eyes, and then I hear Matt calling out, "Daddy…Daddy."

I'm up and in his room in a flash. His "big bed" is simply an oversized crib with sides that can be elevated. He's standing up and calling to me but not in a whining or frightened manner.

"Daddy, breakfast," he exclaims when I enter his room.

"Breakfast, Matt," I respond, stumbling into the rocker I left adjacent to the bed and had not noticed in the faint light of dawn. He gives a joyful squeal at my clumsiness, as if I'm performing part of a Three Stooges routine.

It's 7:00 a.m. by the time I finish cleaning and changing him, and the first ferry from the mainland is still a couple of hours away. While at Cranston, I had reverted to my old habit of picking up a copy of the *Providence Journal* to read with breakfast. I normally go for a run when I awake, and then near the end of my route, I stop into a convenience store to get a copy. After a light breakfast, I suggest to Matt that we take a run down to the harbor to pick up a paper. He appears game, although I am sure the main attraction is to spend time with his dad. At eight o'clock, I begin to organize the jogging stroller, packing it with a few snacks, diapers, and a change of clothes for Matt. We are on the road in thirty minutes, under a partially sunny sky with the thermometer already pushing sixty. There is next to no traffic as I begin the three-mile run down to the ferry landing at a comfortable ten-minute pace. As we pass the turnoff for the Southeast Lighthouse, I have the familiar urge to tell Matt that he was conceived beneath the stars as Maura and I made love on the grass, our movements following the ebb and flow of the nearby surf.

The ferry's landing whistle blows as I make my way up Spring Street into the small town center. I jog out onto the pier while the passengers are debarking. There is a small knot of islanders, anticipating when the first bundle of newspapers will be tossed off. Rather than wait for the papers to be placed into the dispensing machine in the Block Island Ferry office, we each drop our money onto a bundle as we pull copies free. I catch up on local gossip with a few of the other islanders while scanning the headlines. Matt gets plenty of compliments and basks at briefly being the center of attention. As I begin to make my way off the wharf, I hear my name called. It's Kathy, and she's approaching me with another woman.

"TC, what are you doing here? I want you to meet someone," she exclaims as they draw near.

My immediate impression of the woman approaching me with Kathy is that she is sturdy. She is not so much pretty as handsome with square shoulders and dark-black hair flecked with a few strands of gray pulled back into a ponytail. Before I can study her more closely, Kathy is in my arms. "TC," she whispers in my ear, "Woody and I can't thank you, and we can't thank Maura enough."

The other woman immediately crouches by Matt's stroller to take his extended hand.

"How you doing, big boy?" I hear her ask while Kathy embraces me.

"I'm Mattie, and I'm three," he declares as Kathy releases me.

I'm slightly disoriented but manage to get out, "I'm glad I could help, Kathy," as her friend begins to rise. It is a relief that the emotions I feel are not as powerful as those I felt last night when speaking with Woody.

"TC, this is Nancy Gardner. We were at Connecticut College together," Kathy says by way of introduction.

Her eyes are a watery turquoise blue set off by dark eyebrows. A small and slightly upturned nose enhances the eyes as her most dominant facial feature. "Black Irish," I say spontaneously.

She smiles. "You're not the first to say that."

"And this is his son, Matt," Kathy continues. "TC is Woody's best friend, and they'll be catching dinner for us tomorrow while we take care of this little guy, right, Mattie?" she concludes by kneeling next to the stroller. Kathy has been the next most constant female figure in Matt's life after my mother, and he's pleased with our dockside encounter.

"Do you want a cup of coffee, or do you need a ride?" she asks.

"We're fine," I reply. "We still have a few more miles to cover. Don't we, Matt?" But he doesn't respond, and I expect he would prefer to be spending time with Kathy rather than being pushed along the streets of Block Island.

We amble down the pier together, and then the women veer off to the parking area. From behind, my view of Nancy as sturdy shifts to shapely as I watch her from the rear. Her legs are beautifully formed, and there is a definite sway as she moves farther away, with her ponytail and hips bobbing and swaying in a captivating unison.

"Sweet!" I observe to Matt as I first check if he needs to be changed and then jog out of town. I consider taking a route that will bring us by Dodge Cemetery to stop by Maura's grave but opt not to, the extra half hour being a lot for Matt. Instead, I take a shorter route that passes the airport. Rather than heading directly home, I detour into the airport diner for a more substantial breakfast, where I'm able to get an outdoor table so I can read the paper and Matt can watch the occasional plane take off or land. By the time we get home, it's been close to a three-hour trip with our two stops. Matt stayed awake the entire time, often singing or simply making various noises as we rolled around the island, and now he is ready for a nap.

"What did you think of Kathy's friend?" Woody asks as we start out of the harbor the next afternoon.

"I only spoke to her for a few minutes, but she seemed nice enough."

"She likes kids, and she's got a great ass," he pronounces while opening the throttle slightly after we pass the outer breakwater.

"I never noticed."

He chuckles. "That's right. You've never seen her with kids, have you? Seriously, TC, she's all right. I've known her as long as I've known Kathy. I met them at a Coast Guard Academy dance. The academy used to send a bus over for the Connecticut College girls, and I was there for an advanced navigation program after Cape May. We were told the dances were for academy cadets, but we all went anyway. She studied architecture at Yale but dropped out and finished at Michigan. She's a big Frank Lloyd Wright fan, and Yale was too utilitarian for her with all that form-follows-function BS. She was working in Chicago, but I'm not sure if she still is. She's from Mystic, Connecticut, and is considering coming back this way. She's here to see her parents, but she may also have an interview or two lined up. Her old man was some type of manager at the GE Electric Boat Yard in Groton.

"We got the tour while I was at the academy; you'd get a kick out of it. Submarines aren't exactly the classic boats Izzy and your dad worked on but incredible stuff. She saw one guy for a few years but ended up being more serious than he was. He couldn't take the plunge, so she pulled the plug. Her biological clock is ticking away, too, and she knows it. It's sorta what Kathy and I are dealing with, but she doesn't have a guy, which puts her a step further behind us."

"You have her bio down fairly pat," I comment.

"It's Kathy. She's been scheming to bring the two of you together for a while, but the opportunity never arose. I told her I'd give you the rundown, so now I've done it. Hey, what will be, will be. Anyway, we have some fish to kill before I can turn this crate around, so hold on."

As Woody finishes speaking, he leans on the throttle, and the twin Mercs explode, lifting the *Klown*'s bow as we begin to bound and crash our way through the surf.

"Beer," I scream above the roar. Woody nods, and I make my way back to the cooler secured by the stern.

In no time, we are trolling along a shelf off the southeast side of the island. We are using lures, and on my first cast, I recollect the dream I had a week earlier of fishing with Woody or someone else for stripers with live eels. I awoke on the upper deck of the ferry as the ship's horn blew. An eel had wrapped itself around my arm at the end of the dream, and inadvertently I again check my right forearm to confirm that there is no eel lurking there. As I glance down, I hear Antonio Lopez's voice from two nights ago: *Hey, Doc, any chance I can come fishing with you on Saturday?*

"You okay?" I hear from Woody and realize I had momentarily drifted off in my mind.

"Yeah, I'm set. A couple of dreams I had recently just came back to me. We were fishing for stripers in one, and then there was an inmate in another dream, asking if he could come with us."

"That's fine by me, TC. Those guys are human too."

I laugh. "That's not what I mean. The guy's still in prison. In fact, he's in the isolation section, so he's not going anywhere anytime soon. He been in for four years and used to be a commercial fisherman out of Newport."

"Hey, if he gets released, I'm cool with bringing him out with us."

Before I can explain further, my attention is drawn to a roiling upon the surface fifty meters off the port side. "Woody, port side," I almost whisper as if the fish were listening to us.

"I'm on it," he replies after a glance, angling the Whaler near a school of stripers in a feeding orgy.

CHAPTER 4

1

After my second trip to the DSU, it dawned on me that the unit was permanently short staffed, and if I expected to see Lopez in the interview room for privacy, I'd have to wait for an extra officer each time I went there. Certain that the wait could be anything from fifteen minutes to hours, I again elected for the kneeling position by his door and chatting through the food slot. Having been officially served with his ticket, he tried to explain his behavior and hoped I had information on when his D-board hearing was. The most serious charges were assault of a staff member and holding a staff member against their will. Boden wasn't a regular DOC staff person, but as a contractor or someone working within the facility, any assault on her was viewed the same way as it would be as if she were a staff person.

"I told you I didn't do anything to her," he whispered into the slot, with both of our heads tilted to the side, a mere six inches apart from each other. His warm, rancid breath broke across my face like a light surf lapping the shoreline.

I nodded, fighting back the urge to recoil.

"If I did anything, they'd have charged me with indecent A&B or rape. I told you nothing happened, Doc."

"But it may have been something for her," I ventured.

"Bullshit!" he hissed. "You get my drift. I didn't touch her. I tried to get her to shut her big fat trap, and that's it. Will she be at the hearing?"

"No idea, Tony." Yet I did know. Boden desired for it all to disappear, as much or more than Lopez did. She had accepted Olken's offer to consult, which was an offer to move on. I had sent my regards to her via Olken but never heard back. I can still see her on the gurney whispering, "Thanks, Tom," as the EMTs wheeled her away. I expect that vulnerable woman has disappeared, and any remembrances of the events, or of that vulnerability, may not be welcomed.

"Maybe it would be better if she did come; it would be proof nothing happened. What do you think? Do you think it would be better if she came?"

"I really have no idea. But what the ticket is for, is what you must focus on. They won't change the charges up on you at the D-board."

"Yeah, you're right. Fuck it! I bet it's better if she doesn't show. That's probably best, eh?"

Our conversation was circular, and my knees were hurting, so I told him about fishing and the feeding frenzy Woody and I saw, hoping to break the cycle.

"Oh, man, that's something," he observed. "Have you ever seen sharks feeding?"

After I told him that I hadn't, he recounted a few stories of watching porbeagle sharks chase fish up and down the water column out on Georges Bank and how they dealt with sharks whenever they brought one in as part of the bycatch. "We always kept them; we kept everything. By the time you got any of them free, they were half dead, anyway. Hey, they're going to die in the ocean if we toss 'em back, or we can make a few extra bucks by keeping 'em. The captain had a false wall welded in the hold. We stuffed the small stuff and bycatch we wanted to keep in there."

I wondered what else got stuffed behind the false wall in the hold but didn't ask. It was a common trick. I once spoke to a guy who worked a tanker.

He told me all the crew shared one large cabin so that the other rooms could be welded shut. All the oil pumped into the tanker was metered. Once the massive cargo tanks were signed off on, they then filled the sealed compartments up with oil, reversing the procedure at the other end, first offloading the metered oil and then their personal stash.

The third time I stopped in to see Lopez, I asked the block officer if I could use his rolling desk chair.

"Why?" he asked, clearly puzzled.

"I've been kneeling on the concrete for the past two weeks, and I've done enough penance."

"Hey, Doc, why not?" He laughed. "If you gotta talk to a bunch of douchebags, why not be comfortable doing it?"

I didn't respond to the officer then and didn't plan to today if I get a similar comment from whoever had the post in the DSU, but the only thing the officer on today says after he nods his okay to my request is, "I'd stay away from 22. He tried to toss some piss out on first shift when they were passing out breakfast. He's a little buggy and needs a tune-up."

"Thanks. Who is it?"

The officer scans a clipboard and then responds, "Jamal Rivers, Black guy, awaiting-action status on a D-report. He ripped up his cell after having a beef with his roommate. He's new, first state bit. Pretty much a punk, if you ask me. Roommate was an older guy."

I nod at the officer's assessment and then ask him about the smell. The air is staler than usual, and there is a rank, foul quality to the scent. I am used to the mixed aroma of urine, feces, and disinfectant that permeates most medical units to some degree or other, but this is different, unfamiliar. There is a metallic quality as if someone had been welding inside the unit.

"One of the air circulators is down."

"Can you open any of those transoms?" I ask, motioning to the line of windows that run ten feet above the cell doors for the length of the unit.

"We used to have electronic controls for them, but they got welded shut six months ago for security reasons."

"Who could ever get up there?"

He raises his eyebrows and smiles. "Monkeys?" It's as absurd to him as it is to me.

"Hey, don't worry, Doc. There was a guy from facilities here this morning. They pulled out the unit and said we should be back in business in a week or two."

"Or three or four," I add. "Is the AC linked to the circulators?"

"Right again. It's shut down until the circulator is fixed. They're both on a common feed of some sort and can't be run individually."

I sigh. "Unless they figured some way of diverting the line."

"Hey, at least we don't have to live here," the officer says as I begin to push my chair down to Lopez's door.

It's my fifth time in the unit, and already numerous inmates have figured my schedule out. "Can you see me too?" a half-dozen voices call out as I make way down to number 15. The air has an acrid, metallic aroma, and I expect that facilities must have done some welding or used a torch of some type to cut loose the broken unit. With summer approaching, it's not hard to guess how miserable the place will be with no fresh air. Thankfully, the small control room is located inside the block. The officer on the post won't want to sit in the stench any more than any inmate does, and the officer's union will have more oomph than the cons ever would in getting something done.

Lopez is standing and gazing out the narrow, heavily screened window when I arrive. He jerks around at my tap on the door and smiles broadly. By the time I unsnap the food slot, he is already kneeling on the opposite side.

"I wasn't sure you were coming. I forgot what day it was and wasn't sure if you'd be here today or tomorrow. I had my D-board. I got eighteen months of seg time, Doc. This month counts, so that leaves seventeen months, but I'll wrap up before that." He's breathless as the words tumble out.

"That good, Tony."

"Good! Are you crazy? It's great! Like Tony the fucking Tiger says,

Grrreeeat. She didn't show or even send a statement. The lieutenant said it was because I came out peaceful. They gave me more time than my sentence in case I get a new bit on top of this one. Then when it was over, he told me he doubted they were filing new charges. Those bastards would break a leg running down to file if they could. I bet that bitch told them not to do it. Christ, I really didn't do anything, you know, any sexual thing, and I could of. I could of have if I wanted to, but I just wanted her to stop ragging on me."

He is almost hyperventilating. He gets up from kneeling on the concrete, paces back and forth in his cell twice, and then collapses back to his knees.

"Are you okay, Tony?"

"Yeah. Yeah. I'm good. I'm good. I haven't had anyone to talk to in this shithole. You're the first person I told. I had to tell someone. I had to get it out. I could have been smoked. Not picking up a new case—the lieutenant said that's the big thing. What do you think? Do you think she'll press charges?"

"I'm not in that loop," I lie, having had a discussion with Vos about it after my weekly meeting at Adams. We hadn't spoken of it when I met with Olken, Vos, and a few others working on the field test, but I did later with Vos and Olken privately. Boden hadn't attended the meeting, although Olken had informed us earlier she would remain a consultant to the project. Alain told me she did decide to pursue an academic career, and then, when we were meeting in his office, he asked me if I believed she brought the situation upon herself.

"Not in the sense of her being responsible for what Lopez did," I replied. "But from what he told me, she missed numerous cues that he was escalating. She may have been more focused on completing the interview protocol than on the patient and didn't realize he was starting to melt down."

"So you're saying yes," he pressed.

I hesitated. "Yeah, I guess so, but that doesn't sound right to me because we can't excuse Lopez's behavior. Still, if she didn't push him, I doubt he'd have flipped out."

"Would you say that in court?"

"What do you mean, would I say it in court?"

"If the DA prosecutes, will you say she helped bring this upon herself if it goes to a trial?"

"I guess if I was asked, I'd have to say what I saw, as would Craven and some of the other officers who were there."

"Who's Craven?"

"Paul Craven. He's a captain and led the hostage negotiations with me. He was in charge of the tactical unit. He positioned the officers inside the building and snipers outside prior to my speaking with Lopez."

"There were snipers positioned?" Alain asked, unable to keep the incredulity out of his voice.

"Two, with scoped high-power rifles. They had a bead on Lopez the entire time I spoke to him."

"They would have shot him?"

"If the hostage was in severe danger, we would have had to."

"On whose orders?"

"Paul and I would have made the decision together. He was in radio contact with them the whole time, and we had a periscope camera observing through the window. All the information was processed in a makeshift command center and filtered to Paul. If there was an emergency, he'd have gotten my attention."

"The whole thing was an emergency, wasn't it?"

I can tell Vos is viewing me in a completely different light. It's not so much due to his words but to the tone and cadence of his words.

"Alain, we have to be ready for any contingency. If it appeared that her life was in imminent danger, we would have given the order to shoot. But it never remotely got near that point. He immediately engaged and almost as quickly showed an interest in resolving the situation amicably."

"Amicably?" he interrupted.

"I guess that's the wrong word, but it was clear he wanted out of the room. My job was to ensure her safety, and to do that, I had to get him out.

Every situation is unique. Paul and I had frequently drilled on hostage situations. Each one is a different scenario with various possible outcomes. It was clear almost at once she wasn't in danger."

"She was tied up," he interrupted again.

"She was tied up with her own stockings, but as a rule, we don't shoot people in the head with a high-powered rifle for tying someone up. We try to end the situation with as little violence as possible," I responded, becoming a bit irritable myself.

"What if he didn't come out? What if he wasn't amiable or amicable or whatever?"

"Then Paul and I would have dealt with that. Shooting him is the absolute last alternative in a hostage situation, and we never got to that. In fact, we never even got remotely near that."

We sit in silence for some time before Alain speaks. "I spoke to Andrea, and she knows none of this. She has no idea there were snipers outside with guns pointed in. After she got out of the hospital, she met with detectives and elected to pursue criminal charges. She wanted him in jail—I mean, in jail longer. Anyway, when Ralph spoke to her this past week, he pointed out that a trial included testimony from all present and that you appeared inclined to say she brought the situation upon herself."

"He said what?" I exclaimed.

"He said that in court, you may say she brought the situation on herself. You just told me the same thing, TC."

"That doesn't mean I'm absolving Lopez of responsibility. If she wants to press charges, she should."

"For this to go away will be the best alternative. Andrea can avoid a court appearance where her professionalism may be called into question, regardless of your testifying or not. And Ralph can avoid any negative publicity for Adams, particularly as the study is now up and running."

"What about you?" I asked.

Vos shrugged. "I wanted to hear from you. Now I believe it is better for her to let it go. It will muddy the waters if she pursues legal action, and she can get on with her life."

"Is there a risk she may sue Adams for placing her in an unsafe work environment?"

"Based on what you said and what else I have heard, she was the one who overstepped the boundaries. She placed herself at risk. That would all be revealed in a lawsuit."

On my way out of Adams's offices, I stopped in to see Olken.

"My goal was to protect her from a potentially painful situation," he said to explain away his behavior with Boden.

"I think your goal was to protect Adams, and you used me as a foil with Boden to prevent her from pursuing any criminal charges."

"That too," he agreed. "But who is best served by having her pursue criminal charges, which may in turn force you to say in an open courtroom setting that she was a poor clinician and therefore contributed to Mr. Lopez's behavior? Even the most incompetent public defender would make that connection. It's best for all that she's gone. She has an excellent severance package and will still retain her authorship position on any published papers related to this study."

I was still irritated but held my tongue. It was logical, eminently logical, but I didn't take kindly to being used.

"Have you found an apartment yet?" Olken asked solicitously.

"I haven't been searching that hard."

"Please feel free to use that same office if you wish to check additional listings, but if you're not in a rush, reconsider that condo option. They are an exceptional value."

"I'll consider it," I replied curtly, leaving his room irritated and unsatisfied.

2

"Do you think the DA will press charges? I haven't seen any detectives. If they planned to press charges, I'd have been questioned by now, right?" Lopez asks, even pleads, breaking into my thoughts and bringing me back to his cell door in Cranston's Departmental Segregation Unit.

"It's not my thing, Tony. Why don't you ask your caseworker? One is supposed to stop by here weekly. Ask him?"

"The guy's a cunt," he spits out. "You know that. He's as useful as tits on a bull. Can you look into it for me? Please?"

He's right, of course, and I do know it. The DSU caseworker is useless. If he shows up for his weekly rounds, that's a lot, and it's usually only to drop off mail at the guard post. I doubt he has ever bothered to walk down the tier or kneel by a con's door. No one likes the place. There is an ordeal element to each trip, as a simple fifteen-minute check on Lopez inevitably evolves into a two-hour voyage down desolation row with all the other guys pleading to be seen.

"That's not my job, Antonio. I'd have no idea where to begin or who to call." I use his full name, an unconscious move to create distance between us.

"The DA, call the DA or the police, the state police. Will you call them for me?" he begs, his voice steadily rising. "Please, I need to know what's going to happen."

"I can't—"

"Shut your big mouth, you crybaby!" Another inmate hollers out from a nearby cell, cutting me off in midsentence.

"Hey, fuck you, asshole!" Lopez screams, spraying spittle through the narrow opening in his fury.

"Jesus!" I cry, pushing myself away from the door and wiping my face.

"Oh, no, Doc! I'm sorry! I'm really sorry! You'll still come back, won't ya?" Lopez whines, transmuting from a raging maniac to a child, fearful of abandonment, in the space of a millisecond.

"I'll be here, Tony. Next week. Same time, same channel," I say, cleaning the saliva from my face with the sleeve of my shirt.

"Hey, I'm sorry, Doc; I really am. That asshole pissed me off. Let me get you some toilet paper to wipe off with. You're coming back, right? You won't forget me?"

"I'm all set, Tony, and don't worry. I'll be here."

I snap his food slot shut to cut off his next apology and then push my chair away from his door toward the center of the tier. I had made a list of eight other guys who requested to be seen when I was last here. I start to make my way down the names and realize that the second con I see, an older Providence guy I have spoken to twice previously, is the person who screamed at Lopez.

"That Cape Verdean diddler is a piece of work, Doc. I get tired of listening to him. He wails his ass off half the night like all the other boneheads in this place. A bunch of pussies, none of them can do time. I don't want to hear it. Hey, did I tell you my daughter graduated? You have to see this."

When he goes to his cot to retrieve a letter, I steal a glance at my list, having already forgotten his name.

"This is her, and that's my ex. She done real good for herself. She's a great kid, man, a great kid," he says, passing the photo through the food slot.

"You must be proud, Mark. She does look like a great kid. What's she planning to do now?" I reply while studying the picture of a cute young girl in a blue graduation gown, standing next to a beaming obese woman holding the girl's graduation cap.

"She got into the St. Joe's nursing program, but it's three years and eight grand a year. If she can get a loan or something, she might go. When I was out there, I'd piss through eight grand in a week, but now I don't even got a pot to piss in. Ah, screw it! Complaining doesn't help."

"Hopefully, she'll figure something out," I say as I pass the snapshot back.

"Yeah, maybe she'll go to hairdressing school. Her mom's a hairdresser. People are always getting their hair done. See you next week?"

"If you're here, I'll be here."

He laughs. "I got a long paper route, pal, and it's all uphill. I'm two years down in this block with two to go and five more on top of that when I wrap up the seg. I'll be here."

I continue rolling down the block, and when I arrive by 22, I remember what the officer said about the new guy in there. All I can see is a long white cylinder stretched out on the bed, so I tap on the door and then open his food slot.

"Jamal Rivers, I'm Tom Phillips, a psychologist. How are you doing?"

The tube begins to shift, revealing a dark-brown shoulder followed by an arm raised from the bedding. "Fuck off," I hear muffled by the bedclothes as the middle finger in his hand pops up.

"Take care," I call back in and then click the small door shut.

The walk back to the ATA is depressing. I save visiting the DSU until my last full day at Cranston. The sooner I can get to Block Island, the sooner I can shake off the despair and contamination I carry out of the building. As I make my way across the prison yard, I envision Nancy Gardner's rear end swaying from side to side before me as her ponytail bobs up and down. I held her briefly at the end of our dinner a few weekends back and kissed her lightly on the lips, but she has been occupying more and more space in my mind ever since. We trade emails and texts almost daily, and I have become increasingly interested in making a trip to Oak Park, Illinois, to see Frank Lloyd Wright's early studio and examples of his work. Envisioning her is significantly more pleasant than the grim concrete, stone, steel, and brick that currently envelop me.

At the ATA, we are completing our third full week and seem to be off to a good start. The unit is now full and is no longer labeled the Zebra House by the inmates. Several minority guys, particularly drug dealers, both Black and Hispanic with some history of violence, signed up to help us fill out the count. Much to Vos's and Olken's satisfaction, we decided to expedite the admission process rather than drag it out over five weeks. The common theme among each con interviewed is that they hope participation will help them at their parole hearing. The management of aggression is secondary to most, and when I have brought this up at the weekly meeting at Adams, both Vos and Olken minimized my concerns. "We have objective measures to assess their aggressive impulses along with the placebo controls," one or both of them explained. They stressed that it is a double-blind study, so neither the subjects nor researchers know who is being given Eumonia and who isn't. Vos reminded me that Olken is the one person with access to the key that identifies who took which med and he is not involved in the data analysis.

Nonetheless, both Lincoln and I have our misgivings. Cons are always trying to get over, and in their minds, the stakes on this are potentially high. If they believe that the successful completion of six months in the Alternatives to Aggression program can lead to a few months off their sentence, then they'll do everything in their power to present well. On Tuesday, we shared our misgivings with Jim at our weekly supervision meeting.

"Of course, the cons will try to present well if they believe it can help them get out early," he concluded. "Any of us would. In the end, what difference does it make? Who cares if it's the drug, the groups, the privileges, or whatever? If it makes life easier for us, that's good. No one gets hurt. I don't see it as a problem."

That night I decide to call Nancy. For some stupid reason, I have limited myself to calling her just once or twice a week and then only from Block Island.

"Tom," she says as soon as she picks up, likely recognizing my number on her cell's display. The lilt in her voice brings a vision of her to my mind. At dinner Woody and Kathy called me TC, but for some reason, she stayed with Tom. I never asked her why or told her to call me TC. I liked her calling me Tom. It made our relationship different.

"Are you back on Block Island?" she asks, her voice an ocean breeze evaporating away the despair of the DSU, which still clings to me like a clammy coating of sweat.

"No, I'm still at work. I leave tomorrow after a meeting at the drug company. How about you? Are you still at work?"

We chat for a half hour, and when I tell her my misgivings at how smoothly things have begun on the unit, she laughs. "We should all be so lucky that our main complaints are that things are going too smoothly," she observes. "Why don't you interview a couple of the men that participate to see how they view the program? It's not as if that would confound the research design."

"I meet with the two social workers each week in supervision, and they are convinced all is fine. They love their jobs and are surprised at how motivated many of the prisoners appear to be. We're completing our third week and only now came up to full census, so it may simply be an initial honeymoon period."

"Whatever it is, if your job is to run the program, then you need to look into it."

"I expect it's more of a gut feeling."

"Maybe, but I doubt it. From my experience, most gut feelings are rooted in some type of assessment or belief, even if it's an unconscious one. We're rational beings, right?"

"I'm not fully sure on that. What about love? Is that rational?" As I listen to the words flow from my mouth, I'm surprised and slightly taken aback.

A thousand miles away, Nancy pauses. "Good point," she says softly. "Love is…ah…I guess love is in a class by itself."

There is a poignant pause until I move the conversation onto a new area.

The next day I call the ATA first-shift supervisor shortly after she comes on at seven o'clock and ask her to hold Mario Zorello back from his job in the print shop. I have an hour until I leave for my meeting at Adams, and Zorello is the guy with the most status in the unit and one of the inmates admitted in the first group. I can interview him before I head out and then see a few other guys when I get back from the island.

"Buongiorno, Doc. What can I do for you?" Mario asks as the escort officer turns to leave.

"Morning, Mario," I reply, getting up from my desk to shake his hand. "Have a seat. I wanted to ask you a couple of questions about how you're doing. It's a new program, so I plan to meet with a couple of the guys to see what they think of it."

"It's working for me. I can't tell you what any of the other cons might say, but it's working good for me."

"What's working, Mario? What are one or two things that you see as working the best?"

"I can't say for sure. It might be those pills, the Eumonia. They may be helping me. No one's pissed me off in the past few weeks; I'm calmer. I don't feel pissed off inside."

"Was that a problem in the past?"

He shrugs. "I can't say it was a big problem, but, hey, shit happens."

"What kind of shit?"

"Just plain old shit, as in excrement. Don't people ever get up your ass and need to be straightened out? That the kind of shit."

"I'm still not certain of what you mean. Can you give me an example?"

He sighs. "Come on, Doc. If I say I'm doing better, I'm doing better. You got it. What else do you want me to say?"

His last words convey an unspoken emphasis that this part of the conversation is done, but I decide to push a bit more and ask again for an example.

He leans back in his chair pensively, appearing to organize his thoughts, and then leans forward. "Okay, you know I'm not big on Blacks. They do their thing, and we do our thing, but on the whole, it's best if we each keep to ourselves. Whenever I've been down, I always stick to my own kind. I had a single room back in the camp, right?"

He pauses, and I nod in agreement to his question.

"Now," he continues, "I'm sharing space, and I'm in groups with them and Puerto Ricans, and I find out they aren't so bad."

"What if you had a minority guy as a roommate?"

"That is not a good idea. It is not an idea for you to entertain, not at all. I'm okay with them in the same unit, but I'm not looking to get married, capisce?" He raises his thick eyebrows as he finishes, and a slight chill passes through me.

"I'm not saying we're planning that, Mario. I was simply raising it as a question," I explain almost apologetically.

"Hey, if it's a hypothetical question, then hypothetically, I'd do fine. I've gotten by in the unit, and if I had to, I'd get by with that too. What else can I help you with, Doc?"

The aura of threat is gone, passing as quickly as it did when I first interviewed Zorello. He is again an older genial Italian gentleman sitting and idly chatting with me.

"The pills, Mario. You said you believe they are helping. Why do you think it's the pills?"

"Nothing else is different, so I guess the pills are making me feel better."

"What about the therapy groups, the anger management class, the substance abuse group, the mindfulness group, the individual counseling? How helpful is all of that? Perhaps it's the therapy and not the medication that's helping you."

"Be serious. Those counselors are kids. You actually think they can help me? They have no idea where I live. They try, but they're children. I go to the groups you ask me to go to, and they might help a little. But for me, I suspect it's the pills."

"Half the pills are placebos, so there's a fifty-fifty chance you're not taking Eumonia."

"That means there's is a 50 percent chance that I am taking Eumonia," he counters. "I don't particularly care what I'm taking, but I am taking something that makes me feel better, okay?"

His voice raises slightly, and the sense of threat again enters the room. Often, I have seen inmates posture, but this is different. There is a deliberateness. Zorello has greater command over the shifting faces he can present than the average con.

"You seem to be getting a little angry now, Mario," I observe.

"Frustrated, not angry," he declares after a brief hesitation. "You're not hearing me. We're on opposite sides of the river."

"Then help me ford it," I request, and the threat I sensed a moment earlier has now totally dissipated.

"You tell me you're curious as to how this thing, this Alternatives to Aggression program is going, so you decided to interview me and a few other guys. I tell you I'm feeling better, less aggressive. I believe it's the medication, but you, you're not sure, so you keep asking me the same questions. Therefore, I believe you're listening to me with some preconceived idea, and that idea keeps you from hearing me. You can ask me these questions all day, Doc, but I'll still feel what I feel and think what I think. So it makes me frustrated that I have to repeatedly say the same thing."

"How far did you go in school, Mario?"

"I graduated from Classical in '65. Why?"

"Why didn't you go to college? Most guys from Classical went on to college, didn't they?"

"You didn't answer my question. Why are you interested in my education?"

"I was struck by how well you summarized our conversation. It made me wonder about your level of education, that's all."

"You thought, *This Zorello, this con, he's got half a brain.* Is that what you're saying?"

"Yeah, I guess that's part of what I thought, but not in a demeaning way. I appreciate your logic."

"I must say, Doc, you should know better than that," he replies with a wry smile. "Didn't your mother teach you to not judge a book by its cover? I attended Providence for two years, but they weren't teaching me anything I didn't already learn at Classical, except Greek philosophy, so I dropped out to work in the family business. Does that settle all your little curiosities?"

"Did you ever consider reenrolling?"

He laughs at my question. "What, are you studying to be a guidance counselor now? I've been busy the last thirty or forty years. In Italian we say, *La speranza è l'ultima a morire*—hope dies last. So I'll keep working this Alternatives to Aggression program, and who knows? It may help me get out a few weeks or months early. Then when I wrap this bit up, I'll retire and go back to Providence College. How's that? Would that make you happy? I have to get to the print shop unless you have any more questions."

There is a condescending, dismissive quality to his words, but I decide not to pick him up on it. "I'm fine, Mario. I'll catch up with you later," I reply and then get up to escort him back to the entry area.

3

Zorello is right, I decide on the ride over to Adams. It's a mistake I've made numerous times: underestimating the potential of an inmate. They all have dreams and abilities that have often been derailed by the lack of opportunity coupled with an abundance of easily available drugs. My mother taught me not to judge a book by its cover, but I continue to do so. When he said he left Providence College to enter the family business, I knew he meant to work his way up in the Patriarca crime family, which he has apparently been quite successful at, if but a small percentage of the rumors are true. His shifting presentation with me was controlled and intentional. That he has difficulty modulating his anger I find highly suspect, although I believe he can and has used violence in pursuit of his goals. Yet it would not be violence arising from some type of distorted or paranoid ideation, which may be amenable to treatment with Eumonia, but rather, purposeful violence to make a point, protect an investment, or for some other particular reason. When his affect changed as we spoke, even the threatening demeanor, I believe it was all intentional. Nonetheless, if participation can help him get out of prison a few months early, who am I to protest? Additionally, his involvement gave a green light for other White guys to sign up and possibly some of the Blacks and Hispanics too.

I arrive early at Adams and use the spare office to check my email online, and then I glance at the apartments available on craigslist. For some reason, I don't feel the imperative to get out of the warden's house that I previously felt. I also haven't had the urge to drink anything beyond beer for the past couple of weeks. I expect it's a combination of my inherent miserliness at not giving up a free place to stay and the newly developing relationship with Nancy Gardner. One major reason to get out of the prison housing was that I didn't appreciate anyone snooping around the place, but now I don't have any empty whiskey bottles or anything else to hide.

Olken enters the office and notices that I am scrolling through the listings. "Any luck at finding a place?" he asks.

"I haven't been looking that hard," I confess. "I'm settling more into the warden's house at Cranston, and it's free."

"If you're in no rush anymore, a condo on the Woonasquatucket may work after all."

"It may," I reply, giving the idea more serious consideration than I previously had. Having a place off the island would be good, regardless of how long I stayed working at Cranston.

"Alain's ready whenever you are."

"I'll be right there," I acknowledge and begin to log off the machine.

In the meeting, I again bring up my concerns that inmates may try to present well if they believe it can help them get out early. "It may be a type of enhanced Hawthorne effect," I speculate, referring to a series of studies done to improve worker productivity at the Hawthorne Works in the late 1920s. No matter what intervention the examiners introduced, such as better lighting, redesigning the workspace, and so on, productivity increased. Gradually, it dawned on them that the increases were not due to the interventions but due to the workers being observed or studied.

"These inmates all realize they have been singled out to be in a special study of Eumonia; plus, they believe if they do well, which means report fewer aggressive thoughts or feelings, they may get out of prison faster."

"That second part is simply not true," Vos objects. "We make it totally clear in our informed consent that participation will have no bearing on their incarceration."

"No matter how clear you make it, that doesn't determine how they will perceive it," I counter. "They're in prison, and they all want out. Why do you think it's standing room only at the AA and NA meetings? Each inmate gets a day a month of goodtime, which is time taken off their sentence, if they attend four meetings a month. They aren't there to get clean; they're there for the goodtime. It may be merely a quarter of a day per meeting, but it's time. The guys in the ATA are all short, with two years or less on their sentences. If they believe they can shave a couple of months off that by participating, it's a huge motivator."

"Your implication is that the motivational factor may confound our results, but all our measures have established independent validity. That validity cannot be confounded by motivation," Vos stresses.

"It's not a validity issue or something you can pick up with any type of psychological test that includes a lie scale. I interviewed a guy today who meets our criteria and was one of the first to sign up. He's brighter than most participants, if not the brightest guy in the program, and I have no doubt he has a history of violence, although it's not what he's incarcerated for. He said his aggressive impulses have significantly decreased in the past three weeks, and he believes it is due to the medication."

"What's your point?" Vos asks, the frustration evident in his voice.

"I don't believe him. I think his main motivation is to get our early."

"But that's purely speculative," Vos presses. "The subject is saying he is having an initial positive response to the Eumonia, and of course, we don't even know which medication he is taking. But putting that aside for the moment, he believes it is due to the medication. Did he indicate any changes in his ideation?"

"He said he was racist but was not as bothered by racist thoughts now as he has been in the past."

"Who is it? I may remember him from the initial interviews?"

"Mario Zorello."

Alain reflects for a moment and then says, "Yes, I saw him. If I'm not mistaken, you had misgivings about him from the onset. Wasn't he one of the persons you identified as involved in organized crime?"

"He is allegedly a higher-up in the Patriarca organization, but that's not why I had misgivings. He's been convicted of no person crimes, and I was concerned that the program may get a reputation that it was only for White inmates. That was an initial problem, although that is no longer an issue. The program is diverse at this point and representative of the prison population. But when we spoke, I got the distinct impression he was trying to shape his answers to highlight the effectiveness of Eumonia. Anyone who reads the informed consent should realize what we are trying to do, and he was trying to make it appear successful."

"Isn't it possible he is telling you the truth?" Vos suggests. "It is the answer that conforms most closely to the data. If he is an experimental subject, then he should have been at full therapeutic blood level for the last week to ten days. Why were you interviewing him to begin with?"

I briefly ponder his question before responding. "You don't realize the degree of motivation a favorable parole hearing with the accompanying possibility of an early release can have for an inmate. If you requested that guys stand on their heads for an hour a day and then attest that it has changed their lives for the better, it wouldn't be a problem if they believed it could help them get out of the can."

"But we're not asking them to stand on their heads," Alain says slowly. "We're asking them to participate in a highly controlled study to determine if taking a particular medication will improve their mood and cognition, allowing them to better manage any aggressive impulses."

"Tom," Olken says, breaking into the conversation. "You have to trust us. This is our area of expertise. You're right; it is the first field study we have done within a correctional environment. Your expertise is helping us navigating the nuances of such an environment, and that is greatly appreciated. We will evaluate the points you have made, but from the research perspective, they are variables we cannot control and therefore study limitations that we will acknowledge. All studies, including this one, have certain limitations."

I am glad Olken intervened, as I was beginning to get irritated with Vos, particularly with a paternalistic attitude I had not previously noticed in him.

"Ralph is correct," Vos adds. "All studies do have limitations. I have devoted three years to the Eumonia project, so I can get a bit hyperprotective. Obviously, I hope this field test will have positive results. Nevertheless, even in light of my admitted bias, I believe we have an excellent design. The limitation you pointed out of subjects shaping their responses in hope of some secondary gain, such as an early discharge from their incarceration, will have to be noted."

"I may be overreacting a bit." I concede, feeling more at ease.

"I have one concern, and it relates to a question Alain asked you a moment earlier," Olken says, studying me intently. "I realize that you may have to interview inmates, Tom, in respect to the secure and safe operation of the ATA. We wish to avoid a second major security breach at all costs. It would jeopardize the entire study, and we remain indebted to how you managed the situation with Andrea. Yet I do have misgivings as to your interviewing Mr. Zorello or any other inmates regarding the program and specifically in respect to the effectiveness of Eumonia. Those interviews may contribute to some shaping of subjects' responses. That is part of what I meant by trusting us. We need to trust that you will provide a safe environment and coordinate the counseling intervention components, but you need to trust that we will conduct a safe and ethical clinical trial."

I ponder his word for a moment and then respond, "I can understand that."

4

For one of the first times, I wish I were on the high-speed ferry back home, making the crossing in a half rather than a full hour. As a rule, I enjoy how long the standard ferry takes, allowing me to transition from my professional mainland self to my more enduring island personality. It's not a conscious transformation, but I can almost always feel it taking place as the ship plies the waters between Point Judith and the terminal on Block Island. Today there is a slight chop, and the catamaran-style hull of the high-speed boat would have banged and crashed its way for the entire voyage, but at least I'd get home quicker. There is an additional delay at the pier while the deckhands debate how to best position the weight of the three tractor-trailers waiting to embark. In the end, I have to move along with a couple of other cars, so the trucks, a type of rolling ballast, can be centered on the lower car level. It is a necessary safety consideration, but it postpones our departure by fifteen minutes.

Once I am situated on the upper deck, I begin to relax, leaving the mainland tensions and concerns behind me. Olken was accurate in his assessment: misgivings or not, I do have to be less controlling and let them do their job.

Under a moderate wind, the sea runs at five to seven feet with the breeze snapping whitecaps, which briefly linger and flicker atop the rolling water before merging back into the surf. A slight mist works its way to the upper deck as a familiar briny scent fills my nostrils. The distant band on the horizon is the island coastline, which will grow more distinct as we voyage on. I settle in on one of the metal benches with my back leaned against the bridge tower and punch in Kathy's cell phone number.

"TC," she says after the first ring.

"How's he doing?" I ask.

"Why don't you ask him yourself?" she replies.

Woody had the varicocele procedure four days earlier at Yale New Haven Hospital. They ended up doing surgery—not the outpatient embolization treatment, because an MRI showed that the cluster of veins was larger than the surgeon initially suspected. He spent one night in the hospital and then an extra day at a New Haven hotel. Because of how strongly the surf was running. Kathy didn't want to risk the crossing in a heavy sea for fear that the jarring may loosen his stitches. When I spoke to Woody two nights ago, we agreed her fears were unfounded but decided some things were better left unsaid.

"TC, my man, I feel great," he exuberantly shouts into the phone. "What's your poison? Do we go after blues or stripers tomorrow?"

"You're not going anywhere tomorrow," I hear from Kathy's alarmed voice in the background.

"Just kidding, just kidding," Woody is saying to her as I hold on the line.

A moment later, he is back on with me and more serious. "Actually, I'm feeling okay, a lot better than I was the day after the surgery. Those sawbones always lie when they say you may have some slight discomfort. Today is the first day I haven't taken any of the Percocet I was given, but I needed them majorly the past three days. I'll still be on restricted duty for a while, so why don't you stop in with the little guy?"

We chat for a bit more and make tentative arrangements for me to swing by with Matt on Saturday.

"Come early, and we can all watch cartoons together." He laughs before saying goodbye and handing the phone to Kathy.

"TC," she says softly, as I expect she is making her way into another room. "I can't tell you how grateful we are to you and Maura for this. She's been on my mind so much since Woody told me about the money. I visited Dodge yesterday and left a miniature purple azalea by the grave. I hope that was okay?"

"Sure, Kathy," I say, touched and taken aback. I was half expecting her to bring up Nancy, not my wife. "Maura loved azaleas, and purple was one of her favorite colors."

"I know. It's past its prime, but there are still plenty of blooms on it. You can decide where to plant it if you want. I was uncertain if the cemetery allowed small bushes by the graves and would never plant anything without your permission, but I thought the colors were so much her."

"I appreciate that, Kathy. I'll take a ride up after we land. That was really nice of you."

"It was the least we could do. What you did was really nice, TC—more than nice."

I'm tongue-tied until Kathy fills the momentary silence between us. "We'll be seeing you and Matt Saturday morning?"

"Definitely. We'll be there at nine thirty, okay?"

"See you then, and thanks again, TC."

Fortunately, my car is among the ones that debark before the tractor-trailers, and I am making my way out of town shortly after the ship ties up. Rather than heading for my mother's house, I drive directly to Dodge Cemetery. The plant Kathy left is in fuller bloom than I expected, reminding me more of a bougainvillea than an azalea. "That's for you," I say to the dark granite stone with both my wife's and dad's names incised in it. "It's from Kathy in appreciation for the money we gave her so Woody could have surgery to increase his sperm count. Kathy thinks I got the money from an insurance policy you took out after you became pregnant."

The sea shimmers in the distance as I stand by the grave, noting that among the stones, there are numerous small evergreens and bushes planted adjacent to other monuments. Kathy has placed the azalea by the front of the grave, and I shift it over to the left side and then stand back to study it. The black granite beautifully sets off the purple. "The azalea looks good there," I say aloud. It is a question as well as an observation, and I half expect Maura to respond, but she doesn't. Spying an equipment garage a few hundred yards away from me, I begin to jog down to see if I can borrow a shovel from one of the groundskeepers. No one is around, but I scavenge a shovel with a broken handle from a junk pile, along with a couple of plastic water bottles. I fill the containers from a spigot on the side of the building and then make my way back to the plot with the shovel and water. I have a hole dug in a few moments and then carefully position the azalea within it before gradually refilling it with earth and saturating the small bush with water. I then return to the shed to dump the shovel and water bottles back onto the trash heap.

As I approach Maura's grave, the azalea's blossoms form into a small flock of purple butterflies cavorting in the summer breeze. "I met another woman I kind of like," I say. "She's an architect and went to school with Kathy. Her name is Nancy Gardner. Matt met her, too, and they hit it off well."

The air has tailed off to a soft zephyr, and the speckles of distant white-caps have disappeared. A ship's whistle blows, and anyone making the crossing now will have a smoother sail than I had. The fickle sea can change its mood in but a few minutes.

"I have to go pick up Matt," I say as I turn for my car. I'm expecting a sign or response, but there is only the soft breeze threading through the newly leafed trees.

It takes all my strength to hold the boom steady as a following wind fills both the mainsail and jib. The wooden hull lifts, and we begin to skip atop the water's surface.

"Dad, we're flying! We're on the back of the wind! We're flying," Matt cries out joyfully. "Do you think we'll see any mermaids?"

"I hope so," I holler as the boat lifts free of the sea and soars into the air. Sailing through space, I'm amazed that I can still control our direction with the tiller.

"There's a mermaid! I saw a mermaid," Matt squeals, leaning out over the port side gunnel.

I peer down and see a beautiful woman sitting upon a boulder with the surf breaking against the rock. Mussels and golden starfish are woven into her long black hair, with strands of glimmering pearls falling into the cleft between her exposed breasts. She smiles invitingly from her ocean perch while the luminous green scales of her fish tail twinkle beneath the midnight sky. Matt is gone from the boat as I shift the rudder to bring the small craft about.

I awake with a strain in my groin and an erection throbbing against my pajamas. I sink back onto the pillow to try and reevoke the image of the woman on the rock in my mind, but the urge to use the bathroom is too strong, and I stumble from my bed to the john.

I have begun to read *Peter Pan* to Matt, and as I stand at the toilet urinating, I realize his words in the dream are taken from early in the book when Peter brings Wendy to the window for their first leap into space. He tells her as they stand by the window's ledge that she will see mermaids.

Making my way back to bed, it is not Peter Pan or the flying sailboat or even Matt's joyful screams that hold my attention, but the glimmering mermaid with the upturned breasts. Her hair was dark and luxuriant, with shells and sea creatures woven into the flowing locks. Maura's hair was auburn with golden highlights, whereas Nancy's is a richer black. I try to envision either of them as the mermaid and fall into a mesmeric sleep with beautiful women floating through my mind.

"How would you like to learn to sail today?" I ask Matt as we have breakfast.

"Yes, Daddy" is his immediate response. He has been on the ferry numerous times to visit Maura's grandparents on the mainland and loved to romp about on the ship's upper deck, but the first time I took him out on Woody's boat, he was uncomfortable with the roar of the motors when they were opened to barely a quarter of full power.

"Let's go to the Great Salt Pond, but only if I can find someone else to join us," I explain, and he heartily agrees, although I doubt he fully understands. I call around to a couple of guys, but none are available. Finally, I give Kathy a ring and ask if she can free herself from her nursing responsibilities long enough to go for an hour-long sail with Matt and me.

She is initially concerned for Matt's safety, but once I explain we will stay within the pond by New Harbor, she consents. "Woody's climbing the walls and driving both of us nuts. We'll meet you by the public launch area at two."

I swing by Izzy Fellows's boatbuilding shop at 1:30 p.m. He has already attached the *Lir*'s trailer to his pickup and has it waiting for me outside his shop. The Whitehall's mahogany hull glistens under a new coat of varnish, and I realize it is the boat from my dream.

The large shop doors are swung wide, and Izzy comes out as I'm securing Matt's car seat in the truck.

"We're going sailing, Mr. Fellows," Matt announces as Izzy draws near.

"So I hear," he says. "Your dad is getting you started young."

"Kathy Kent is meeting us there, and we'll keep it in the salt pond for an hour or so," I reply to his unasked safety question.

Izzy nods his agreement with the plan and smiles. "Good way to get the little guy started."

We do a quick check of the boat, and I pull the jib bag out from the bow, telling Izzy we can leave it at the shop since I don't plan to use the forward sail.

At the landing, I step the mast and get the small craft rigged out. The whole time I work, Matt is inside the hull and continuously questions me on each task I complete.

Kathy pulls in a little before two o'clock with Woody in the passenger's seat. They park off to the side, and there is an obvious hitch in Woody's step as he approaches me, noticeably dragging his left leg.

"Have you recovered enough to be out?" I ask.

"Why not?" He laughs and begins to trot across the remaining thirty feet between us.

"You idiot," I say as he gives me a big hug.

"Not fully a hundred percent, but I'm getting there. If the plan is to float around in the pond, I'm sure I can handle that." Then, looking at Matt standing in the boat, he says, "How you doing, sailor?"

Matt excitedly begins to jabber about sailing and an assortment of other things as Kathy comes up by the side of the Whitehall and lifts him free of the boat.

While they back away, I nod to the pickup. Woody reads my mind and makes his way over to the driver's side. "You're all rigged out?"

"Set to go," I confirm as he jumps in and starts the truck. In a flash, we have the boat floated off the trailer, and I pull myself over the side as Woody parks.

I use one of the oars stowed on the floorboards to maneuver along the dock and then secure the bow and stern lines to the carved oaken cleats Izzy made for the *Lir*. The pond is glass with a mild breeze that barely kicks up a ripple. Nevertheless, we briefly debate the wisdom of Woody joining with us until Matt cries out, "When are we going sailing?"

His question brings an end to our bickering. Kathy agrees to Woody's coming as long as we don't go into the open water and immediately turn back if the wind picks up.

It's a perfect day to introduce Matt to sailing. It would be impossible to lay the boat down, even if I tried. We more float atop the water with an occasional gust of air slightly filling the sail and wafting the musty smell of the salt marshes over us. The tide is outbound, and as we reach the far end of the pond, I momentarily worry that I may have to drop the two oars into their locks to row against the ebbing flow that could pull us into the open water. Catching the wind as best I can, I'm able to tack my way through the stiffest current without resorting to the oars. As I coast gradually along the opposite side of the pond, my cell goes off.

Woody casts me a glance, probably remembering the last call I got when we were out on the water.

"Tom Phillips," I say into the receiver.

"Tom, it's Tony Vorenzi. How are you?"

It takes me a moment to register the name of Senator Poletti's chief of staff. "Ah, hi, Mr. Vorenzi," I half stammer while trying to get my bearings. "I'm fine. I'm fine. How are you?" Both Kathy and Woody are staring at me, and I make an Alfred E. Newman *What, me worry?* face of incredulity. I haven't the slightest idea why he is calling me, and it's made all the stranger because of how incongruent the call is with my surroundings.

"That's good. I'm glad to hear that. Why I'm calling is that Dr. Olken mentioned to me that you may be interested in a Woonasquatucket condo. That is Senator Poletti's district, and I wanted to reach out to a potential new constituent."

"Oh, thanks. I'm—"

His laughter cuts me off. "Just joking there, Tom, but as you may know, we are very involved in the entire river development project. In light of how helpful you have been to the Adams study, including your management of that hostage situation, I would like to introduce you to one of the key developers of the residential space. Are you free after the weekend, say Monday afternoon?"

"I'm not certain I'm in the market for a condo."

"No problem! It never hurts to look, and certainly no commitments, but allow me to make the introduction as an expression of our gratitude. Anything you do or do not negotiate with the developer is strictly between the two of you. I have your email and will send you the exact time. I expect it will be between three and four. Have a good day."

He has cut the connection before I have a chance to respond.

"What was that?" Woody asks, observing my puzzled countenance.

"Tony Vorenzi, Senator Carlo Poletti's chief of staff," I say. I then go on to explain the relationship and why he called. By the time I finish, we are approaching the landing.

"Do we have to stop?" Matt asks as I bring the sailboat alongside the wharf while Woody drops the safety bumpers and then steps from the boat to secure us to the pier.

"That's it for today, champ, but you did great, and we'll go out again," I explain. I expect him to protest, but he doesn't as I lift him from the seat and pass him up to Kathy, who is already on the dock.

Once Woody has the trailer backed down and into the water, I unlash the *Lir* and, using one oar, guide the boat over the submerged conveyance. Wading into the water, I retrieve the winch cable and snap it onto a bronze eyebolt embedded in the stem. As I begin to crank the Whitehall, Woody wades in next to me and asks how serious I am about buying a condo in Providence.

"Not much at this point. I wanted to get out of the prison housing a few weeks back, but now I don't feel the same imperative; plus, it's free."

"Some of those mills are beautiful and built a damn sight better than anything made today. It may be worth taking an inspection tour, especially if you plan to keep working there for a while."

"Maybe," I reply noncommittally. "How are you feeling?"

"Like a million bucks." He laughs, and then just as quickly, his eyes mist over. "Thanks, TC. I mean it. You can't understand how important this is to us. It would have taken me years to save that kind of bread."

I catch myself from saying, "No problem." It's too trite and easy. "What are friends for, Woody? You'd do the same for me in a heartbeat."

4

Matt is definitely getting more attached to me, as my mother has predicted. I push him about the island in the running stroller a couple of times while I am home, and he never once asks if we can stay at my mother's house. On Saturday afternoon, I take him to his first playdate with a day-care friend, where I sit chatting with the one other father and a group of mothers on a patio as our kids play in the yard. It seems strange to me, and I can't remember if my parents ever had playdates when I was a toddler. When I later ask my mother, she tells me that she used to drop me off at other kids' houses to play or have kids over to our house, but that it was never organized in any type of formal manner. She is a little puzzled that I stayed while the kids played. When I explain that I thought it was expected because all the other parents did, she is still more perplexed. "When I dropped you off to play with other small children, it was so I could have time for myself and get something done, not kibitz with the other parents," she observes.

At dinner, I mention the call from Vorenzi and the possibility of buying a condo in a newly renovated building on the Woonasquatucket.

"How long do you plan to keep working at the prison?" she asks.

I shrug noncommittally. "I expect I can stay there as long as I feel like it, but I'd have to move back into a state position."

"Is that what you want?"

"It's a possibility," I reply. "The project I'm working on is going well, and if the results pan out, corrections will likely continue to operate the ATA once Adams is out of the picture. Or they may ask Adams to administer the unit."

"Didn't you say that was their initial plan?"

"It was Adams's original idea, but corrections nixed it, and then the hostage situation pushed it way to the back burner. Still, Adams has serious political backing, and if the results are positive, they may again try to take control of it. The whole field of correctional healthcare management is an area they hope to expand into, in addition to developing meds."

"Could you work for them? Have you given that any thought?" she asks.

"Not a lot. They have implied—or their president, Ralph Olken, has implied—that there may be a position available for me if the clinical trial is successful. He's told me they appreciate my correctional experience and how important that will be to them whenever they get approval to market Eumonia for use with inmates. It's a small company, but I still would have problems working for any drug company."

"There are no predictive studies that show serotonin levels to be associated with depression or other mood disorders," she says, drawing on her education as a nurse practitioner.

"I know that," I agree. "And there aren't any that link dopamine levels to schizophrenia predictively, yet that's how all the antidepressants and antipsychotics work. One way or another, they increase the amount of those neurotransmitters in the brain. I'm sure Eumonia has a mix of serotonin and dopamine enhancers. If they can show that it reduces aggression in prisoners, they'll be sitting on a gold mine. Half the parole boards in the country will make being on Eumonia a condition of release for guys with a history of violence. Yet to me, it's all a big house of cards, when placebos may work almost as well as the meds."

"A big valuable house of cards," my mother adds.

Once we're back at my place and Matt's asleep, I give Nancy a call. After we chat for a couple of minutes, I ask her if she has ever worn her hair long.

"Up until five years ago. Why?"

"I had a dream a few nights ago, and there was a mermaid in it with long black hair—"

"A mermaid?" she interrupts with a minor fit of the giggles.

"Yeah, a mermaid, and don't laugh. There was also a flying boat that I was sailing through the sky in with Matt. We saw the mermaid down below us sitting atop a boulder in the sea."

"Are you saying that I looked like the mermaid?"

"Not exactly, but she did have long black hair, and I don't know a lot of other women with black hair."

"I remember from an undergraduate psychology class that water was frequently a feminine symbol. What do you make of that?" she asks.

"I thought it was more a symbol of the unconscious, the ocean we originally evolved or emerged from."

She laughs. "An amniotic dream! But am I stranded on a boulder in your unconscious, or am I swimming there?"

"Swimming," I say immediately, taken with the image of her paddling around or even skinny-dipping in my mind. "You're undoubtedly swimming about in my unconscious. Yeah, that's it. That makes sense to me."

"So if I'm swimming through your unconscious or some aspect of your feminine side, why are you flying above me? Why aren't you landing?" Her voice is soft with a new seriousness to her inquiry.

"Good question," I say slowly. "But I want to. I want to come down, to know you more."

We are both quiet for a few moments until I say, "Tell me more about Frank Lloyd Wright."

"It would be best for you to come out here sometime to see his work for yourself."

"I'd enjoy that," I reply reflectively. "Would you be okay with my being there for a couple of days? Could you get some time off?"

"I'd make the time. We can go out to Oak Park, do an architectural tour of the city, and possibly visit the Art Institute."

"That sounds like a lot."

"It's only a half-hour ride to Wright's studio. We can do that one morning and still have plenty of time to see the city. It's easily manageable, but simply hanging out is nice too."

"I'll check if I can take a few days off. It shouldn't be a problem; I'm a contract employee and have a somewhat flexible schedule, but I'm more interested in the first part of my question. How would you be with my coming out?"

"I'd like it. I'd like it a lot."

Warmth suffuses me. I envision it instantaneously traversing the thousand miles of phone lines between us or bouncing off some satellite to fill a void within.

"I'd like it too," I respond into the silence between us. "My mom's schedule is fairly free. I'll check if she can watch Matt and get back to you."

"You can bring Matt if your mother is busy. He could get to ride in a real plane instead of a flying boat."

"He'd enjoy that, and I appreciate the offer, but I'd rather spend the time alone with you. I'll speak to the superintendent on Wednesday and give you a call after that."

We chat for a bit more, and as I'm about to hang up, she says, "Tom, you know I grew up in Mystic, and my dad worked at the Electric Boat Yard?"

"Sure, you mentioned it. Or maybe Woody did. Why?"

"One day when we stopped to see my dad at the yard, there was a nuclear sub in dry dock for repairs. I forget its name, but it was a sturgeon class. To me, she appeared like a massive, beached whale. To the fore, a beautiful mermaid was painted on one side. Her golden hair flowed back as she gradually—and now I would say, *seductively*—made her way toward the bow. My dad told me the sailors cavorted with mermaids when they were at sea. That wasn't his word, "cavorted," but that's what was in my imagination. I believed him and was fascinated with mermaids for years. As a preteen, I collected *Aquaman* comics, and when that movie *Splash* came out, I was in my early teens and must have seen it half a dozen times."

"I never thought much of mermaids until this dream," I say after considering her words. "But suddenly, they have become a major interest of mine, particularly the cavorting part. I'll call you in a couple of days."

"I'd like that," she says to close the conversation.

That night I hope and half expect to dream of Nancy, but I don't, or else I don't remember the dream. I generally take the noontime ferry back on Sunday, but I'm having trouble getting myself ready to leave. On Sunday, my mother and I take Matt to the 9:00 a.m. Mass at Saint Andrew's summer chapel on the Old Harbor. It is a quaint structure a few blocks from the ferry terminal, more of a seaman's bethel than a full-fledged church.

At breakfast, my mother asks me what was wrong.

"Nothing. At least nothing I am aware of. Why?"

"You seem preoccupied," she observes.

I shrug and immediately feel about three years old. I glance at Matt to my right and realize he's the three-year-old, not me. "I met this woman, Nancy Gardner, a couple of weeks ago."

"Kathy's friend." My mom helps to fill the gap in our conversation.

"Yeah," I say, unable to remember if I had already mentioned Nancy to my mother or if she and Kathy have been kibitzing. I can't remember, and in the end, it doesn't make any difference.

"She and Kathy were at Connecticut College together, and I kind of like her. I can't say what it is, but something's there." I decide not to mention that she's been floating naked through my mind since the mermaid dream of a few nights earlier.

"What does she think of you?"

"I can't say exactly. She's never been married, has no kids, studied architecture at Michigan after graduating from Connecticut, and works for an architectural firm in Chicago."

My mother is chuckling by the time I finish.

"What's so funny?" I ask irritably.

"I asked you what she thought of you, not for her curriculum vitae."

"Oh," I respond sheepishly. "I'm fairly certain the feelings are mutual. I haven't asked Kathy or anything, but I'd say she's interested in me."

My mother laughs again. "I'd hope so. Any woman in her right mind should be interested in you. You're smart, you have a profession, you're independent, you're kind, and you have the cutest son in all of Rhode Island. Right, Mattie?"

Matt smiles and squirms in his booster seat at the sound of his name before crawling onto the bench cushion between us and up onto my lap.

"What are you planning to do?" my mother asks more seriously.

"Her family is from the Mystic area, and she comes back periodically…" I trail off without answering the question and then continue, "I'm thinking I may take a trip out to the Windy City."

"Soon?"

"Possibly."

"Do you need me to watch Mattie?"

Hearing his name, Matt glances up at my mother.

"Daddy has to go to work, and you're going to get to spend a few days with Nana," she explains.

His face begins to grimace until finally, he blurts out, "I don't like work," while clinging to me tightly and burying his face in my neck. "I don't like work," he says a second time, his voice muffled against my skin.

"I don't like it either, big guy," I coo softly. "I don't like it either."

My mom's eyes have fogged up. "He'll be okay," she whispers consolingly.

Instead of driving right back to my mother's house, we take a detour by Dodge Cemetery so I can show my mom the plant Kathy gave me and where I placed it.

"It's beautiful!" she exclaims, kneeling to study the blooms more closely. "That was nice of her."

"I gave them some money so Woody could have varicocele surgery. They've been trying to have a child for some time, and his sperm count has been too low."

"Was the surgery successful? If I'm not mistaken, the research results are mixed."

"That's why I gave them the money. His insurance refused to cover it. Woody told Kathy that Maura had taken out a million-dollar policy after she got pregnant, and I wanted to do it in her name. Otherwise, he didn't think she would have accepted the gift. It was done last week, so he may not have had a sperm count yet."

As we chat, Matt plays in the grass with a yellow Tonka truck he carried over from the car.

"The woman from Chicago, Nancy…do you plan to go out there soon?"

I nod. "As soon as I can get loose from work."

"I'm certain they would both like that," she says, nodding to the grave.

The stone bears the names of Maura Phillips and Francis Phillips etched into its black granite. A summer breeze presses the azalea blossoms to the marker and riffles the leaves in the trees. My father has been dead twenty years and my wife three, yet Nancy is the one now alive in my mind.

"It may be as soon as a week from now," I say.

"For how long a visit?"

A month, I want to say. "I'm not sure. Four or five days. Instead of going into work, I'd go there. I can leave on a Thursday and return on a Tuesday or a Wednesday and then take a couple of more days off here before I go back in. I'll talk to Superintendent Dwyer this week. The unit is running smoothly, so I doubt he'll have any objections."

CHAPTER 5

1

I delay at my mother's house to spend time with Matt, intentionally missing the noontime ferry, although I did first call the unit and was told that all was running smoothly. When I leave, I'm relieved that Matt is busily playing on the floor and does not appear particularly upset by my departure.

"I told you he would be okay," my mother says as I give her a goodbye kiss and then start for my place to pack a small bag before driving down to get in line for the 2:00 p.m. boat. On the crossing, I make a second call to the sergeant running the shift and am again reassured that all is quiet. A third or so of the inmates have or have had visits, and the remainder are sleeping, watching TV, playing cards, out in the yard, or engaged in some other activity prisoners use to kill time. I know few are reading or engaged in any trajectory of behavior that may help them stay out of prison in the future since, ultimately, incarceration is a mind-numbing and motivation-killing exercise.

Sitting on the upper deck, I have an urge to call Nancy again but decide not to. As great a catch as I may be in my mother's eyes, I have no desire to be a pest in hers. Reclining on a metal bench, I close my eyes as the sun bakes down upon me. The slight tremor working its way up from the ship's massive twin diesels gently massages my body. The image of making love to Maura beneath the star-filled sky by the Southeast Light fills my mind. It was over three years ago, and we were both convinced it was when Matt was conceived, except it wasn't Matt. It was Estelle, Estelle Phillips. *We can call her Stella*, Maura said at one point after her intuition inaccurately convinced both of us that a baby girl was growing within her. Her name was for the stars of the Milky Way that spanned out as a wedding canopy above us while we made love in time with the rolling surf on the outer edge of a great celestial disk. Lying still, I reexperience the shock of being told at the Rhode Island Hospital Trauma Center that my son was safe. I had no idea what the doctor or nurse or whoever told me was saying. We were having a daughter, but I didn't care about the kid; I wanted to see Maura. When I told her we had a son as she was being rolled off to emergency surgery, she immediately accepted the news. *Take care of our son* were her last words to me as they rolled her out on a gurney.

It's three years. It's time to move on.

A blast of the ship's whistle brings me back from the semiconscious state I have been lulled into as the boat crossed to the mainland. Swinging my legs around to sit up, I feel a slight mist somehow brought up from the sea lightly splash my face. I step to the rail as the captain powers down by Point Judith's outer breakwater. Scanning the massive stones of the jetty for a welcoming mermaid, I find only a few kids fishing in the midafternoon sun.

The voice again echoes in my mind, *It's three years. It's…* but it is overwhelmed by the second whistle and announcement for drivers to return to their vehicles.

"Enough already. I get it," I say to the voice. "I am thinking about it."

I make it to Cranston by four o'clock and decide to check on the unit and sort through my email before heading over to the warden's house. Crossing the makeshift visiting area we have set up in the entry, I notice everyone is White. Visiting time is scheduled from one to five o'clock, and there are commonly a dozen or so inmates who have family that come in. Seeking out the shift commander, I ask him if he has any idea why there are so few visits.

"Can't say. Not sure, but my guess is Zorello. Last week he complained that the little kids bothered his visit, and then this week, all the Black and Spanish cons' people with kids came in around one and were gone by three when Zorello's people showed up."

"Not all the Black or Spanish guys have kids. I didn't see any minority guys out there."

He shrugs. "Zorello's a racist pig. He probably didn't want any of the brothers near him. Most of these guys are two-bit drug dealers who only signed up for this unit because he told them to anyway."

The sergeant's words take me aback but don't totally surprise me. It was not long after I spoke to the super, some of the Adams people, and others regarding the lack of diversity in the unit that many Black and Spanish guys made inquiries. There are no secrets in a prison and I'm certain that word was circulating in the camp that the Alternatives to Aggression program wanted to balance its racial composition. While Lincoln and I were strategizing on engaging some of the high-profile minority inmates to give the ATA an unofficial approval, Zorello may have been putting out the word on his own to get some guys in there, which was what the sergeant inferred.

"You think he got some of those drug dealers to sign up?" I ask.

"Who knows, Doc? His group is supposed to control much of the heroin and cocaine that makes its way into our community. The Spanish guys tend to work their own side of the street. Their dope comes up the New York, the Spanish Harlem route. Most Blacks use a local distributor like Zorello, so they owe him. Therefore, when Mario Zorello says to do something, people do it. If he put the word out for some Black or Spanish guys to sign up, some would sign on the dotted line the next day—one hand washes the other and all that."

"Yeah, sure," I reply. "Is there anything else happening?"

"Not really, Boss. We're just all doing our time. Seven years left for me until I max out my retirement, and then it's sayonara."

I ponder the sergeant's words as I start down the corridor to my office.

They make sense, especially the likelihood that Zorello called in a couple of favors to get minority guys to sign up for the program. It wasn't a hard sell. As soon as the rumor made it into the population that you could get some time knocked off your sentence by participating, we had a waiting list. Perhaps all he did was let that word out of a potential early parole for participants. Nevertheless, the possibility that he or anyone else was informally playing with the visiting schedule was a different matter. It wasn't acceptable and had to be immediately addressed. I consider paging Lincoln at home to see what he knows but decide against it.

Scrolling through my email, I see there is one from Anthony Vorenzi. He is confirming a four o'clock time for the Monday meeting. We will get together at the former Providence Brass Works, and he has attached a link to Prestige Construction, the developer's website. Perusing their materials, I get a brief history of the industrial development along the Woonasquatucket, which emphasizes how solidly the buildings were constructed to accommodate the machinery of the times. In particular, the Providence Brass Works building has a slate roof, which has been fully restored, along with a significantly ornamented brick front facade. It backs up to the river, and the long-range plans for the area call for the restoration of a small canal out to Providence Harbor that the new owners will be able to access. It will be a mixed-use development with the first floor housing some small businesses or restaurants and all the upper floors residential. A banner floats across the top of the screen as I read: *Let us build your dream.* The exposed brick, decks with river views, and future canal project are all appealing to me. Studios begin at $150,000, with one-bedroom units in the mid-to-upper-$200,000 range range. I shoot Vorenzi an email confirming I'll be there at four o'clock. After checking the Monday schedule, I send a note to the first-shift commander asking him to hold back Zorello from his job assignment in the morning, and then I head out.

2

My legs are a little stiff when I go in on Monday. The previous night I did a ten-mile run, keeping a steady seven-minute-a-mile pace the whole way, and right after getting up today, I did another strong eight. That was a rigorous eighteen miles within a twelve-hour time span. Out on Block Island, I haven't been pushing myself, largely because I have been pushing Matt most of the time. It's harder to get into rhythm with the stroller. The faster runs feel good, although my thighs are burning slightly when I enter the unit. After reviewing the second- and third-shift reports, I call the gate officer and ask him to bring Mario Zorello down to my office.

"Buongiorno again, Doc," he says upon entering. "You planning to make this a regular thing between us?"

"Not a regular thing, but I am interested in how you are doing."

"Like I said the last time, I'm doing fine. This place is helping me. What else can I say?"

"Do you still believe it's mainly the medication?"

"I believe that's your job and that of the other doctors to figure out, but if you ask me, then yeah, I think it's the medicine, the Eumonia."

I nod at his response and then say, "I came by yesterday afternoon near the end of visits and noticed you in the visiting area with someone. It was after four, and the only people out there were you and a couple of other White guys."

I pause, and Mario fills in the momentary void. "Are you asking me some type of question or what?"

"I was wondering what happened to all the other inmates who had visits."

"We made an accommodation, Doc, if that's what you're wondering. You're the one who put us in this place with a real small visiting room and only two vending machines for our people. It gets crowded in there, so we decided that it might be better to have two shifts for visits. That's all."

"Who's the 'we,' Mario?"

He lifts his eyebrows as if the question is completely ridiculous. "Who do you think the 'we' is?" he asks rhetorically. "It's us, the inmates. I brought it up to the other cons, and they agreed that it made sense."

I sneeze twice as he is talking, and it takes me a moment to realize that it may be because of the cologne he is wearing, which gives off a heavy scent that I had not previously noted when we met. Excusing myself, I study Mario more intently while blowing my nose. His slightly graying hair is neatly combed, and there seems to be a light behind his dark eyes that flickers off and on with the intensity of his emotions as if controlled by some internal rheostat. He's wearing the standard state-issued garb, but it looks neater on him than on others. For generations, inmates have altered their state-issued clothing to mimic fashion trends. The baggy state jeans are often pegged, pleated, or otherwise altered by inmate tailors to fit particular tastes. It's harder to do much with the blue work shirts, but some guys convert their open collars to button-downs or add cowboy or other stitching designs on the fronts. Any type of gang representation, including keeping one's pant leg rolled up in a certain manner that identifies you as a particular gang member, is verboten and leads to a ticket. Inmates can have their own undergarments, but jewelry, except for watches, wedding rings, and medals, is forbidden. The medals concession was made as part of a lawsuit in which religious discrimination was asserted by a group of prisoners who claimed they weren't allowed to wear crosses and other religious items around their necks. This, in turn, has led to periodic disputes between the inmate council and prison administration on the size of allowable chains and medals prisoners can wear. Jim's policy is that no medal over an inch-and-a-half long or in diameter is allowed and that chains must be twenty-four inches or less, with each inmate allowed to wear only one chain at a time. The wedding ring policy has morphed into each prisoner's right to wear one ring after numerous guys claimed that a regular ring was actually a wedding ring. Again, any "wedding ring" deemed to indicate gang affiliation is confiscated and earns the wearer an immediate ticket. Watches are at the discretion of the inmate, although most guys stick with the cheap plastic Timex variety available in the canteen to avoid having other inmates target them for their timepieces.

Zorello's jeans appear to be more denim slacks rather than state issue, pleated and neatly pressed. His shirt is state issue with no fancy adornments, although his T-shirt is clearly not provided by Rhode Island Corrections. It is a lustrous royal-blue-silk item, and his circular gold medal almost shimmers against the rich backdrop.

"Tell me about this accommodation," I say once I have finished blowing my nose.

"Not much to tell, Doc. That visiting area gets crowded, and last week it was real bad. Some little Black kid spilled his tonic on my visit, and I didn't appreciate it. Later I suggested it may be best to split the time up. All those that got little kids use the space from one to three, and those of us that have no little kids use it from three to five."

"I didn't notice any Black or Spanish guys out there at four when I came through?"

He smirks and twitches his shoulders at my question. "What can I say? Guess we don't reproduce as quickly as they do. I've certainly done my part, and I hope the same is true for you. You got any kids, Doc?"

"We're going back to the regular schedule next Sunday, Mario. It will be open visits from one to five, and it makes no difference if there are kids or no kids," I say, not answering his child question.

"That may not be a great idea, Doc. If I remember correctly from those Greek philosophy courses I took during my Providence College days, Aristotle said that all things should be done in moderation. You're making a decision that is immoderate."

"How so?" I ask, slightly irritated at his patronizing tone.

"You want us to be less violent, right? That's a main goal of this Alternative to Aggression thing, right?"

I nod, and he continues. "This situation comes up where this kid, and it's this Black kid, and I told you already I've had my troubles with them in the past, and this kid, he spills soda on my visit, who happens to be my sister. There was a time when I may have let the father of that kid know that I wasn't real happy that he wasn't watching his kid, and he wasn't watching his kid because he was trying to feel up his girlfriend, which also didn't make me real happy, since that, too, was happening in front of my sister. At one time, I may have told him in a manner that makes sure it never happens again."

"You may hurt him, you're saying," I interject.

"That's what you're saying. I'm saying accidents happen, and maybe he has an accident. But now I'm not there. I'm not thinking of him getting hurt. What's on my mind now is how can I make the situation better so this won't happen again, not how do I get revenge or anything like that. So I make nice with some of the other cons I live with, and we make an accommodation. No one gets hurt, and everyone is happy."

"And my decision is not moderate because?"

"Your decision is not moderate because you are acting against your own best interests. I dealt with my aggression. You're trying to help me do that. This unit is trying to help all of us do that, and we did it. It may be the pills, it may be those groups or the therapy, but we did what you asked us to do. We made an accommodation, and no one got hurt."

"That makes sense, Mario," I comment. "But the problem is that you're a prisoner here, and you don't make the rules; you follow the rules. Whatever position you have had in the past to make rules, either in another unit or on the street, you are not in that position now. If you want to bring an idea up, then put it through channels, and we'll consider it. But as of now, we're back on the old schedule."

I can see that when I stressed he was not the one making the rules, he winced slightly as a flame of anger pulsed behind his eyes and died away almost as quickly.

"Hey, you're the boss," he says into the lull between us. "But as I said, I don't believe it's a wise decision. The cons may just decide they prefer to split visiting time up anyway."

"They might," I agree. "But if I hear they do it because you're pressuring them or any of your fan club is pressuring them, then you're out of here, along with any thoughts of an early parole."

"You may benefit from a little of this Alternatives to Aggression thing for yourself, Doc, to go threatening people like you are," he observes.

"That's not threatening you, Mario," I reply coolly. "Threatening is telling you I intend to have you strip-searched each day so a CO can stick his finger up your ass to see if you have any contraband in there. That's a threat, and that's not what I'm doing. I'm telling you you're a convict in this program, not an administrator. If you wish to submit a suggestion or anything else to me, then you're welcome to do so. But next weekend, we are returning things to the way they were. I think you should be getting back to your work assignment at this point."

He regards me steadily while he rises from his seat. "Like I said, you're the boss." He then turns to leave.

"Mr. Zorello, one second," I call as he approaches the door, having momentarily forgotten I must escort him to the entry area that leads into the prison and his job at the print shop.

He turns to me with venom in his eyes, which he quickly covers. "Yeah."

"I need to escort you to the trap," I explain, rising from my seat.

"Right," he says as I approach him. Any trace of the rage I saw seconds earlier has been wiped away.

"Have a good day," I say while opening the door at the end of the corridor for him.

"Sure, you too, Doc," he says casually as he enters the control area that leads into the prison proper.

I am uncertain why he made me so angry. The sense of entitlement he exudes, believing that he can change the rules to his liking, is part of it but not all of it. I believe he is getting over on me despite everything, and I can't stand that feeling. It's not grounds to toss him out of the ATA, and I suspect the problem is more with me than Zorello. As a rule, I enjoy the verbal give-and-take that I can have with a bright inmate since it is not the norm. The average inmate's intelligence quotient runs ten points below that of the normal population, with their verbal skills even worse. Fahad Milton, the lead suspect in Leon Alexander's murder, is a Muslim of African American descent. He was one of my star pupils when I coordinated the Medical Assistant Training Program in the hospital unit. We disagreed about many, if not most things, but I always enjoyed our interactions. He was easily my intellectual equal, but due to a range of circumstances, including the situation he was born into, he's doing double life, and I go home each night.

Zorello is different. He is equally bright but entitled and used to being in charge; plus, he has remarkable control of his emotions, way beyond anything I can muster. When he turned to glance back at me from the door, he could have killed me as casually as squashing an ant. I had crossed an unacceptable boundary. It may have been reversing his decision or threatening him, as he called it. Yet when I got to the door, his demeanor was totally changed and relaxed. Fahad may have killed twice and possibly three times, but Zorello was more lethal.

3

The interaction lingers with me until the early afternoon, when I leave the unit to meet Vorenzi. The former Providence Brass Works is a magnificent structure with a prominent facade that is more imposing in real life than the images displayed on Prestige Construction's website. As with many older buildings, the brick courses are laid perfectly level. So often, in newer construction, a dye of a similar hue to the bricks is mixed into the mortar to hide today's poor craftsmanship, but the immigrant Italian stonemasons who worked on this foundry didn't require such tricks. Ornamental arching granite lintels grace all the front windows and top the entry.

Arriving early, I decide to stroll around the building and am struck by the brickwork on the northern side. Evidently, rather than toss out any of the misshapen or odd bricks, the masons integrated them into the sidewall, where they are not so readily apparent. Hundreds of bulging, buckled, and over- and undersized bricks are all neatly fitted into the masonry. The men who did the work clustered the blemished or distorted bricks together in a dozen or so distinct areas, making the side into a massive rouge mosaic sculpture. It may have been done for reasons of economy to not waste the bricks, but the result is strikingly beautiful. A cyclone fence extends out from the end of the side thirty or so feet down to the bank of Woonasquatucket, preventing me from making a full circuit. I work my way down toward the river and look back. The pipe scaffolding assembled against the rear of the building is dotted with guys busily at work. Spaces for oversized windows and sliding doors have been cut into the exterior wall, and half have already been installed, with the doors leading to decks that face out to the river. If the river weren't so shallow, it would almost be possible to leap from the upper decks into the water. I remember the banner running along the top of Prestige's website: *Let us build your dream.* I could live here, I decide, as I make my way past the construction rubble to the building's front.

There is a small office right inside the entryway. As soon as I say I am waiting to meet Anthony Vorenzi, the receptionist immediately tells me she will call the building manager, and almost instantly, a guy near my age in a white hard hat emerges from a side door.

"I'm Edward Lorenz, the project manager," he says effusively as if we are long-lost pals. "Mr. Vorenzi called and notified us that you were coming. It's Dr. Thomas Phillips…am I correct?"

"Yes. I was supposed to meet Mr. Vorenzi here at four."

"He is running a little late but asked me to show you some of the units. He mentioned you may be in the market for a studio or one-bedroom condo."

I nod, and he continues. "This river area is going to be a magnificent development, and I believe the Providence Brass Works building will be the centerpiece. We have already sold fifty percent at preconstruction, but quite a few of the better units are still available. Do you work with Dr. Olken? He purchased one of our first units, and we expect to collaborate with Adams Pharmaceuticals when they move their corporate offices and manufacturing here."

"Adams is moving their offices into here too?" I ask.

"Oh no, no," he clarifies. "The first floor is strictly boutique commercial, with one or two bistro-type eateries, with the upper four floors all luxury residential. Adams is considering the former Zelden Mills building less than a quarter mile away for office space. You and Dr. Olken could walk to work together from here."

I can't envision myself accompanying Ralph Olken to work every morning but don't mention that to Lorenz. I don't even mention that I am not an employee of Adams.

"Please," he says, passing me a hard hat similar to his with PRESTIGE printed above its tiny visor in bold letters. "Building department regulations," he explains as I position the plastic cap on my head. "We can take the freight elevator to the top floor and then work our way down."

Lorenz leads me to an antique lift, which is little more than a wooden platform surrounded by a heavy wire cage. "Believe it or not, she's over a hundred years old and still runs perfectly," he says, raising the wooden gate. "Once the major construction is done, we'll install two modern units in this same location. Until then it's a big help and has saved us north of ten thousand dollars in crane fees.

"Let's take an initial tour to give you an idea of the layout, and then I'll show you a building plan when we get back to my office. Do you prefer a unit with a street or a river view?"

"River, but right now, I'm looking, not buying."

"No problem, no problem. This building virtually sells itself. We have a model one-bedroom that is nearly complete. Our timetable calls for formal occupancy in six months, and I'm pleased to say we're running right on schedule."

The model is on the riverside and is the one I noticed from the ground where the windows and deck slider are already installed.

"It's beautiful," I remark as we tour the unit. "How much is this one?"

"This unit is in the upper end of the one-bedrooms, listing nearer to three hundred thousand than two fifty. It's a corner, which increases the square footage, and for display reasons, it has the upgraded granite counters and designer cabinetry. But since Mr. Vorenzi has recommended you and your linkage to Adams, I expect an offer in the two fifty range may be viewed favorably."

"Do you have any idea on what the condo fees may be?" I ask in spite of myself. I came mainly because Vorenzi more or less insisted, but now the idea of having a place in Providence has grown in its appeal.

"They have yet to be fixed, but as a newly renovated building, there will be no surprise assessments for bad roofs, leaking pipes, and all the other horrors condo owners can be blindsided by. I expect the fee will run between six to eight hundred a month, but parking is included."

His phone goes off as he completes the pitch, and the girl in the front informs him that Vorenzi has arrived. We take the stairs, and on the way down, I can study a bit more of the construction. The heavy beams and brickwork make it clear that the original Providence Brass Works designer built it to last.

Vorenzi is standing outside the first-floor office, and he beams as we approach. "Edward, I hope you were able to find a suitable unit for Dr. Phillips," he almost crows, taking Lorenz's hand warmly in his before turning to shake mine. He appears to be in full political glad-handing mode as he pumps both our arms. It's a side of him I have never seen.

"Your father, he is well?" he asks, turning back to Lorenz. But without waiting for a response, he continues, "Riccardo Lorenz has been a long-term supporter of Senator Poletti, and his firm, Prestige Construction, does the best work in the city."

Lorenz laughs. "Thank you, Mr. Vorenzi. My father is well and sends his warmest greeting."

"So what do you think?" he asks me. "Dr. Olken highly commends the help you have provided, and he mentioned to me last week that you may be interested in a condo. Will the Lorenz family be able to sell you one?"

"They are quite beautiful, but I'm not sure I want a place in Providence. I'm only contracted with corrections for six months to a year."

"We looked at the one-bedroom model unit on the top floor," Lorenz interjects.

"How much is that one, Edward?" Vorenzi asks.

Lorenz hesitates briefly and then replies, "We'll put it on the market at three hundred, but my dad may entertain a somewhat lower offer."

Vorenzi nods pensively as Lorenz speaks and then says, "I have to run back to the capital. Why don't the two of you continue the tour? I just stopped by to say hello, but now duty calls. Dr. Phillips, can you accompany me outside for a moment? And Edward, please give your father the senator's best."

There is a black Escalade parked by the entry. As we descend the few steps to the street, Vorenzi asks what I thought of the unit.

"It was beautiful."

"Good. I'm glad you liked it. We are in the process of evaluating Prestige to be the lead developer of this river project and the entire Knowledge District. When this field trial confirms the effectiveness of Eumonia, Adams will be in a better financial position to make a relocation commitment. We remain grateful for all you have done to bring that to fruition, particularly in your handling of the hostage situation, which could have derailed the trial or added months of delay. If you are interested, you can have that unit for one twenty-five. Why don't you go back in and talk with Edward? But don't discuss a sale price; I'll handle that directly with Riccardo. One hand washes the other, Dr. Phillips, and you have been exceptionally helpful to keeping us on track."

As he finishes his little speech, he motions to a Providence cop, who opens the back door to the SUV. After Vorenzi climbs in, he lowers his darkly tinted window while the cop circles to the driver's side. "Again, make nice with Edward, but if there are any negotiations, let me handle them directly. Who knows? We may be able to get the price under one twenty-five if all continues to go well."

I go back inside, where Lorenz is waiting. We spend ten minutes studying the detailed plans while he continues extolling the building's various amenities. Once he finishes, I ask him what the other one-bedrooms have sold for.

"There is some variability, but they have all closed at between two hundred twenty and three hundred thousand. The less expensive ones are on the street side and don't have decks."

"I'd want the river side," I say spontaneously.

"Then you're in the two fifty to three hundred price range."

"Would that model unit be less because it's a model?"

"I doubt it. The foot traffic for the model is minimal, and it is on the corner with every upgrade we offer, but I'll check the price with my father."

"That's okay. I need to consider the whole thing. I wasn't thinking all that much about a condo recently. Let me get back to you, and maybe we can do another walk-through."

"Please do, and call me at your convenience," he says. We shake hands, and I head out to my car.

Vorenzi indicated he could get me the unit for what appeared to be half of Lorenzo's best price. Of course, that was somewhat contingent on the field trial turning out well.

I saw an inmate years earlier who had managed one of the big downtown Providence's parking garages. He located the parking ticket print shop and ordered a few rolls of tickets identical to the ones his company used. Once the garage was full, he removed the company's roll from the machine and inserted his own tickets. He and his cohorts next filled all the ramps in the garage, adding up to an extra hundred cars per day. The company was happy because their garage was always full, and the guy brought in nearly an extra hundred thousand a year for himself and his crew. The parking inspectors, however, had issues with his loading up the ramps. The guy told me he always kept a variety of catalogs in his office, and whenever an inspector brought up packing the ramps, they would spend some time paging through the catalogs. If the inspector indicated he was interested in something from a particular catalog, such as a large-screen TV or custom fishing gear, my guy then made the items appear at the inspector's house a few days later from an anonymous donor. No one ever spoke of a bribe, and the charade of plausible deniability, which Dick Nixon and Ollie North immortalized, was kept intact.

On the ride back to Cranston, I decide that Anthony Vorenzi, very nicely and very tactfully, offered me a bribe. Possibly, it was simply business as usual, which in some respects is even worse. Similar to the con running the garage scam, nothing was said directly, and all remain able to maintain their little cloaks of plausible deniability, but I know what I felt, and it felt like a bribe or an insurance policy that things will work out for Adams, a simple quid pro quo—and worst of all, it was appealing. I'd own a riverfront condo with eventual canal access to the harbor. I could continue to maintain my Block Island house and commute into the city to spend three or four nights there per week.

It is still light out when I turn into the prison drive. Rather than going out for a second run to unwind, I decide to get in some range time. I feel the need to hold and shoot a weapon. Hopefully, it will help clear my mind; plus, I require the additional hours to keep up my marksmanship qualifications. At my request, the range officer passes me a Colt 2000 and a target. After 9/11, you could select a blank target or one with Osama bin Laden's face glued on the front, and then after we invaded Iraq, there were three choices: Osama, Saddam, or blank. I always took the blank. The Colt feels a little clunky in my hand, and after two magazines, I turn it in for a GLOCK nine-millimeter. The new gun's abraded grip with front finger contours fits my hand better than the Colt. After firing off three clips, I feel much better.

Later that night, I get a call from Woody. "Medical report," he announces as soon as I snap open my cell.

"Were you in New Haven today?" I ask.

He laughs. "On second thought, let's make that a partial medical report."

His voice is infectious, and I'm laughing along with him. "Okay, give me the partial medical report."

"All systems are fully functioning. This boy is firing on all cylinders, TC, but no word yet if he's shooting blanks or the real McCoy."

I don't remember reading any mention of impotence being a possible side effect of the varicocele surgery, but I realize if someone took a knife to my groin, that would be a major concern, regardless of what anybody said.

"Halfway there, my friend!" I exclaim. "When do you go in for your next sperm count?"

"Not for three weeks, but I had to tell someone. It's been kind of eating away at the back of my mind that he may have cut something he shouldn't have when he was chopping around in there. Now to a more interesting topic…tell me what's been happening with you and our Miss Nancy Gardner?"

"Happening how?"

"Come on. Kathy's been burning up her minutes with calls back and forth to Chicago for the past week or two. I'm sure they're not planning a trip for walleyes in Lake Michigan, so tell me what's up."

"We've been chatting now and then, getting to know each other."

"Are you planning a trip west anytime soon?"

"Who said anything about that?" I grumble.

"Easy, big boy," Woody cautions. "No one said anything about anything, but you don't have to be a genius to figure out a visit may be in the cards."

"Sorry, it's been a long day. But, yeah, it's a possibility. I may not have mentioned this, but I am extremely interested in the work of Frank Lloyd Wright."

"Kiss my ass, sailor!" He chuckles. "You never heard the name until a month or so ago."

"Believe it or not, I have heard of him. But you're right; Nancy did significantly heighten my interest."

"Hey, TC, it's been nearly three years. Maura would want it," he says more seriously.

"Yeah, probably," I reply noncommittally.

"Not probably, pal—definitely. She was a good girl and loved life. She'd want that for you, not to see you out on some rocky shoal tending a lighthouse."

"Christ, Woody, you're beginning to sound like my mother, except she merely implies things instead of saying them directly."

"I was never much for subtlety, which you should have figured out by this time. Anyway, why don't you tell old Woodrow what's happening at work that's making the day so long? Maybe I can float over and straighten things out for you."

"It's nothing. The unit has thirty guys and as many staff. There's always some issue popping up."

"If I can help, call me, and I'll be there with a helping hand. Got to run, but I wanted you to know that I'm hot to trot."

"That's great news, although I'm not sure Kathy agrees with me."

He laughs. "She agrees, pal. Ends up that she was as worried as me that there might be some erectile issue. Seriously, thanks again. You'll be back on Thursday?"

"It's still the plan. I'll call you once I'm on the boat."

"Great. I'll catch you then."

After I click off, I remember Maura chastising me for holding too much in. *You have no professional peer group in the prison. You need people to talk to and process things with.*

She was right, and it is still a problem.

4

On Tuesday I meet with the two social workers for our weekly supervision session. They both remain enthusiastic and see the inmates as motivated to participate in the afternoon groups. One of them has prior corrections experience, and she sees a marked difference in the level of motivation among the ATA participants than she had previously noted in the general population. We do a brief review of the status of each inmate in respect to their involvement, and when we get to Zorello, the social worker who is his primary therapist notes no unusual behavior.

"It's hard for me to believe he has ever had a problem with aggression. He always presents in such a calm manner, and there is no reported history of substance abuse," he explains.

"How do the other group members respond to him?" I ask.

"Pretty much like anyone else. Possibly they are a little more deferential because of his age, but that's about it."

"Have you noticed anything different in how he relates to Black or Hispanic guys?"

"He doesn't reach out to them, but that's true for most. I've yet to see a minority inmate challenge a White inmate or vice versa. People tend to stay in their own lanes."

"I ask because when he signed up, he said that he had a problem with minorities," I explain.

"One of my guys, Leroy Brooks, said they had a minor beef last week when his son spilled some soda near Zorello during a visit," the other social worker mentions. "I guess Zorello got angry, but Brooks said they worked it out later."

"I heard about that," I acknowledge. "They worked it out by splitting the visit time into two shifts. This past Sunday, those with kids came in from one to three and the others from three to five. Zorello more or less imposed that decision on the unit, and when I told him it wouldn't continue, he wasn't pleased. I believe there was also a racial piece to it, but he'd never admit that. Keep your ears open. My guess is he's going through the motions."

Zorello's therapist laughs. "What else is new? All these guys are going through the motions to one degree or another most of the time, but that doesn't mean they don't benefit from the program."

I smile. "Your right, but still keep your eyes open."

Later in the day, I remember Woody pointing out my tendency to isolate myself akin to a hermit lighthouse keeper out on some treacherous shoal or rock formation. The thought is immediately replaced by the dream image of a mermaid lounging on a boulder amid a rolling sea, but this time the woman is positively Nancy Gardner. Her hair streams out behind her like the locks of the mermaid painted on the steel skin of the sturgeon class sub she described seeing as a child at the Electric Boat Works in Groton. A few days off and a trip west would do me good.

That night I give Nancy a call. "How serious were you about my visiting pretty soon?" I ask after we chat for a bit.

"How serious are you?" she asks back. "Weren't you planning to check your work schedule and then get back to me?"

"I see the superintendent tomorrow for our weekly meeting and intend to ask for his approval to take a few days off. If it works out, how soon can you get free?"

"I'm already here. There are no pressing projects I'm working on. I'll make the time."

I hesitate briefly and then say, "Is next week too soon? What if I'm able to get the time off right away? There is nothing special I'm needed for here either. What if I came out, say, a week from today, next Tuesday?"

"You may pay a premium for a ticket on such short notice, but if you came out on Tuesday, I'll take the next few days off and then the weekend if you stay that long."

"Yeah, that long sounds perfect," I reply.

"Southwest flies into Midway from Green, and their short-notice fares are generally the best." I hear hopeful anticipation woven into her words as she surely heard in mine.

"I've been thinking of you a lot, Nancy. I hope we can get to know each other better. I'll check tomorrow with my boss and then see if my mom can watch Matt."

"I look forward to seeing you too. If your mom can't watch Matt, you're welcome to bring him."

"I appreciate that, and that's one of the reasons I want to come. The two of us are a package deal, and I'm sure you realize that. But if my mom's busy, Maura's parents will jump at the possibility to spend a few days with their grandson."

When I mention Maura's name, I'm struck that I have no pang of guilt or other emotions. We have never talked of Maura. She has always lingered in my mind when I've spoken to Nancy but never in any type of taboo or negative manner.

"What? I missed that," I say, realizing I have been momentarily lost in my thoughts as Nancy was speaking.

"Do you maintain regular contact with her family, with Maura's family?"

"Not as often as I should," I admit. "They have a hard time getting out to the island. My mother and I have given them an open invitation, and we have plenty of space to put them up, but it hasn't worked out as easily as I had hoped. He's still working, but her mom, Matt's grandmother, is generally free."

"They may prefer a specific invitation rather than an open one. Possibly, they could stay at your house when you're out here? Then Matt can be near them and your mom, plus the things he's familiar with."

I puzzle over her words for a few seconds before responding. "I like that; it's an excellent idea. Once I clear it with the super, I'll call Ellen—that's Matt's grandmother—and check on her schedule. I'll try and coordinate a time when she can come out to Block Island in the next two weeks or so. I don't think she's doing a lot, so hopefully, next Tuesday will still work."

"I'll be here, Tom."

A storm kicks up that night, and lying in bed, I listen to the wind creak and force its way through all the old sashes. In the netherworld between sleep and wakefulness, I envision myself soaring above the sea in Izzy's Whitehall, scanning the waters below for the mermaid on the rock. I spy her in the distance and adjust the tiller to bring the *Lir* around for a closer pass. The wind fills the small boat's mainsail and jib as I come about while the woman's hair streams out behind her, and it is Nancy, not a mermaid, standing amid the waves. Still partially awake, I wonder if I can maneuver the boat to swoop down and lift her from the surf.

A familiar voice rises from my unconscious and jars me awake. *Hey, Doc, any chance I can come fishing with you?* It's Antonio Lopez.

Fully awake, I lie still as the wind gusts outside. Lopez has chased the image of Nancy Gardner from my mind. She is sleeping in a warm bed in a Chicago apartment or condo, while I lie in the house the former wardens of Cranston State Prison lived in, and Lopez languishes behind walls of concrete and steel, with the only rustling of air audible to him being his breath.

Unsuccessfully, I try to reevoke the image of Nancy in my mind but am unable to as I fall into a restless sleep.

5

Lincoln and I spend an hour together Wednesday morning, first reviewing the most recent shift reports and then discussing the unit in general. When I fill him in on my conversation with Zorello, he is not the least surprised.

"That's Mario, but I'm more concerned that none of the officers noticed it and stepped in. The shift commander should have immediately figured out something was up when he saw how the visitors came in. I'll speak to him. When I left on Saturday, no one mentioned revising the schedule."

"When I spoke to Zorello, he told me that all the cons had reached an 'accommodation.' The guy royally pisses me off, and he knows it. At one point he told me I may be able to benefit from the ATA programming."

Lincoln chuckles at the last comment. "We knew from the start that it was questionable to take him in. He pretty much ran his unit in the camp, and there's no reason he wouldn't expect to do the same thing here. Most screws are fine with it because he makes their lives easier. He keeps the static down, so any unit he's on has fewer incidents. If we were to put it to a vote, I expect both the majority of cons and officers to opt for his revised schedule."

I weigh Lincoln's words. "Yeah, I thought about that too. If all the inmates agreed to do it, why rock the boat? But it was the way he did it that got to me. Let's see what Jim says when we meet with him later. I'd also like to take a couple of days off next week if that's okay?"

"I plan to be here," Lincoln says. "There's nothing special on tap, right?"

"Just the usual visit from the Adams nurse practitioner to do interviews and some blood draws on the ones that are scheduled."

"Why did they end up backing off on the medical director issue?" Lincoln asks.

"Obviously, their last one didn't work out too well," I say, remembering the Boden mess.

"You're right on that, Cap," Lincoln agrees. "But is it enough to have that NP coming in once or twice a week?"

"It should be. I meet with them weekly for a couple of hours to keep tabs on things. Part of the idea of an on-site part-time medical director was for them to gain the correctional management experience. Now they are primarily focusing on the meds, and informally I provide them with consultation related to the correctional management issues."

Lincoln nods. "I'll be happier when they're out of here. No matter what we say, all the cons expect they'll get a jump on their parole date or something else out of this. When that doesn't happen, watch out."

I shrug. "Supposedly, the pills they're taking will prevent that, at least for half the guys who are getting the real thing."

That afternoon we have our regularly scheduled meeting with Jim. After we give him a general rundown, he brings up the situation that took place with the visits but doesn't mention Zorello's role. I'm not the least surprised at the question. Jim has his ear to the ground, paying special attention to any incident that may affect the institution's functioning. It is unlikely Zorello spoke directly to him, but more likely, the information was conveyed by someone in the print shop where Zorello works, either by the instructor or one of the officers who monitor industries. After I give Jim a brief rundown, including Zorello's role, he asks what I think of the split visiting idea.

"It may not be a bad idea," I admit. "But it should have been presented through channels. The way he did it irritated me."

"That's Mario," Jim says, echoing Lincoln. "When he signed up, he helped us fill the place, so now he expects to run it, or at the minimum, to have some influence on how it's run. Guys like him help with climate control. You know, with him in a unit, there will be no D-reports. What if you formed a small inmate council for the ATA? He is sure to be elected. Then we could consider any ideas, such as revising the schedule, that they propose. I can't see any reason not to open Saturdays for visits and eventually one weekday evening. The cons will feel like they're getting something, and that can reduce the risk of any potential disturbance or bad blood. Christ, when we were initially planning this, some people were asking for conjugal visits. Opening the extra day demonstrates that we are listening."

Lincoln and I ponder Jim's idea for a few moments before Lincoln responds, "I think that's workable. How about you, TC?"

"I can see a mini-inmate-council, and I have no issue with the increased visit schedule. The more we can get family in, the better. I guess it's the feeling that Zorello is getting over on us that I need to deal with. But, yeah, let's do it."

We continue to review other issues related to the ATA, and as the meeting winds down, the super asks if he can see me.

Once Lincoln leaves, Jim asks if I had threatened Mario in any way.

"No," I reply immediately. "He complained I was threatening him, and I told him threatening him would be forcing him to be strip-searched each day and throwing a cavity exam into the bargain. He irritates me. He is so entitled and figures if he decides to shift things around, no one will care. I may have been a little out of bounds, but it wasn't intended as a threat."

"Telling a con you can arrange to have him strip-searched and get someone to stick their finger up his ass isn't exactly being hospitable."

"Come on, Jim! You know what I'm saying. He may also be faking his response to the meds—if he's even taking them. He's already told me a couple of times that he views Eumonia as the best thing since sliced bread."

"So what if he's trying to get over? You should leave the sorting out of that to Adams. That question belongs to them."

"Right! They told me they have different tests to determine who is scamming them and who isn't, but I don't trust them either. This is their first time working with cons, and they want it to succeed a little too much. Christ, Vorenzi arranged for me to see one of the buildings that is being turned into condos on the Woonasquatucket because Olken told him I may be looking for a place in town. He offered to have them knock a hundred grand or more off the price. I got the distinct feeling it was a bit of a quid pro quo. I help Adams run their field test successfully, and then I get a special deal on a condo. The whole thing stinks."

"It's politics, TC. Vorenzi is doing the same thing Zorello is doing—you scratch my back, and I'll scratch yours. Zorello keeps the incidents down on his unit, and he expects a little slack. You grease the wheels here for Adams to make certain things run like a clock; then Vorenzi does you a favor. His boss is banking on that Knowledge Zone or Knowledge District, or whatever he's trying to pull off in those old factories, to work out. That's a multimillion-dollar development, so he asks the condo guy to cut you a deal."

"I still don't like it."

Jim laughs. "It's the way of the world. You do need some time off. You've been totally focused on this Alternatives to Aggression unit for the past three months. Recharge your batteries. Lincoln can hold down the fort. Why not take a week or two?"

"Are you asking me to take the time or ordering me to take it?"

"Come on, TC. You've never threatened anyone in your life; even in jest, you never have. You could use a break, so take some time off. Zorello is a pain in the ass, but you don't tell a guy you plan to have him strip-searched because he pisses you off. You're too valuable to this project. Why don't you take two weeks?"

The resentment I feel at Jim's suggestion takes me unaware. I was planning to ask him for the time off, and now that he is offering it to me unsolicited, I'm irritated. I decide that I must need a vacation more than I realize.

"Two weeks? You want me to take two weeks?"

"It's your call. Your staff is in place, and we'll be able to manage for two weeks. You've been putting in plenty of time, so I'll make sure you get paid. Why don't you start now and take off the rest of today? You can still make a late ferry."

"I promised Antonio Lopez I'd see him weekly and still haven't been up the DSU this week. I'll do that and then knock off for the day."

"You've got to let things go. Lopez will get by; he has for years. There is no real reason you have to keep seeing him in segregation. He wouldn't do the same thing for you. Leave today."

"I also still have my weekly meeting at Adams tomorrow. I'll stop by the DSU now to see Lopez, talk to Lincoln early tomorrow, and then be gone for two weeks after I meet at Adams."

"I like that plan," Jim says, getting up from his chair. "Tell Lincoln I'll give him a buzz to go over the schedule for the time you're away."

On my way to the DSU, I'm still a little put out with Jim. I want the time off but resent being told to take it off. Crossing the large common area for the max unit, I'm again struck by what a waste the entire high-security setup is. Guys continue to mill about, watch TV, and play cards as I make my way toward the entrance to the DSU. The AC has yet to be fixed, and the segregation area is bleaker and more dank than usual. The semirank aroma of too many men packed into a steel-and-concrete container greets me as I approach the security post by the gate leading into the cell area. As usual, they are running short staffed with only one officer on.

"AC still down?" I ask the CO occupying the post.

"They'll get to it any day now, Doc." He laughs. "You here to see your usual crew?"

"Yeah, Lopez and a few others," I reply. "I'll be between an hour to ninety minutes."

He nods to one of the rolling desk chairs while saying, "Be my guest."

As I take the chair, I'm tempted to ask him if I can steal one of the half-dozen assorted pine-tree car deodorizers that are now decorating the small control room, giving the air an odd balsam-vanilla aroma.

The half-light of the unit reminds me of the dreamscape from the prior night's fantasy when Lopez so rudely disturbed my flight over the stranded mermaid. Arriving at cell 15, I peer into the stained window above the food slot. Lopez is sitting on the edge of his bed in his skivvies, intently staring at the wall rather than being asleep. He immediately jerks up when I tap on the glass, and I hear a muffled, "Hey," from inside the cell.

Sitting back down in the chair, I unsnap the food slot and call in, "Antonio, how are you doing?"

"Good. If I stay cool, I get a TV next week," he says, kneeling by the door.

"That's great!" I exclaim, aware that inmates who have no incidents for four to six consecutive weeks are given a tiny black-and-white set. They only receive three or four channels, but it is a major incentive.

"Yeah, you can go buggy in here, Doc. It's a zoo at night. There's always someone losing it."

"How about you, Tony? How are you doing?"

"The first few weeks were bad, real bad. But now I'm doing okay. Hey, any idea what's happening with my case? No one has come to see me yet, so I'm thinking I won't get no new charges. What did you hear?"

"Like I told you before, it's not my thing. You need to ask your caseworker."

"I told you before, he's a useless cunt, that caseworker." He begins to giggle. "A cunt," he repeats, his voice rising. "A big fat useless cunt. He's a useless cunt." And now he's screaming.

"Antonio!" I call loudly through the slot. "Cool it. Chill."

He stops as suddenly as he began. "Oh man, I'm sorry. You're coming back to see me, right?" He whimpers. "You're going to come back to see me. I didn't mean to go off. It gets to me sometimes, Doc. I'm okay now. I'm okay. You'll come back, right?"

"I'll come back, Tony. I'll be away for the next two weeks, but I'll come see you as soon as I get back."

"I'm sorry, man. You're not leaving because of me, are you? I wasn't yelling at you. It's just that caseworker is useless. He's totally, totally useless! Tits-on-a-bull useless!"

"Take it easy, Tony," I say steadily, trying to avert him from a second escalation. "Are you sure you're okay?"

"Yeah, yeah, I'm set. I'm good to go." His voice has steadily lowered in intensity.

"It's tough."

"Yeah, but I can do it. You don't have to worry on me, Doc. I'm straight. It gets me sometimes, but I'm straight."

"You sure you're okay, Tony?" I ask again, deliberately using his name over and over again to keep him oriented.

"You'll come back and see me?" he asks, and I can tell he's struggling to keep the pleading out of his voice.

"I'll be gone two weeks, Tony; then I'll be back. Blues and stripers are running now, and I have to see what I can catch. Who knows? I may even sign onto one of those big boats you used to work on and check out the scene on Georges Bank."

"I can tell you one thing," he says slowly. "It's a lot better than life here, a whole lot better."

I begin to worry I have pushed him into a melancholic mood as he pauses, but then he picks up the conversation and tells me another fishing tale from his days on the trawlers.

When I get to Mark's cell a few doors down from Antonio, he cautions me. "Your little friend down the tier has lost it at night a couple of times."

I shouldn't discuss one inmate with another; nevertheless, I say, "He's scheduled to get a TV soon."

"That might help. He's a whiner, but he'll probably be okay when he gets to watch *Judge Judy*."

"You get any more pictures from home?"

"Not this week, but did I show you the ones from my daughter's graduation?"

"I think so, but I wouldn't mind seeing them again." It's a lie, yet it doesn't trouble me. I'm certain from my previous visits that he will take pleasure in recounting his daughter's accomplishments.

After we chat for a bit more, I tell him I'll be away for a couple of weeks.

"Enjoy your time off, and thanks for stopping by. It helps talking to someone with half a brain. It's kind of a novelty around this joint, and I appreciate it. I'm being serious here, boss; I seriously appreciate it."

"No problem, Mark, I'm glad to be able to do it. I'll see you in two weeks."

As I pull back and prepare to shut the slot, a wrist and hand stick out of the opening. Touching or shaking hands with an inmate, particularly via the food slot, is heavily frowned upon in the DSU to prevent an inmate from jamming or injuring the other person. I hesitate a second but then grasp Mark's hand while our eyes lock through the safety-glass panel.

"Thanks, man," he says again with tears in his eyes.

"Two weeks," I say before releasing his hand and snapping the door shut.

Near the end of my round, I get to cell 22, Jamal Rivers's cell, and see a figure sleeping on the bunk. I start to bypass him but then decide to try and say hello, especially since I'll be leaving for a while. I tap on the door, and the figure begins to unwind the bed linens, gradually poking his head out from the wrappings. It's not Jamal but a young White guy. "Yeah?" he calls from the bed.

"Sorry, wrong room," I call back, and he immediately begins to rewrap himself in the sheets.

When I get back to the gate officer, I ask what happened to Rivers.

"He bugged out last weekend and got sent down to the ranch for a tune-up."

"What happened?"

"I heard he threw a nutty Saturday night, smashing his mouth against the side of his bed and banging his head on the wall. Not too swift—the son of a bitch is concrete. I guess he knocked out three or four teeth. There was still blood all over the place when I came in on Sunday. He acted the hard-ass, but he couldn't even manage a couple of weeks in seg. As far as I'm concerned, he was a punk and got what he deserved. His ticket was for beating some old guy."

"Will we get him back?"

The officer shrugs. "Where else will he go? Once they get him tuned up and filled with the right pills, he'll be back. He's still awaiting action on the ticket. We're not about to forget that just because he bugged out."

6

Traversing the max unit from the DSU, I'm preoccupied with the Rivers situation, uncertain whether he will get the right care at the Rhode Island State Hospital or whether I could have done any more for him in isolation. He refused to see me each time I stopped by his door, and I never pushed the issue. As soon as he waved me off or gave me the finger, I was on my way, as happy to be rid of him as he was to be rid of me.

I'm still sorting out my thoughts when a familiar voice intrudes. "*As-sa-laam alaikum*, Doc."

Turning, I see a slender Black man in his late thirties wearing a white kufi skullcap beaming back at me. "*Wa-alaikum salaam*, Fahad!" I exclaim. "God, how are you doing?"

"I'm like the lost tribe of Israel roaming in the desert, except I only have a year left till I can get back to the land of milk and honey, not forty."

"I see you've been reading your Old Testament history," I say.

"The Prophet Mohammad said that the Bible is a holy scripture too, so I've been catching up on all my holy reading. I've had plenty of time to kill."

At his use of the word *kill*, I cringe slightly within. Corrections and the Rhode Island State Police all believe Fahad murdered Leon Alexander. The state police theory was that he believed he was doing me a favor by killing the pickup driver who had slammed into Maura's car. Initially, they viewed me as an accomplice and came out to Block Island to quiz me at the New Shoreham Police Station. A week or so after that initial questioning, I was brought into the state police headquarters and held for a few days while they evaluated the evidence and threatened me with charges, hoping to force me into making some type of deal or confession. It was a surreal period. I was glad Alexander was dead, although I was doubtful Fahad did it. The adjutant general of the Rhode Island National Guard, Wendell Brady, who is also an attorney, was the person who convinced me that it was possible and even probable that Fahad was the murderer. I called him after the state police questioned me for the first time, and he had agreed to represent me. Aware of who Brady was, the state police brought me in on a weekend when the Guard had a major drill scheduled.

Later, as we sat in an interview room talking, it was General Brady who pointed out that because of how I had helped Fahad, and particularly the respect and trust that I had for him, he may have seen the murder of Alexander as a favor or type of obligation to me. He asked me if I would kill to help or protect other guys in my Guard unit. Without hesitating, I responded I would if I had to. "I would too," he concurred. "Mr. Milton may be much more attached to you than you are to him. It's not that different. He's helping someone he respects and who respects him, at least in his mind. We make a somewhat similar commitment to the men and women we serve beside."

Now I was seeing Fahad Milton for the first time in nearly three years. I knew he was in the max unit, but it never occurred to me that I may run into him one day on my way to or from the DSU.

Studying him a second time, I am uncertain as to what to say. The surprise and joy I initially felt have been tempered. I start to speak but catch myself before asking what happened.

Anticipating the question or reading the perplexed look on my face, he says, "You don't want to know. There was a lot of confusion."

"You didn't have to do anything. I didn't need you to do anything," I say in spite of myself.

He shrugs. "What happened, happened. But you're back, and rumor has it you have a new job working for the Zorello brothers."

"What do you mean?" I ask, intently interested in the comment. Fahad was the informal imam of the Muslim inmate population until he came into max and remains one of the two or three most influential Black inmates in the camp. He was exactly the type of person Lincoln and I originally tried to recruit to the ATA to have that minority seal of approval. Instead, we ended up with Zorello and the gangster seal. Ideally, it would have been best to have both, but it wasn't to be.

"You're running that alternatives program with Lieutenant Grant, right?"

After I nod, he continues, "If Mario Zorello and his friends signed up, it's for a reason. Mario don't do nothing he don't make money at, in the joint or on the street." His words are clear, firm, and determined.

"A lot of the guys who signed up expect it will help them at their parole hearing."

"Will it?"

"It might—but not that much," I concede.

"Then that's not why he's in there, Doc. He's getting something out of it, and my guess is money's involved. I've known that crew for going on twenty years, long before I came behind these walls. He's running something, and it's not small time. Roosters don't just one day get up and start laying eggs."

"Maybe he is trying to get better control over his aggression."

Fahad beams, like when we first met, and chuckles. "I hope you don't expect me to agree."

I smile along with him. "I guess not."

"Keep your eyes open. He plays hard, but his head can get too big. He thinks all the brothers are like the ones who work for him."

"I really can't talk about another inmate, Fahad," I say, realizing I have already crossed several boundaries.

"You know, you don't have to keep coming by to see that Cape Verdean, Lopez. He wouldn't do the same thing for you," he says, apparently changing the subject.

His words mimic Jim's from an hour or two earlier and take me aback. As I start to form an answer, he continues. "But it's good you do it. He's a card or two short of a full deck, and you may help him from ripping out. In Islam you are doing *amal saleh*, good deeds. The Koran says that upon those that perform good works, Allah will bestow his love."

"Thanks, Fahad. I appreciate that."

"You taught me to do amal saleh in the medical assistant program. When I changed a patient's sheets or cleaned a bedpan, that was my learning good works. I was building my faith and never knew it."

"That was a good program," I acknowledge. "You guys made a big difference in the hospital unit."

Fahad nods, responding with measured words. "I can't say what Zorello is doing, but keep your eye on the money end. I'll stop you on your way through again if I hear anything else. He's a most serious dude, Doc. Remembering that is a must. I'd hate to see you get burned and have another decent program go down the tubes like the MAST one did. One hand washes the other, brother."

I want to tell Fahad not to worry and remind him that I can't discuss another patient, but I don't. I thank him.

He smiles. "It was good to see you. *As-salaamu alaykum.*"

I take his hand a second time and say, "Peace be with you, too, Fahad. I'm off for two weeks, but I'll keep in mind what you said."

I take a step away and then am struck by a thought. Turning back, I call out to Fahad, who stops less than five feet away.

"You said working for the 'Zorello brothers.' Mario is the only one here that I know of. Who are the brothers?" I ask as I draw close to him for a second time.

"Ricky and Angelo," he replies. "There are two sisters, but I forget their names. They were from the Atwells Avenue area, Holy Ghost Parish, before they moved out of the downtown. Ricky was the youngest and the one I knew the best. He ran their businesses, probably still does—construction, trash, restaurants, any place you can move a lot of cash. They ran ice cream trucks when I was a kid. It's how I first met him, helping on a truck. Ricky was okay. He could care less about the color of your skin; green—that was the one color he saw. Angie worked mainly out of Hartford for the Patriarcas. I never met him. One sister…I think it was Martha. Yeah, definitely Martha. She worked with Ricky. She was decent too. Mario was their street guy. He generated the cash, mainly through drugs, protection, gambling, prostitution, and an occasional truck hijacking. On the whole, they stayed away from anything that would get FBI attention, like banks, armored cars, or other big-ticket items. As long as they kept their dealings to the Providence PD, they were fine. Those cats grew up with half the cops and bought off the rest. That's why the feds were unable to get Mario. It was a good business plan; all those nickels and dimes add up."

"What did you mean, 'I was working for the brothers'?"

"A figure of speech, I guess. If Mario is running some type of game and using that alternatives program to do it, then his family is involved. None of them operate solo. It's why they've been so successful. They're part of the Patriarca family, but for the Zorellos, it's more of a franchise, like McDonald's. They pay their dues or whatever you call it and get to keep their own operation. Ricky runs under the radar and pays his bills on time. Since Mario's the street guy, he's always showing off his balls, but it's an act. He's a control freak.

They don't joyride. Mario didn't join that program for the fun of it. There's a destination. If he thought it may get him out a few months early, that's possible, but you said that's unlikely. He would have been hip to that when he signed up, so it's not why he's there. I'm not sure why he signed up, but I expect his family is involved, and someone's making money. And if money is involved, those Zorellos will do whatever they have to do to protect their investment."

I consider his words for a while and then say, "Thanks, Fahad. You gave me something to think about. I appreciate it. I'll be back in two weeks. If you have any other ideas, let me know. Take care of yourself."

"You too," he replies. We shake hands for a second time and then go our separate ways.

As a rule, I don't look into an inmate's criminal history to any great degree. Unless they're a sex offender, it doesn't have a lot of bearing on their treatment. But with a sex offender, there is frequently a perversion or addictive aspect to their behavior. Therefore, understanding their offense history can be an integral aspect of treatment in helping them break their offense cycle. Nonetheless, when I return to my office, I go online to find out what I can of the Zorello family. A short Wikipedia page is devoted to them. It is linked to the more extensive Patriarca crime family entry, but otherwise, there is little else. The page confirms Mario has two brothers, Riccardo and Angelo, and two sisters: Martha and the one Fahad couldn't remember, Maria. It notes that Mario and Angelo are linked to organized crime through the Patriarcas, but it does not mention any other family members' involvement. Overall, Mario and Angelo are presented as minor figures. It confirms what Fahad said about them focusing on less noticeable criminal ventures and trying to stay out of the spotlight. I pull Zorello's DOC folder and see that his criminal history conforms with this by being relatively minor. I am struck by his elegant American Spenser script that I note on several of the documents he had to sign when he entered Cranston. The elementary school I attended on Block Island as a child drilled us in penmanship using the Spenser method. While penmanship classes have fallen out of favor in most schools, I am proud of the hand I developed in childhood and can see Mario Zorello has also cultivated an admirable and individually stylized script, the flourish of which is remotely familiar to me.

That afternoon I decide to go down to the Cranston High School track for some speed work. I have been getting in the mileage on my morning runs but feel the urge for a second workout. Now that I have time off starting tomorrow to visit Nancy in Chicago, I am reluctant to go. I know it is due to a variety of factors. The biggest is Jim telling me to take the time. That automatically tripped my resistance. After leaving the max unit, I should have gone to his office to brief him on my conversation with Fahad Milton, but I didn't. He will hear about it at some point from one of the officers who was on the floor. While we had not previously placed any restrictions on my contact with Milton, it was kind of a given. I knew he was in the max unit but had not expected to see him. Jim and I both had not considered that the entry into the DSU was inside the max facility, which increased the possibility that I'd run into him when I went there to see Lopez.

The second thing is the whole situation with Zorello and how I let him get to me. Fahad's certainty that Mario was involved in the ATA for some reason I did not grasp resonated with me. If I told Jim, he'd say I was paranoid, not to mention he'd be pissed that I was chatting with Fahad Milton.

I slowly rotate around the cinder oval, integrating a hundred-yard wind sprint into each circuit. On my fifth revolution, a vision floods my mind just as I'm beginning to pick up my pace for the dash down the track's straightaway. Veering onto the grassy center of the ring, I try to reconstruct the image in my mind.

7

Turning off my radio, I drive in silence over to the former Providence Brass Works, hoping the images, thoughts, and ideas eddying about my brain will organize themselves into a clear pattern. Parking out front, I can see the building is closed up and the work crew gone for the day. I'm chilled by the sweat I generated on the track, so I pull on a set of cotton warm-ups as soon as I step out of my car. Circling to the rear of the building, I follow the temporary chain link fence that extends down to the riverbank. The construction area remains visible in the last light of day, and I can easily make out the bright-red dumpster that had jogged my memory. The elegant script on one side proudly displays *Z Brothers*. The *Z* has the distinguishing slash through its diagonal line that I had noted on Mario's signature a few hours earlier. I study the lettering and realize it may be a coincidence, but I don't believe it. The Zorello brothers are involved in the renovation project. They appear to be providing the disposal services, but I wonder how else they are involved in the whole Knowledge District development.

I slowly make my way back to the car, but the whirlpool within my mind has not subsided. Researchers stress the importance of listening to the data, and this data points to the Zorello brothers being linked to the renovations along the Woonasquatucket River, which in turn is linked to Senator Poletti and Anthony Vorenzi, who are linked to Adams Pharmaceuticals and, particularly, to Adams Pharmaceuticals having a successful field test of Eumonia to anchor the river development project, which is linked back in turn to one of the Zorello brothers, Mario, who happens to think that Eumonia is the latest miracle drug. The pieces fit together, yet I have no idea what they make.

Twenty minutes later, I am backing into a space on Benefit Street. I take a casual walk past the building that houses Adams's offices, and they appear to be empty. Letting myself in the main door, I make my way up to the second floor and into the Adams suite. I am uncertain what I should be searching for, but if there is anything to be found, I expect it will be in Olken's office. I make my way down to his room, flick on the light, and go behind his desk. The two display terminals gaze up at me from beneath clear panels fitted into the smoked-glass desktop. Vos was right; Olken does like his toys. The terminals instantly come to life and silently rise from the plane of the workspace when I press his computer's on switch. The word *user* appears on the left screen, and I type "rOlken" into the empty box, knowing that all users on the Adams system, including me, use their first initial and last name for logging on. A second box immediately appears with a request for a password. I remember that the password Olken used, when signing me onto Boden's computer under his name, contained letters followed by numbers. I stare at the display for a few moments and then glance around the room. As my eyes fall on the framed Boston Marathon number, I recall that when I asked him for his time, he promptly responded, "Three hours and fifty-six minutes." After a momentary calculation, I type "Boston262236." It is the marathon distance and his time in minutes tagged onto Boston, but it doesn't work. I continue to ponder the framed number on the far wall and type in "Boston26.2236," representing the marathon distance at 26.2 miles accurately, but again the screen cycles back to the password request.

"Third time's the charm," I say aloud and then type in "Boston26.2.236" to separate the mileage from the time.

"Good evening, Dr. Olken," a slightly seductive, metallic voice announces from speakers embedded somewhere in the desk.

I automatically respond, "Good evening," and then click on "Accessories." Opening the computer, I go into "My Documents," which neatly lays out over thirty folders. I randomly click on two folders, and they both contain numerous subfolders, and within many of the subfolders are additional folders. His computer is organized in the same orderly manner as his mind. Pushing back the chair slightly, I study the folder list, uncertain which area to examine first. Finally, I open the Eumonia file. There are numerous folders, including four labeled "Field Test." Knowing that the Cranston site is the fourth field test of Eumonia, I open the subfolder identified as "Field Test 4."

It's the one for the Alternatives to Aggression program. Within a background subfolder, I skim a series of memos written by Olken to Poletti with a cc to Vorenzi and others. They all essentially confirm Adams's commitment to the project and present optimistic projections of how successful they expect Eumonia to be. Olken or someone else did extensive homework on the growing market they believed corrections represented if the field test results are positive. Olken also expressed his desire to be part of the Knowledge District plan for the Woonasquatucket area. Within the folder are letters or memos he generated and those he received back and copied into the folder from the emails, allowing me to get a sense of the correspondence.

I next search for documents in which Poletti's name is in the file name. The screen displays roughly a dozen items. Clicking through them, I can see they are similar to the memos I scanned, in which he generally makes nice and expresses his appreciation for the senator's advocacy or where the senator responds, indicating his support. A second search of files related to Vorenzi lays out a more extensive correspondence. The tone of the letters and memos is both more casual and detailed, with particulars related to Adams's plans and commitments, such as moving its operations to the renovated Zelden Mills, which is explicitly indicated. One memo is related to financing and how information should be presented to the Adams board of trustees at a pending meeting. It differs markedly from the few others I have reviewed, so I peruse it more carefully. Looking at the top of the document, I see it is from Martha Vorenzi, not Anthony. The file is labeled "From M Vorenzi" rather than "A Vorenzi," and I realize my search has identified documents related to two different people. I search for M Vorenzi files and see that Martha Vorenzi is a member of the Adams board of trustees and intimately involved in the company's financing.

Studying one memo, I hear Fahad's voice in my mind: "One sister…I think it was Martha. Yeah, definitely Martha. She worked with Ricky." Returning to the general folder list, I open the one designated "Financial." Doing a content search of the folder for Martha Vorenzi, I see numerous files appear on the screen. Scanning down the list, I see a half-dozen documents identified as "HG Loan Agreement," followed by a date. Rapidly paging through them, I note it is clear that a major financer of Adams is Holy Ghost Investments, of which Martha Vorenzi is the president. She is both a trustee and an investor.

I remember Fahad's comment that Mario was in ATA for the money, and I wonder more about Martha Vorenzi and whether there is any way to confirm she is his sister, as well as determine what her relationship is to Anthony Vorenzi. Once I shrink the open files, I go online. Googling "Holy Ghost Investment" uncovers various Catholic sites related to spiritual growth and the power of prayer, but no finance company. A search of Martha Zorello is equally fruitless. After a pause, I go to the *Providence Journal*'s website and search for her there. Olken's machine is remarkably fast, but it still takes a few seconds before it displays the May 1967 marriage announcement of Anthony Vorenzi to Martha Zorello, who were married at the Holy Ghost Church on Atwells Avenue. The wedding photo confirms the link, showing Senator Poletti's chief of staff as a younger, more vigorous man.

More pieces shift together, and it appears evident that Adams is bankrolled in part by the Zorello branch of the Patriarca crime family. There is something karmic to the whole thing, where criminals hope to back the development of a drug that will be used to sedate other criminals, or at least make them more tractable. But it is not as if the Zorello brothers will be atoning for their prior actions by helping others. On the contrary, they are in the mix to make money, as Fahad pointed out, and they are positioned to make a fortune. I can't help but smile to myself. I have no idea if it is illegal, but at the least, there are ethical questions.

Closing out of the internet, I switch back to Olken's file list. Reopening "Field Test 4," I go into the data folder. Within it are various files set up in Excel and SPSS, the Statistical Package for the Social Sciences. I scan the documents, and it appears that Olken has created multiple data records. I go to the same files in "Field Test 3" and see a parallel process. Each subject is identified by FT3 followed by a number. It's been nearly ten years since I ran any SPSS data analysis in graduate school, but it is clear that numerous analyses were run on the various data sets based on the statistical tables that were generated. Opening the properties tab of a few tables, I can see Olken originated them. It appears he did a preliminary data analysis before shipping the files off to the statisticians. That is not necessarily a problem, but maintaining what appears to be multiple and differing sets of raw data is. Without further investigation for confirmation, it nevertheless appears that Olken may have fudged some of his results.

Reportedly, the mid nineteenth-century British prime minister, Benjamin Disraeli, said, "There are three kinds of lies: lies, damned lies, and statistics." My Boston College statistics professor stated that on numerous occasions. It was a two-semester course, and he spent most of the first semester forcing us to read professional articles from a range of disciplines to develop the critical skills essential to being a competent researcher. First among those skills was being able to identify bogus, shoddy, or deceptive work. "Just because it's been subject to a review process doesn't mean it's gospel," he often said, pointing out how many peer reviewers volunteered their time and may be half asleep when they were reviewing articles. Olken's multiple data sets and analyses have my antennae vibrating.

It certainly would not be the first time data was manipulated, but concerning the amount of money riding on the results, it was an issue and was nearly undetectable. If Olken was playing with the data, he was doing so with the raw material before it was shipped off for analysis. The statisticians had no idea the numbers they were working with had been through a preliminary analysis and then revised to get the predetermined outcomes. If any other researcher asked for the raw data, they'd be given the same numbers the researchers were. To be extra thorough, Olken would have to amend any test or lab results for subjects. Yet, in light of his role at Adams, that wasn't difficult, and considering the sample size, he could easily manage to get the results he preferred by simply shifting a patient or two between the control and study groups as needed. For a sample of thirty, as was being run at the ATA, it may mean exchanging as few as two non-Eumonia-responding subjects out of the intervention group for two subjects who appeared to be improving, to be shipped in from the placebo group. To do that, he merely had to find some way to relabel the lab work of the subjects being exchanged.

Rocking softly in Olken's chair, I am pondering ways to manipulate data and how to get past any reviewers who insisted on seeing the raw data itself. It was an unlikely scenario for most researchers to contend with, but it was a contingency that had to be dealt with if you were fudging results. Suddenly, I am aware of a sound at the front door and automatically reach down and turn off Olken's machine. With a soft hiss, the two monitors disappear into the dark-glass desktop.

<h1 style="text-align:center">8</h1>

Olken is standing by the open doorway a moment later, slightly winded from his dash up the stairs.

"What are you doing here?" he shouts, trying to regain his breath and master his emotions simultaneously.

"Checking craigslist for apartments," I say, listening to the footsteps of others approaching down the corridor.

"You're lying," he spits out. "I followed you on my mobile."

Tightly gripping the phone, he aims his arm at me accusatorily. "You've been into my records."

"That too," I reply. He has not left the doorway, and now Vorenzi and the uniformed cop who was with him at the brass works fill up the space.

"You want to tell us what's going on, Dr. Phillips, that got Dr. Olken so upset at dinner?" Vorenzi asks as he moves into the room, followed by the cop, who I notice is a sergeant.

"I needed a computer and borrowed his," I reply while Vorenzi and the cop move to either side of the desk. "It's the fastest machine in the place."

"How did you get my password?" Olken blurts out from the entry.

"You showed it to me the other day when you signed me onto Boden's machine."

"I did not," he insists, sounding almost like a child whining. Both the cop and Vorenzi glance at him, and I'm tempted to say, "Did too," but catch myself.

Instead, I respond, "Then how do you think I got it?"

"I don't know," he angrily retorts.

"No one particularly cares how you got the password," Vorenzi interrupts. "Dr. Olken indicated you accessed his files, including Adams's financial records. Why were you doing that?"

"He spoke to me about a job, and I'm interested in knowing how solvent the company is before making a decision. I figured the best way to do that was to check the financials Dr. Olken kept."

While answering, I push the chair back slightly from the desk. The cop, who is to my left, immediately tells me to stop moving and remain seated.

Almost as if magically, Olken has become insignificant, ceasing to exist in any meaningful manner. There are now three people in the room: Vorenzi, the cop, and me. If I'm to get out in one piece, the way is through them.

"So how did the finances look?" Vorenzi asks.

"I didn't understand them all that well, but from what I saw, they appear fine. If the Eumonia field test works out, I expect they'll be even better."

As soon as I began to speak, I heard Fahad Milton's voice in my mind for the second time in the past fifteen minutes: "I can't say what Zorello is doing, but keep your eye on the money end." It made me add the second sentence to my response on how financially successful Adams would be if the Eumonia trial at Cranston came out positive.

"Adams does have a lot invested in that trial," Vorenzi acknowledges in carefully measured words.

Now I feel we're down to two people in the room. This time when I get up from the chair, the cop stays mute. I see a silent glance pass between them as the officer backs up slightly. Olken remains by the door, but all my attention is on Vorenzi.

"I'd like to do all I can to guarantee it's a success," I say to him. The cop has moved to the side, allowing me to pass to the area in front of the desk.

"What do you mean?" Olken puts in, breaking the link between Vorenzi and me.

"Shut up, Ralph," I say in as controlled a manner as I can muster before Vorenzi has a chance to respond.

Vorenzi nods to the cop, who strides across the room and motions for Olken to sit in one of the side chairs.

"Now why don't you be a little clearer in what you're trying to say?" Vorenzi instructs me.

"It took me five minutes to see that Olken was fudging the data on Eumonia. How long do you think it would take anyone else?"

Olken begins to say something, but the cop places a heavy hand on his shoulder as Vorenzi simultaneously tells him to be quiet.

"I really don't have anything else to say," I reply to Vorenzi's question on what else I want to add to my comment.

"He can't be trusted," a new voice says. I rapidly scan the room but see that no one else has entered.

When the phrase is repeated for a second time, I see that the words are Olken's. He's leaned back in the chair with the cop to his side, staring directly at me. "You're bluffing."

The configuration of the room has shifted in a manner I had not expected. Olken is more deeply involved than I suspected. By the tenor of his correspondence and my general take on him, I had guessed he neither realized the flaws in his research were readily discoverable nor that his potential investment partners may be linked to organized crime.

"What do you mean?" Vorenzi asks, directing his question to Olken.

"The research is totally legitimate," he contends. "Eumonia is a remarkably effective medication, and it does reduce aggression. I fully expect the clinical trial at Cranston to be successful, confirming our previous studies."

Vorenzi shifts his gaze from Olken to me and then back to Olken.

"If the trials have been so successful, then why have you been running multiple sets of data with a preanalysis before it gets sent to the statisticians?" My question is directed to Olken but is equally for Vorenzi's benefit.

"That's a standard procedure for—"

"That's a lie, and you know it," I interject. "Any reviewer would hang your ass out to dry, leaving you and any of your investors on the street."

"That's ridiculous," he responds with equal force. "It hasn't happened yet, and it never will. Adams follows the highest standards in medical research. Our backers' investments are at no risk whatsoever."

The initial part of what Olken said was directed at me, whereas the second segment of his response was for Vorenzi's benefit, and Olken couldn't help looking directly at him while he spoke.

Initially, I saw the negotiations as between Vorenzi and me. Now, I see it as between Olken and me, with Vorenzi as the judge.

"If your boss has made a major bet on this guy, he may want to reconsider it," I say. Vorenzi holds up a hand to quiet Olken, who begins to interrupt me, and I continue. "Adams is a house of cards, and I'm not the only one who can see that."

Vorenzi ponders my words for a few moments and then says to Olken, "We have nothing to worry about?" It is evident from the tone of his voice that it's a question.

"Nothing whatsoever," he replies. "The research is gold standard, and your investments are safe."

From Olken's words, I realize that he is fully aware of the link between Vorenzi and Martha Vorenzi of Holy Ghost Investments. Yet I remain uncertain of whether he is aware of the criminal link, but nothing would surprise me at this point.

Vorenzi's response isn't directed to Olken or me but to the cop. "Get him out of here," he says, motioning with his head to me as he makes his way to the opposite side of the room where Olken is seated.

"That's fine with me. I've had enough of this place," I say, starting toward the door from the far side of the desk as the officer moves to intercept me.

"I want you to come with us so we can talk this through some more," Vorenzi says, looking over to me from where he is with Olken.

"That's fine with me," I say casually, as Fahad's words echo in my mind for the third time: "And if money is involved, those Zorellos will do whatever they have to do to protect their investment." Those words and his assessment that half the police in Providence were in the pocket of one Zorello or another have me worried about where we are heading.

"Damn!" I think and simultaneously say aloud as the cop nears. He glances up at me, puzzled, and his expression rapidly changes to one of extreme pain as I kick him in the groin with all my might. He folds toward me, and I bring my hands together to form one giant fist, which I slam down on the base of his neck. The force causes him to crash into the desk, shattering its top, and then ricochet onto the floor. He is slightly stunned, and I expect he will regain his footing shortly. He has taken two major blows, but in real life it is a lot harder to knock a person unconscious than on TV. While he's falling to the carpet, I am moving right along with him. His holster has a rotating safety hood holding his pistol rather than a snap band, and I am able to slide the gun from its leather casing quickly. Keeping an eye on the other two who are starting toward me, I can tell by the familiar feel of the grip that it's a GLOCK nine-millimeter, the preferred weapon of law enforcement officers. I step away from the body, snapping the firing pin safety off as I lift the gun. "You've crossed the Rubicon," a voice cautions in my mind.

"So what?" I scream in response and squeeze down on the trigger while raising the weapon higher. I hear a slight click as the trigger safety gives way and the firing mechanism engages. The thing roars like a cannon in the small room as the bullet crashes high on the wall. "On the floor!" I holler. Olken immediately collapses, but Vorenzi sprints for the door. I could easily hit him but don't, turning back to the cop, who is now on his knees. I back away slightly and then bring my arm around to ram the butt of the pistol into his head. He collapses, dazed, a second time, while Olken remains unmoved on the rug. Placing the weapon atop the desk, I retrieve the cop's cuffs, quickly haul his hands behind his back, and jam on the bracelets.

Momentarily, I survey the chaos that I have created in the last sixty seconds. "You need a plan," a voice says.

"Yeah, yeah, I know," I say and see Olken's eyes shift toward me to see who I'm speaking with.

"Don't get me mad," I growl while trying to organize myself and assess alternatives. My National Guard training mantra enters my mind: *Prepare, prepare, prepare, and then expect the unexpected*, and it is immediately followed by *Secure the area, and protect the hostages*, which I recognize as a maxim from hostage training.

Slamming the door shut, I lock it and then scan the room. I spy a four-foot wooden cadenza on rollers, which I push to the door and then flip on its side. "Door secure," I tell myself and hear the cop groaning behind me. Grabbing the lamp that was on the credenza, I yank it from the wall and turn back to him.

"Don't move, either of you," I say in the most menacing voice I can muster while glaring at Olken and stomping a foot on the center of the cop's back, forcing him to the ground. I then place the gun down for a second time and use the electrical cord to bind his legs.

"You're a dead man," he half gurgles and curses as I bind the line securely.

"We'll see about that," I respond, searching the room for a second lamp. Instead, I unplug Olken's sleek, modern desk lamp, hook a length of the cord under his face, and then haul it back to force it into his mouth before tying it off.

"I've heard enough out of you," I say to the cop and stuff the gun into the waistband of my sweats.

Less than three minutes have gone by since I initially kicked the sergeant in the balls. The room is secure, and the hostages are safe. "Now you have to figure out how to get out of here," the voice tells me.

"Ralph, do you want to get out of here alive?" I ask.

He looks up at me from the floor and nods.

"Good. I do too. Is there anyone else with Vorenzi?"

"One other guy who stayed in the car. He may be a plainclothes officer?"

"They will be at the door straightaway. No matter who comes to that door, you will not speak unless I instruct you to. Do you understand that, or do I have to gag you too?"

After he nods, I ask him to slide his cell phone across to me. I noticed he has been clutching it in his hand the entire time.

I study the phone for a second and then punch in 9-1-1. As soon as the operator asks how she can help me, I say slowly and deliberately, "This is Thomas Phillips. I am in the Adams Pharmaceuticals offices on Benefit Street. I have taken two persons hostage, including a police officer. I was forced to do this because my life was in danger. I did this only to save my own life. Please get your hostage team here ASAP, and please play this message for your lead negotiator. I want to end this peaceably."

She tries to say something, but I cut her off because someone has begun to hammer on the door halfway into my minispeech. "I have to go. Please get here as soon as possible," I say and then click off.

"What do you want?" I yell at the door while removing the gun from my waistband.

"Why don't you come out from there, Phillips? You made your point about Olken playing with the data, so now we can settle this between ourselves without calling the police. None of us need any bad publicity."

It's Vorenzi, and I'm about to tell him I already called the police but catch myself. "How do I know I'll be safe?"

"You'll be safe. We all want to avoid bad publicity."

"Give me time to think," I call back. Then, turning to Olken, I softly ask if the windows have any type of coverings.

"Semi sheer sunshades," he replies.

"Lower them," I order.

The cop on the floor began to squirm at Vorenzi's voice, but all he can manage is a couple of grunts and groans with the electrical cord laced through his mouth.

"What are you doing, Phillips?" Vorenzi asks.

"I'm still thinking."

"Think quick, or we'll be calling the cops, and that won't be pretty. I won't be able to help you once they get here."

"Shut up and give me a minute," I scream, trying to sound frazzled.

The whirring stops as the room-darkening shades settle into their positions while Olken continues standing by the windows, appearing completely befuddled.

"Holy Ghost Investments, your primary financial backer, is a Mafia front company linked to the Patriarca crime family through Martha Zorello Vorenzi. I found that out, and they want me dead," I say quietly as Olken's visage transforms from one of befuddlement to being dumbfounded.

"That's why I called 9-1-1 and they didn't," I add. "To get out of here alive, you must do exactly what I say."

"Are you coming out, Phillips?" Vorenzi screams from the hallway for a second time.

"I'm still thinking!"

"Finish thinking now, asshole, or else I'm calling 9-1-1. And like I said, I won't be able to protect you from the Providence PD when they get here. They don't take kindly to their own being hurt."

As Vorenzi was carrying on, I surveyed the room. Turning to Olken, I quietly say, "Drag the cop to the front of your desk, and then stand in the corner on the opposite side from me."

I want none of us visible through the window. The desk will hide the officer, and Olken and I will be in opposite corners.

The cop groans as Olken drags him the few feet necessary to position him against the desk.

"Ralph," I call softly over to him as he stands up. "I am an excellent shot. Tell me when you will speak."

"Only when you tell me to," he replies.

"Now get into the corner, and stay standing against the wall." I motion with the pistol to where I want him. "I'm doing this so no one will mistakenly shoot you through the window." The rising scream of sirens punctuates my words.

"Hey, Anthony," I call out. "Don't bother calling 9-1-1. I already did it for you."

"You little—"

But his words are cut off by the rapid report of another gun as a series of bullets slam into the door.

Vorenzi is screaming, but now it is at the guy out there in the corridor with him.

9

The squad cars' pulsing blue-and-red lights cast their faint hues into the office. After taking another inventory of what's inside the room, I move a standing lamp near the entry and turn it on while also prying a chair against the credenza. Vorenzi is still yelling outside as I work, but I block him out.

"Ralph," I call to Olken.

"Yes."

"I'm turning off the overhead lights. The one light on will be this lamp, okay?"

"Yes."

"You still want to get out alive, right?"

"Yes."

"When will you speak?"

"Only when you tell me to."

"Good. Remember that. I'll turn the light off in a second. I have no intention to shoot you or the sergeant, but I will if I have to. Do you both understand that?"

"Yes," Olken says, but the cop doesn't respond.

I take three rapid steps away from the door and kick the cop in the gut as he lays bunched against the desk.

"I know you've been listening. Do you understand? I don't plan to shoot you but will if I must."

Once he grunts his assent, I step back to the doorway and snap the overheads off. Immediately, the pulsing red-and-blue lights become more dominant in the room. No one has appeared at the door yet. They are securing the building, identifying sites for their tactical snipers, and trying to find out as much as possible about me from Vorenzi and the cop before making contact. They will have the cell number from the 9-1-1 operator, but I expect the first contact to be from their lead negotiator by way of the door. The one thing eating away at the back of my mind is Vorenzi's comment on not being able to protect me from the Providence cops. Even if I give myself up immediately, getting past that gauntlet alive may prove impossible. He has likely told them I am completely unstable, which, considering the situation from their perspective, wouldn't be hard to believe. That, in conjunction with taking a fellow officer hostage, will paint a massive bull's-eye on my back.

With that thought, I study the large window and try to reconstruct the outside. I remember that Olken's office commands a view of the harbor, so that will hopefully limit the available sniper locations. They may end up positioned in telephone poles with infrared sights, making an accurate shot exceedingly difficult due to the semi sheer shades.

Standing in the corner to maintain Olken in my sight line, I again review my alternatives while awaiting a rap on the door. *Prepare, prepare, prepare, and then expect the unexpected.* After repeating the training mantra a few times, I have another idea. I have to enlist someone else on my side in the pending negotiations, and it must be someone who can say that I am not crazy and someone who has some oomph. I'm about to call Jim's cell and then have a second idea. Pulling out my phone, I scroll down the contact list, identify a name, and hit send.

"Captain Phillips," a voice answers on the second ring, undoubtedly reading my name on the phone's display.

"General Brady," I reply as a huge surge of relief pulses through me. I knew I was tense but had been suppressing the degree of stress until that instant. "I need your help."

"You have it, Tom. I will be happy to immediately reinstate your enlistment," he says with a slight chuckle in his voice.

"I'm serious. I need your help." And this time, I am certain he hears the anxiety and fear in my voice as his tone instantly shifts when he asks what he can do.

"I am in the offices of Adams Pharmaceuticals on Benefit Street by the waterfront. A threat was made on my life because I discovered that Adams's main investor is linked to the Mafia. Some members of the Providence police may be involved and potentially a major political figure. To avoid being murdered, I have taken two hostages and barricaded myself in the Adams offices. One hostage is a police sergeant who I disarmed, and I now have his weapon. The other is the president of Adams. I have already dialed 9-1-1, but I don't want to give myself up to the Providence police."

He has not interrupted me as I spoke, and with each word, I become more relaxed. It feels more akin to a military drill than reality. I partially dissociate from myself, concurrently observing and participating in the experience.

"What can I do?" he asks into the silence between us.

Before I can respond, there is a knock on the door. The taps are so even and normal that my inclination is to say, "Come in." Instead, I say into the phone, "Their hostage negotiator just knocked. I have to respond to him, and then I will get back to you; please hold."

I am unsure whether the general responds to my request as I yell out, "This is Tom Phillips. I am armed with two hostages. I want to come out peaceably. Please identify yourself."

The negotiator on the other side of the door begins to talk, and I interrupt him. "I will talk in two minutes. Please wait."

Then, more softly, I say, "Are you still there?"

"Yes," Brady replies.

"I don't trust the Providence PD. There are undoubtedly a few members who prefer me dead. I'm positive the cop I took hostage was planning to kill me. I—"

This time it is General Brady who interrupts me. "Captain, at ease. What do you need me to do?"

My anxiety had begun to escalate, and I didn't recognize it until Brady spoke.

"The state police—can you contact them for me? The lieutenant who questioned me on the Alexander murder, Michael Cooper, if he's free, but any of them would be good. I want to surrender to the state police."

"I'll call the state police superintendent, as well as make a few other calls. This will take at least fifteen minutes and possibly up to a half hour. I am still at my office and can be there in under a half hour. Can you manage for a half hour if necessary, Captain?"

There is another knock on the door, but this time it is more insistent. "I'll manage," I say, folding the phone closed, greatly relieved the adjutant general of the Rhode Island National Guard is in my corner.

"Two minutes," a voice calls from outside.

"What's your name?" I respond loudly while glancing at my watch. It's 8:32 p.m. I've got to make it to nine o'clock at the latest.

"Daniel Zatek. And yours?" he replies.

"Tom Phillips. What do you prefer to be called: Dan, Daniel, or Officer Zatek?"

He hesitates, and I realize the question has taken him off guard. "Whatever you want is fine," he finally says. "What should I call you?"

"Tom," I answer. "Dan, I'm sure you noticed the bullet holes in the door.

They were fired from the outside. I was protecting myself. I'd rather not yell, so why don't you drop a small mike through one of those holes so you can hear me?"

"Why don't you come closer to the door?"

I realize they will have already placed a camera against the window but have been unable to pick up any of our locations, with the cop in front of the desk and Olken and me both pressed against opposite walls adjacent to the windows.

"I can't do that at the moment."

"Are you hurt, Tom?"

"No, Dan, none of us is hurt, although I have handcuffed and bound the police officer after disarming him."

"On your call to 9-1-1, you said you wanted to end this peacefully. How do you suggest we do that?"

"How about getting that microphone, Dan, so I don't have to yell? It may take us a little while to work this out, and I don't want to lose my voice. You can yell all you want, but I don't want to."

There is a pause as Officer Zatek consults with other members of his team. My main goal is to create a delay. Each minute I can consume gives the state police more time to get here.

"Tom," the negotiator calls in. "We're working on the mike and will have one set up in a couple of minutes."

I'm tempted to tell him to use the one they already slid under the door but keep my mouth shut. Every few seconds, I glance at Olken, who has had his eyes glued on me the entire time. The oscillating blue and red from the squad cars' light bars cast a miasmic discoesque aura over the room. Suddenly my cell goes off, and I immediately flip it open. "Phillips."

"This is Michael Cooper, Captain Phillips. General Brady said you are in an office on Benefit Street with two hostages. I will be there in ten minutes with six to eight troopers."

"Good." I sigh. "You'll see the lights."

"Who were you on the phone with?" the negotiator calls the second I get off the line with Cooper.

"A friend."

"Why did you tell him he would see the lights?" he asks, and I can hear the alarm in his voice.

"I told him where I was."

Now the cop sprawled on the carpet begins to groan. I consider kicking him again but don't dare expose myself by the window.

"What's that noise, Tom?" he asks, his tone again showing alarm.

"It's the bound police officer, Dan. As I said a moment ago, I have two hostages. One is bound. He is not injured, but yes, he is making noise."

"It's best for us to end this sooner rather than later, Tom. I'm negotiating in good faith, but you're calling someone to come here. What do you say we stop things right now so you can be safe, and we can take care of those two people? How does that sound?"

"I like that, Dan," I say, checking my watch and seeing it has only been three minutes since Cooper called. "As the first step, stand down your SWAT team. When I move in front of the window, I don't want to be shot."

"We don't have a SWAT team posted."

"Please, Dan," I say, inadvertently showing my exasperation. "I'm asking for both myself and Dr. Olken. Neither of us wants to be shot, even accidentally. Your fellow officer is on the floor, and they would never hit him."

"Give me a minute, Tom," he calls back.

Turning toward Olken, I say, "We're going to get out, Ralph, in ten minutes, fifteen at the max, okay?"

He nods his agreement, and I say, "Good."

I made the last comment primarily for Zatek, not Olken, certain they are listening with some type of device. The timeframe should give Cooper plenty of room to get here.

"The SWAT team is being moved," Zatek calls back after two or three minutes.

"Great," I respond, checking my watch. Seven minutes have gone by, and I hope the distance whine of sirens is the state police.

"I'm a little nervous I may be shot, Dan. How can we do this without my being shot? What if I come out first but bring a hostage with me? If anything goes wrong, I can shoot that person."

"You don't have to worry about being shot. You have my word on that."

"But I don't know you, Dan, and I don't know if I can trust you. Please talk with your captain. I want to end this peaceably, but we need a plan. You guys talk it over."

The sirens are louder, and I expect my request will eat up all the time until Cooper's arrival. Holding up my hand with my fingers expanded, I call to Olken, "Five minutes, Ralph, and we're out of here, okay?"

"Whatever you say," he responds. I'm glad it was more than a one-word answer, as the interaction was again for the benefit of the Providence cops.

Twelve minutes since Cooper called, and there is finally some disturbance in the hallway. Voices are speaking loudly, although I wouldn't go as far as to call it arguing. After around forty seconds, I hear my name called by a new voice. "Captain Phillips?"

"Lieutenant Cooper, is that you?"

"Yes, I'm here with Lieutenant Zatek of the Providence police."

"Good. Can you find out from Zatek if they have really taken down their snipers?"

There's a delay before Cooper replies. "They're doing it now. Five minutes?"

"There are extra sets of keys by the receptionist's desk so you can unlock the door. I'm being taken into state police custody, right? I can't be taken to the Providence police station. Has that been worked out?"

"We're positioning a wagon by the entrance. You'll go down the stairs and right into the back."

"Lieutenant Zatek," I call after Cooper finishes.

"Yeah," he calls back.

"If Anthony Vorenzi is nearby, you have to get him away. He may have someone try to kill me or Dr. Olken. Is he gone and the man that was with him?"

"He's gone."

While I was addressing Cooper, I was studying Olken. "Dead men tell no tales, Ralph," I say to the look of dismay on his face.

"Snipers down, and we have the key," Cooper calls in after a few minutes.

"Perfect," I call back. "There is a credenza and chair blocking the door. I don't want to move any of it. A few guys should be easily able to push the whole thing open. We'll wait inside for you."

I hear the click of the lock, and someone outside says, "Push!" The furniture begins to inch slowly along the rug like a giant snail. As the door edges open, Olken steps away from the wall by the window he has been pressed up against.

"Wait, Ralph!" I yell, but he doesn't. My words have the opposite effect, acting as a starter's gun. He leaps forward one step and then a second before the room explodes in shattered glass. His body spins in the grotesquely pulsing disco police lights as a second shot rings out and hammers into the wall.

"Olken's been shot," I scream, beginning to crawl over to him on my hands and knees, the GLOCK awkwardly gouging into my gut as I move.

"Ralph, can you hear me? You're going to be okay," I say, wishing I had somehow been able to convey the importance to him of sitting tight. Zatek may have gotten his snipers down, but who knew if anyone else was out there or if one of the SWAT guys stayed in his roost?

The room is rapidly crowding up, and I hear my name as someone grips my shoulder.

"Cooper," I say, immediately forced to the ground with my hands cuffed behind my back.

"We have to make it look good," Cooper whispers as two state cops then haul me to my feet and start to drag me from the room.

"Then you better pull the nine-millimeter from my waistband," I suggest as I turn to see one group of cops untying the sergeant and another huddled around Olken.

EPILOGUE

Undoubtedly, Ralph Olken got the short end of the stick. Besides being shot in the shoulder by an unknown assailant, he lost his medical license and company. On top of that, he was sentenced to three years in federal prison for defrauding the government by the misuse of National Institute of Health funds he diverted to help establish his company and the related tax fraud. The Zorellos, on the other hand, benefited. Holy Ghost Investment was portrayed as a small financial firm deeply embedded in the local community that invested in area businesses. It had been on the state police and FBI radar screens for years, as many of the small local businesses it served were fronts for the Zorello brothers to launder drugs, gambling, and other illicit moneys. But knowing something and proving it are two separate things. In a particularly ironic twist, Martha Vorenzi wrote me a letter of thanks for uncovering Adams's problems and saving them from even greater losses. I saw it as a way to distance herself and her company from Olken while simultaneously appearing as his victim.

Naturally, Vorenzi and the police sergeant adamantly denied they had any intention to hurt me, and none of us was charged with any type of criminal behavior. Nevertheless, Vorenzi lost his job as Senator Poletti's chief of staff but was almost immediately hired to supervise the Woonasquatucket

River Knowledge District development.

"What happened to Mario Zorello and the men that were in the special program you ran?" Nancy asks after listening to my review of what had taken place over the past six months.

"Mario is still in Cranston with less than a year on his sentence. He and the other guys got shipped back to their former units. I took the thank you note I got from his sister as an indication that bygones are bygones, so I'm not worried about Mario holding any type of grudge. That wouldn't be a good business decision."

"You not worried he would come after you when he gets out?"

"Not in the least." I reply. "There's no upside in that for him. For him violence is not gratuitous or impulsive, but goal directed. I expect he's already off to his next project."

"Did any of the social workers or other program staff lose their jobs when everything shut down?"

I laugh. "The opposite! The Alternatives to Aggression program is still there but running with a new name. It's now called Transitions but has the same focus on aggression management. The Eumonia's gone, but the intervention mix we developed to help guys better manage their emotions and behavior is still in place. Lincoln Grant runs the unit, and it focuses on helping inmates being transferred out of the max block readjust to prison life. Reintegration into the regular prison population has been a chronic problem for the men locked in isolation. After months, or even years, in fifteen-hours-a-day lockup in max or twenty-three hours a day in the DSU, people lose their social skills and often become paranoid. Up to 50 percent get into a serious incident during their first two weeks in the general population and end up being shipped back to high security. A certain number never make the transition, so they wrap up their sentences while still in max. Transitions is a six-week intensive program to ease their reintegration into the camp. As a favor to me, the superintendent assigned Fahad Milton to be in the first group. He's already back in the regular institution. Hopefully, they'll run Antonio

Lopez through it prior to his release date too."

"Do you think you'll ever go back to work there?" she asks.

"Who knows? I never expected to return when Jim called me a year ago, but I did. Still, I doubt it. But I do need to do something. I had an offer from the FBI a few years back, and I spoke to them again after this whole thing blew up. The offer is still open, but I'm not sure what I'll do."

Nancy laughs and reaches out to me. "Don't tell me I'm falling for a G-man?"

"Maybe," I say, stretching an arm out to her. But as I shift my weight on the bicycle to reach her, the front wheel slips sidewise on the sand, and I tumble into her bike. Laughing, we crash onto the soft shoulder, none the worse for wear. Light-brown flecks are sprinkled in her dark hair, and the briny scent of the sea envelops us. The image of Nancy as a mermaid fills my mind.

"You would make an exquisite mermaid," I whisper.

"Thanks, Aquaman."

THE END